Dark Game

Rachel Lynch grew up in Cumbria and the lakes and fells are never far away from her. London pulled her away to teach History and marry an Army Officer, whom she followed around the globe for thirteen years. A change of career after children led to personal training and sports therapy, but writing was always the overwhelming force driving the future. The human capacity for compassion as well as its descent into the brutal and murky world of crime are fundamental to her work.

Also by Rachel Lynch

Detective Kelly Porter

Helen Scott Royal Military Police Thrillers

DARK GAME

RACHEL LYNCH

CANELO
US

San Diego, California

Canelo US
An imprint of Printers Row Publishing Group
9717 Pacific Heights Blvd, San Diego, CA 92121
www.canelobooksus.com

Printers Row Publishing Group is a division of Readerlink Distribution Services, LLC. Canelo US is a registered trademark of Readerlink Distribution Services, LLC.

This edition originally published in the United Kingdom in 2019 by Canelo.

Published in partnership with Canelo.

Correspondence regarding the content of this book should be sent to Canelo US, Editorial Department, at the above address. Author inquiries should be sent to Canelo, Unit 9, 5th Floor, Cargo Works, 1–2 Hatfields, London SE1 9PG, United Kingdom, www.canelo.co.

Publisher: Peter Norton • Associate Publisher: Ana Parker
Art Director: Charles McStravick
Senior Developmental Editor: April Graham
Editor: Julie Chapa
Production Team: Beno Chan, Julie Greene

Design: Brianna Lewis

Library of Congress Control Number: 2022939681

ISBN: 978-1-6672-0380-5

Printed in India

27 26 25 24 23   1 2 3 4 5

Chapter 1

Kelly opened her eyes and struggled to remember where she was. She'd been dreaming. Again.

It was the same dream. In it, she walked slowly towards a door – a wooden door that had been bashed in. It was swinging lazily on its hinges, tempting her to go through it. As she approached, closer and closer, her heart beat faster, and although she knew she was dreaming, she could do nothing to wake herself up.

Her hand pushed in vain at the space where the door would be if it were closed tight, and the hinges creaked as the door swayed back and forth, inviting her to go in and take a look. She had no gun, no cuffs, no radio and no time. But she had to keep going. She already knew what was inside; it was the same every time. But each time she still tried. She would never give up. The squeaking door was her only companion as she walked hazily forward, finally making her way into the room.

There, waiting for her, was the victim: a woman about Kelly's own age but who appeared much older. She didn't move as Kelly shuffled towards her on sleepy feet.

The pressure on her throat caught her off guard and struck her with terrifying force. When she woke, she was holding her breath. She could still feel his hands. Air charged into her lungs and she gulped at it greedily. Her heart rate caused her chest to rise and fall, and she took a few minutes to assure herself that it was, after all, just another dream, exactly like the last.

Bastards. All of them.

Her mouth was sticky and she felt the familiar queasiness of a hangover. She'd only been back here five minutes and was supposed to be impressing her new unit. She hadn't got very far, and screwing the local mountain rescue wasn't the kind of start she'd hoped for; but still, it had been a pleasant experience. She looked at her watch: it was still early, and she had plenty of time for a pick-me-up coffee. Then she'd have to get to work.

Johnny slept soundly next to her. His back moved slightly with his breathing, and he was tanned from a long, hot summer on the fells. She'd forgotten how fit the mountains made you. Her stomach knotted briefly. The memory of the last man she'd shared a bed with crept into her consciousness, and it was unwelcome. This was a new start and she wouldn't mess it up.

She hadn't screwed up last time; she'd just trusted the wrong person. Matt Carter.

Twat.

The day Matt Carter hung her out to dry in front of her team, he'd kept his face straight and his eyes away from hers, not even the corner of his mouth moving as she'd been reprimanded for being too much of a risk-taker. Reckless, they'd called her, and Matt never said a word. She'd wanted to scream like a stroppy toddler, but it would've got her nowhere. Instead she left with her pride bruised and her reputation in doubt.

She was tired of London anyway, or at least that was what she told herself every morning when she looked into the mirror and listened to the unfamiliar hush, wondering where all the sirens had gone. If her instinct was interpreted as recklessness, they could shove it. She'd had enough of dead bodies anyway. Enough of sick fucks doing twisted shit to people. The kids were the worst. Images filled her mind: a boy of four lying discarded like waste on the floor of a dirty apartment in Bethnal Green, a rib sticking out of his side, having been kicked to death.

She rubbed her eyes and felt the mascara stick to her lids. As usual, she'd forgotten to remove it. The women's magazines all said it was disastrous for skin – especially ageing skin – but she wasn't very good at taking advice. However, after a night with a man she might want to see again, it was important to look at least semi-seductive, and she wondered where the bathroom was.

She sat up and stretched. She'd leave him asleep, she thought; she could do without being detained by conversation. She looked at him. He seemed like one of the good guys, but it was too soon to know for sure. Naked, she slipped out of bed and didn't bother dressing as she wandered around. The house was small and she found the bathroom easily. She looked in the mirror and shook her head. Christ, she thought. Her eyes were smeared in black and she took a tissue to wipe them. Her hair was tousled and messy, but she had nothing to tie it up with, so she wrapped a towel around it to keep it dry and stepped into the shower.

Johnny was still asleep when she returned to retrieve her clothes from the floor. It took her a while to find her pants, but she eventually gathered everything, then took the pile to another room and got dressed. The clothes felt dirty against her clean body, but she had no choice.

The liaison hadn't been planned; that was what made it so enjoyable.

Her handbag was in the lounge and she used the make-up it contained to bring some life to her dull skin. It wasn't perfect, but she felt satisfied that it wasn't totally obvious what she'd been doing. She felt a pang of shame at the thought of facing her mother, but it was mingled with defiance too. Kelly had yet to find her own place to live and was unused to explaining her every move. She was thirty-six, but lately her mother had made her feel fifteen again.

She hadn't been back to the small terrace in at least five years and it had barely changed. The only difference now was the absence of her father, whose force used to pervade every square inch of it. Now Mum was lost.

Kelly had been pushed by London and pulled by the death of her father. Pushed by betrayal and pulled by duty. The job with the Cumbria Constabulary was a good opportunity and allowed her to escape. She'd jumped at it, desperate to get away. She told people she was going to support her mother but made no mention of the feeling of failure. The dizzy heights of the capital city hadn't delivered a pot of gold after all.

Mum had aged. Her sister, Nikki, had aged. Her friends had aged. Life had moved on quickly here in her absence. She'd missed so much, and now she felt guilty. She wished she could have spent more time with her mother, but her father, the great John Porter, had been all-consuming in his perfection. Nikki had idolised him, but Kelly had competed with him.

'What do you want to join the Met for? Fancy yourself as Sherlock Holmes, do you?' he'd taunted her.

It'd taken her years to finally realise that her father was really not extraordinary at all. He felt the same fears, searched for the same answers and made the same mistakes that everyone else did, but he hid it well, and that was what Kelly had learned to do too. People said it made her hard, but underneath she cried, failed and got damaged like everyone else. Her bullishness made her father smile, but it only made her mother shake her head and give her that look. It could be the smallest thing: emptying the entire contents of her parents' drinks cabinet for her friends when she was fifteen; hitching to Manchester on her own to meet a boy no one knew. She couldn't be controlled and so she didn't fit into anyone's conventions; it made people uncomfortable. Nikki, on the other hand, ticked so many boxes that they had to be stacked up: homemaker, cake-maker, Julie fucking Andrews.

John Porter, Cumbrian Constabulary legend, had stayed in uniform, calling it real police work. Kelly had disagreed and followed the detective route. Her father had sniffed. Mum had worried. And her sister, aping her parents, had rolled her eyes every time Kelly veered further from the sacred path of marriage and children. If only someone would write down exactly what was on that path that was so compelling, and distribute it to all ten-year-olds, then maybe kids would try to stay on it. Or maybe not.

Kelly did fancy herself as Sherlock Holmes. But she was better. And in the Met she'd proved it. Until the last case and a back-stabbing twat called Matt. Matt the twat. Move on.

She filled a kettle and flicked the switch, then looked into cupboards for coffee. Johnny's house was well stocked for a man on his own, and she noticed a framed photo-graph of a girl, aged about ten, sitting on the side. God, he's got a kid, she thought. She wondered if the little girl would stay on the path or wander off it and forge her own. She knew which one she wished for any children of hers. The problem with paths was that you knew where they were going.

She heard a noise and reached for a second cup. She made two coffees, each with a sugar in them, and took them to the bedroom.

'Good morning,' she said, smiling down at Johnny. He propped himself up on one elbow and reached out to take a cup.

'You look fresh. Where are you running off to?'

'Some of us have proper jobs. I'm reviewing cases all day and it's going to be long and probably dull. But first I need to get out of these clothes.' She indicated last night's attire.

She went to the window and looked out, sipping her coffee. 'Nice place,' she said. The familiar caffeine rush soothed her. Silence sat between them and she guessed he didn't do this a lot. She'd been in London for so long that casual sex had become ordinary, pedestrian even, but this was the Lakes, where everybody was married, wholesome and normal.

'How long are you hanging around, Kelly Porter?' he asked eventually. 'Or are you heading back to the big city as soon as your mum's better?'

God, what had she told him? She smiled. 'Christ, I've got no idea. I'll see how the job goes.' A vague recollection of babbling on about her mother being unwell came back to her, and she felt uncomfortable: the paranoid anxiety

6

that alcohol brought with it the next day. It was true, her mother hadn't been feeling well lately, but she was sure she'd exaggerated it. She was fine really.

'Are you sure you need to go straight away?' Johnny pulled the covers back.

She walked over to the bed and began to undress.

Chapter 2

Kelly opened the door as quietly as she could. She felt like a naughty schoolgirl. She even removed her shoes so she could tiptoe in undetected.

When she'd first returned here, three weeks ago, her bedroom was exactly as it had been left when she'd gone off to university nearly twenty years earlier. She'd never come back, except for weekends and holidays.

The first thing she'd done was clear out the room. Old posters, books, and bits and pieces went into boxes in the loft. The space was tiny and she wondered how she'd managed as a teenager. Most of the stuff she'd accumulated during her time in London was left in suitcases under the bed. She asked her mum if she could paint the room.

'What's wrong with it as it is?' her mum replied.

'Nothing, it's just still pink.'

'And what's wrong with that? Your sister likes it; you know she always wanted that room.'

'I'm not Nikki, Mum.' While her sister had played with dolls and worn frills, Kelly had climbed trees and smoked fags with the boys. When her father had painted the room, she'd covered the walls with posters of Nirvana, Rage Against the Machine and the Red Hot Chili Peppers.

Mum didn't understand her music. 'Why don't you like ABBA?' she had asked. Nikki liked ABBA. Nikki *still* liked ABBA.

Now Kelly started for the stairs.

'Kelly?'

Her mother appeared from the kitchen holding a cup of tea and frowning. There was nowhere to hide in the tiny house, and they stood at opposite ends of the hallway that ran the full length of the house, from front door to kitchen.

'Where have you been? I've been worried sick. I got up this morning and went to take you a cup of tea and your bed hadn't been slept in. Why didn't you call?' Her mother's voice rose with each word.

'Mum, I'm not used to living with someone else and explaining my every move. I'm really sorry I made you worry. I'm fine, I just stayed over with a friend; it got late and we shared a bottle of wine.'

That look.

'I called your sister.'

'What? Why?' Kelly was livid. Any moment now, Joan of Arc would waft in with her brood of snot-covered kids and rescue her mother from her wayward, irresponsible daughter. 'You didn't need to do that! I'll call her.'

She rooted for her phone. She'd forgotten she'd switched it to silent in the pub. She had twenty-five missed calls from her mother. She needed to find her own place.

Nikki's phone went straight to voicemail, just as the door opened. Of course, Nikki had a key.

'Kelly, you're OK! Mum was worried sick, weren't you, Mum?'

'Of course I'm OK, I'm a grown-up now.' Kelly tried to smile.

'How about acting like one then?' Nikki fired the first shot.

'How about wearing less make-up?' Kelly responded.

'You're jealous!'

'Fuck off, Nikki.' They'd gone beyond reasonable conversation years ago and simply fired off insults whenever the opportunity arose, but it was always Kelly's fault, according to their mother. At least that was the impression she gave.

'Just stop it, you two! Why can't you be civil to one another?'

They both looked at their mother and hung their heads. Kelly was ashamed. Her mother didn't look right and she didn't know if it was tiredness, old age creeping in or something else. It was indisputable, though, that blazing rows wouldn't help.

'Go and have your fights elsewhere! Kelly, you've only been back five minutes.' She was the easier target because she never answered back, unlike Nikki, who poured honey-coated untruths into their mother's ear.

'Calm down, Mum. I'll go and make you a cup of tea,' Nikki soothed.

Kelly rolled her eyes. 'Like I said, Mum, I'm sorry I made you worry.' She went to her mother and hugged her, and all was forgiven, though no doubt Nikki would stay a while after Kelly left to highlight her errant ways in her absence. Kelly had stopped caring what her sister thought years ago.

She went upstairs heavily, closing her bedroom door behind her, wanting to slam it. She undressed, opened her wardrobe and sighed. She disliked work clothes: they made her feel awkward. She preferred her running gear, or just jeans and a jumper. She pulled on some tights and already imagined taking them off again after another day trussed up like a turkey. She fastened her skirt and tucked in her blouse, feeling like it was her first day at school, when her dad had taught her to do a tie properly on her own for the first time. 'It's too tight!' she'd complained. Her top button never stayed fastened for long.

She checked her make-up in the mirror. It was true, Nikki did wear too much. She looked trashy, like the friends she hung out with, all getting together and moaning about everything and nothing. Kelly reckoned that if Nikki ran out of things to whinge about, she'd write a letter to the council, and eventually the Queen. It baffled her that they were sisters. Nikki's wet dream would be to meet Robbie Williams; Kelly's was to do the Four Peaks Challenge in under twenty-four hours. Nikki wore five-inch heels even when she was giving birth; Kelly still wore the same trainers she'd had in uni. Nikki read Danielle Steele; Kelly read John Grisham. Nikki drove a Fiat; Kelly drove a BMW convertible.

It irritated Kelly that her mother had become primary carer for Nikki's kids. It irked her too that Nikki was advising Mum what to do with the money from Dad's life insurance, and that included taking her and her kids to Ibiza for two weeks. Even something as apparently insignificant as Nikki strutting around in a designer track-suit at the age of thirty-nine got under Kelly's skin, and already the pleasure of the morning was ebbing away.

At least when Dad was around, things were more even. Two against two. Mum wasn't used to making decisions

and taking responsibility, and it made her open to sugges-
tion. Kelly had persuaded her to put what was left of the
money into a bank account, and arranged an appointment
with an adviser to discuss how to invest it and make it pay,
rather than just spending it all. That had caused another
row, or more accurately, a series of insults hurled across
the room until Kelly left to go for a run. It didn't really
matter what she did or said: she was the outsider now, and
therefore easy to blame.

She needed to move out to avoid Nikki, but if she did,
she would leave Mum exposed and lonely. Her mother
had lost the sparkle in her eyes, and she rarely went out
other than to shop or take her grandchildren to the park.
Since her return, Kelly had forced her to go out. They'd
been for coffee and browsed the shops together in Ambleside looking for new walking gear for Kelly; they'd been to
the cinema; they'd cooked together, something Mum had
forgotten she enjoyed. In three short weeks, they'd created
an existence. That all changed when Nikki was around,
but there was very little Kelly could do about it. Nikki had
been here for Mum when Kelly hadn't, and her mother
wasn't a child; she had to make her own decisions. There
was only so much protection and distraction a daughter
could provide. It wasn't Kelly's home anymore; she was
a lodger with no privacy. Nikki could waltz in at any
moment and it made her gasp for air.

She went back downstairs and walked over to her
mum, ignoring her sister. 'I'm sorry, Mum. I'll let you
know what time I'll be home later, I promise,' she said.

'I'm making you a honey waffle, Mum,' shouted Nikki,
prancing towards the kitchen. Kelly sighed and left the
house.

Her black convertible looked out of place on the little street. No one gave it a second glance in London, where three Lamborghinis might be going past in the other direction, but that was the difference between her old life and her new one: perspective. She had to slow down and strip back to basics. The last thing she wanted was to come across as the hotshot from the city who thought she knew everything. She hadn't lost her northern lilt, so that worked in her favour. She belonged. Kind of.

So far, she'd taken it slowly and tried to get to know everyone. She was desperate to get stuck into her own cases rather than looking over someone else's shoulder as she learned new routines. Police work didn't really differ from force to force, but processes did, and she had to get used to them. She'd been patient, and over the last few weeks she'd become more independent. It felt like all she'd done was read case files, but now she'd come up with some solid strategies to move a few of them forward, and this morning she'd share those with the team. She was buzzing at the prospect.

She'd got to know the small squad at Eden House, and she liked them. The two young DCs, Emma Hide and Will Phillips, were hard workers, and DS Kate Umshaw was another solid and dependable local. It was always going to be quiet in an isolated provincial pod like Eden House, and there hadn't been much to do. She'd got used to using first names, except for those senior to her, of course. She'd also been introduced to a few of the better-known local scumbags, though nothing too heavy. The DI helping her transition was Richie Park, and already Kelly rated him. He'd been a detective for twenty years, and he threw instructions about as if he'd been hard-wired to the computer and all the data ever inputted into it. He was a solid operator, and not at all erratic. Kelly admired his discipline. A few times she'd caught herself yearning for a gritty case to get stuck into, but she'd had to rein herself in and realise that life would be different here.

It was a crisp autumn day and she could see all the way to Helvellyn from Penrith. That was a better view than a kebab stand and the smell of piss, she thought. The office wasn't far away and the traffic was non-existent; another bonus of leaving London. Maybe she'd go hiking this weekend.

Chapter 3

The office was quiet, but several of her colleagues were already busy checking emails and making notes. Kelly's last job had been as part of a murder squad of thirty-three officers. Here she'd virtually be on her own, with only her handful of detective constables to help out. But the change needn't be a negative one. She'd been lucky to sidestep to detective inspector and she'd been given a decent reference despite all the trouble in London.

'Morning.' She greeted her colleagues and took off her jacket.

DS Umshaw looked up from her desk. 'Morning, guv.'

As Kelly looked round, she realised that she appeared to be the last one in the office this morning. 'Was there an early meeting I wasn't aware of?' she asked DC Phillips.

'When there's a progress meeting at eight thirty, we all like to come in early to make sure there are no surprises,' he replied. Of course, she thought, impressed. She'd learned that meetings like this usually took place every couple of weeks, unless there was a major investigation on.

She went to the small kitchen to make coffee, and took it back to her desk, where she had a quick look at her emails before going next door to the main incident room.

DI Park opened proceedings. Like a lot of coppers, his voice was devoid of unnecessary emotion, reflecting the way he worked: consistent and dependable. The room was hot, an old heater belting out stifling air. Kelly was grateful for the warmth: she hadn't yet acclimatised to the significant difference in climate between the north and the south, and the temperature had dropped noticeably in the last few weeks.

They discussed several live cases, mostly burglaries and a smattering of assaults. She wanted to jump in, offer to take on the whole lot, but bit her tongue to stop herself. No one liked an over-keen newbie ruffling feathers. Soon she'd be standing in DI Park's shoes, as he was due to move to the Lancaster constabulary. She couldn't wait.

Her mind wandered to one particular new case she'd been given, to go along with a cold case she was working on. She couldn't help thinking about it when she should be concentrating on the meeting.

A baby had been abandoned outside the White Lion pub in Patterdale; they'd found the mother a mile away, curled up alongside a small package of clothes at the foot of a path leading to the old lead mine up past the wind turbines. Both had been taken to the Penrith and Lakes Hospital, where the mother was in a critical condition. The baby, whom the nurses had named Dale, after the beautiful valley in which he'd been found, was thriving, however. The problem was that the woman spoke no English and no one knew who she was or where she came from.

That was what Kelly had been discussing last night with Johnny, who'd been part of the rescue effort to find the mother. Although they'd suspected she might be close by, the fact that the baby had been abandoned near one of the major routes up to the popular Helvellyn range had set alarm bells ringing, and so the Patterdale Mountain Rescue had been called in as a precaution. Mountain rescue guys were all volunteers, and Kelly wondered now how Johnny supported himself. Her imagination fancied him a fugitive sitting on millions, but that was just for story books. She knew he'd been in the army, and so perhaps he had a decent pension.

DI Park interrupted her musings to ask her about her schedule for the day, and Kelly made her first contribution to the meeting. She spoke confidently, but it belied her slight nerves. Park was a decent guy and he'd babysat her somewhat up until now. She wanted to prove to him that she could be left alone. She also wanted to prove that she fitted in. He was off on leave in two days' time, and then she'd be on her own.

'Morning, everyone. I'm still on the cold case that I've been working, I also plan to go to the Penrith and Lakes Hospital at some point to interview the mother of baby Dale.'

Everyone knew the case: it was all over the local news and had even made the nationals. It was a big story but, despite its high profile, no one had come forward with information about who the woman might be. Initially the case hadn't sounded as though it merited the involvement of a DI, but Kelly concluded that Park was testing her. She'd need a few DCs to help out, so that would be her opportunity to make allies and also try out her new authority. 'I'd like to get a language expert in to see her, but she's not in a stable enough condition to be spoken to yet. She's still in shock and dehydrated. As soon as I find out where she's from, I can start to ask some questions.'

Her colleagues all nodded, and Park added the information to his iPad. They all carried them, protected by tough covers, as coppers were notorious for dropping them.

'She'll have to be arrested, but that can wait,' Kelly continued. Abandoning a minor was a criminal offence, which was why it had landed on the desk of a detective. It was her job to find out whether any other offence had been committed.

'As I said, I've also got the Lottie Davis cold case that's been reopened, and I'd appreciate anything you guys remember about it,' she concluded.

A heaviness settled on the room and a few officers bowed their heads. Ten-year-old Lottie Davis had gone missing from Haweswater five years ago. The family had been on a walk to spot golden eagles nesting there – the only ones in England. Haweswater was a dramatically isolated landscape of fells, bogs and heathland surrounding the lake itself, and the family hadn't sensed any danger. Her disappearance had led to one of the biggest public searches in UK history, with five hundred volunteers picking over the surrounding area, but they'd found nothing. The story had captured the hearts of the nation, keeping people glued to their TVs.

'I note here that the dad was a suspect for a while, but I thought he was out walking with them.'

'He was,' said Park. 'I wasn't on the case, but I gather it was more to do with his attempt to omit certain details that stalled the subsequent inquiry.'

'A lot of time was spent building a case against the father, but reading the file, the paedophile angle looks more promising. I'm looking into that, especially the ring in Liverpool: the Harry Chase lead,' said Kelly.

Park nodded. 'Take your time and get stuck in. The fact that the case remains unsolved after five years has frustrated everyone. Especially the mother, of course. She still lives in Ambleside. Merseyside are always helpful; they'll tell you everything you need to know about Chase. Wasn't there some con in prison bragging about it?'

'Yes, it says in the file that during searches for known, active and incarcerated paedophiles, they came across a prisoner in Strangeways who worked for Chase. He allegedly claimed that Lottie had been stolen "to order". The trail went dead, although Chase did serve two years of a four-year sentence for possession of indecent images. He was inside at the time of Lottie's disappearance, but that doesn't mean he didn't arrange it.'

'Wasn't the senior investigating officer at the time DCI Thomas?' Park asked.

'Yes, I've spoken to him. He's retired. That was his last case: not a great way to end a career.'

Everyone nodded in agreement. Lottie's body had been found a few weeks after her disappearance by a fell runner twenty miles away, near Ullswater. She'd been raped and strangled. There must have been a gold mine of forensics, but in the end, no one was ever charged. Kelly knew that she could spend hours looking for mistakes in the initial inquiry, but she had decided she'd rather investigate it with fresh eyes, treating it as a new case.

'Well, like I said, you've got everybody's support,' Park told her. 'It's a case I'd like to see closed.'

The meeting lasted another twenty minutes. Back at her desk, Kelly opened the file and looked at the photo of Lottie Davis. The girl would be sitting her GCSEs now. She made a note of the coroner's name and found his report on the computer.

It had taken three separate lab tests, and a lot of money, to finally isolate DNA on Lottie's body. The information exonerated the father, but it was too late: the suspicion had been too much and he killed himself the following year. Kelly looked up the mother's address in Ambleside. She fancied a drive; it would be good to get out of the office. She called ahead, and Jenny Davis told her she was available to see her this afternoon. Five years was a long time to a police department, but not to the mother of a brutalised child.

In London, Kelly's every move was accounted for, but here officers came and went as they needed to, as long as they informed their colleagues and kept HOLMES updated. The system had revolutionised police work, bringing consistency and compatibility to all forces across the country. Updated daily, sometimes hourly as an investigation moved forward, it had become indispensable.

Kelly packed her things and told Park where she was going. The team had turned their attention to their various tasks, and he had no problem with her being gone for most of the day. There was an absence of the competitive edge that had pervaded her job in London. She was used to the odd detective – usually male – strutting about like a peacock, decrying the flaws of the latest crime drama on TV and offering their own superior theories instead. Kelly wasn't above it. She'd followed the crowd to the pub to discuss cases and watched as old–timers waxed lyrical about legendary crimes. But it was different here.

She left the office and headed to the car park. Her convertible 1 Series would get her to Ambleside, but it'd be a liability on some of the passes, and would attract unwanted attention too. She loved the car dearly, but she knew that sooner or later she was going to have to trade it in for something reliable and sturdy – another thing to add to her shopping list. She dumped her bag on the passenger seat and entered the address into the satnav, then put the roof down.

The wind caught her hair and she turned heads as she sped along. Day trippers waiting for the steamers in Glenridding mulled about in the car park, and walkers trekked with sticks on their way to the countless trails around Patterdale. The area was one of her favourite places to hike: off the beaten track and not chokingly stuffed with tourists like the southern fells. From Patterdale, the whole Helvellyn range was accessible, and she could bag all the Wainwrights between Clough Head and St Sunday Crag in one day.

It had been a long time since she'd driven over the Kirkstone Pass, and she'd forgotten how the tiny inn at the top was hemmed in by rock and cloud in all directions. The isolated pub had been going in some form for five centuries, and a few walkers could be seen on the hills surrounding it, no doubt looking forward to a pint at the end of a long hike. She imagined what it'd been like five hundred years ago, stopping here to break the journey by horse and coach, and whether the monks were inclined to hospitality.

As the sun came out from behind a thick wall of white cloud, she took the road towards Ambleside and her thoughts turned to Jenny Davis. The woman had endured much; Kelly could hardly imagine the pain she must have suffered. She also wondered how Lottie's older brother had coped, losing his sister and then his father. The family had fallen apart.

She parked a little way from the address, ashamed of her car for some reason. It was as if she didn't want Mrs Davis to know that other people still had the sort of lives where they could drive around with the roof down. In her experience, victims' families suffered years of guilt, manifesting itself in the denial of any kind of pleasure. Joyless, that was how they seemed when she visited them. As if someone had inserted a tube and sucked away what made them human.

Kelly had read in the case file that the fell runner who found the girl had a solid alibi, but she'd still pay him a visit later. She needed to revisit every detail as if it was a new inquiry. He lived in Ambleside too, which could be a coincidence or not. As far as she could make out, his DNA had never been taken.

With any crime there was a window of time, known as the golden hour, that gave police the optimum opportunity to solve a crime. With murder, it was usually the first forty-eight hours. Details missed then could never be retrieved, and Kelly's mission was to work out which direction the original officers had gone in, and what had been overlooked. Someone had screwed up royally, and if she could unravel the mistakes and go back to the very beginning with Mrs Davis, perhaps she had a chance of solving the case.

Chapter 4

Gabriela Kaminski walked to her local post office, as she did on the twentieth day of every month. She couldn't afford to send much, but it helped her mother and her brother. Nikita wanted to know why he couldn't go to work in England too, but Gabriela would have none of it. She knew that she could find a ten-year-old boy work here in the UK; that was the easy part. Protecting him was a different matter. Her mother was tempted to send him over, but Gabriela made her promise not to. So far the promise had been kept.

Gabriela had enough on her hands as it was. She couldn't allow Nikita to come. It was out of the question. She'd just have to send more money. She earned five pounds per hour, and if she worked twelve-hour days, seven days a week, she could clear over four hundred pounds a week and send her mother close to a thousand pounds every month. She knew that she could earn more, but she couldn't bring herself to do what the last hotel manager had asked. He'd taken her out in his car for a drive around Windermere and she'd thought it fun, like a little holiday, until he'd touched her knee and offered her one hundred pounds just for one night.

By using her wits and her smile, as well as exaggerating the language barrier, she'd stalled him with promises, given herself enough time to go to her small, airless bedroom at the top of the hotel, pack the few possessions she had, then leave through the garden without him noticing. She'd been lucky. She'd gone to a hotel five miles away where she knew of others like her who worked in the shadows, paying no tax and doing what they were told. Her English was good and so she was a valuable asset front of house, where her neat appearance and pleasant manner fooled the tourists into thinking it was a respectable place. The Lakes was so full of foreign workers, it was hard to tell which were legitimate and which were not.

At the Troutbeck Guest House in Ambleside, she shared a room with two other Polish girls who, like her, were both nineteen. Her intention was to return home after the summer, when the season slowed. She'd have earned enough then to go to Art College. She'd come back again next year by the same route: a car from Lodz to Berlin and then train to Amsterdam, from where the groups of migrant workers hitched, usually through Calais but more recently Ostend. Brexit meant that the cash cow might come to an end at any moment, and she had to earn as much as she could before then. She didn't mind the menial work and long hours, but other girls were seduced by the promise of easy money. Some girls never came home. Some didn't have a choice.

Gabriela had rules: no drugs, no sex and no strangers. She only went places with people she knew, and she only took work by word of mouth. Instinct told her who to trust. She hadn't seen much of the local area, but she had seen enough to understand why people spent so much money here. There were hordes of Americans, Japanese,

Italians, Russians and Australians just dying to give away their cash. They tipped well, and Gabriela knew how to use her smile. It was true what they said about the English: they were the worst tippers and the most miserable of the lot; they were also the hardest employers. Her boss, Mrs Joliffe, exuded the air of someone who should never be crossed. Gabriela didn't mind: she knew where she stood, which suited her well. The hotel was small and the guests were mainly middle-aged couples. She saw very few children, but those she did see, she spoiled. They reminded her of her brother at home.

She thanked the woman behind the post office counter and made her way back to the guest house to begin her evening shift. When she'd first started the long sessions serving meals and cleaning bedrooms, her feet had ached all day long; now, she was used to it. She walked along the narrow street past tourists and hikers. It amused her that they called these pretty little hills mountains, and it made her miss the Slovak border, where she could stand on the summit of Gerlach and see all the way to the Baltic Sea. But it was a pretty little town none the less.

Her shift went by quickly, as always, and an American couple left a ten-pound note under a dish, which she slipped into her pocket. She didn't have a chance to thank them, but she'd catch them at breakfast. On the next table, a man in his fifties stared at her bottom and was chided loudly by his wife.

'Close your mouth, Derek,' she said, her accent crisp, like the Queen's. 'I don't know why we have to be served by people who can't even speak the bloody language.'

'Because, my dear, English people won't demean themselves to do service work any more,' retorted the

25

husband. 'And incidentally, I think her English is very good, certainly far better than your Polish.'

Gabriela hid her smile and the wife fumed. They left no tip.

'Gabriela, can you come to see me when you're done here, please. I have a proposition for you. Ten p.m. in my office.' It was a command not a request from Mrs Joliffe, and it made Gabriela nervous. Neither of her roommates had been at work for the last four days, and she assumed they'd taken some time off: a luxury indeed. It meant she had no one to turn to for advice.

She took a deep breath and willed herself calm. It was only a proposal; she needn't accept. Besides, it could be something as inoffensive as asking her to be a part-time receptionist. That would be nice.

'Of course, Mrs Joliffe,' she said.

She spent the rest of her shift worrying about what the woman could want with her. If she was in trouble, or had brought the guest house trouble in some way, she would just take off and not come back. Her hands shook slightly as she cleared her last table and went into the kitchen to tidy up.

Chapter 5

Just over half a mile away, one of Gabriela's roommates was sitting on top of a fat man in his seventies. He moaned and groped her small breasts as she rode him, and she was glad that she'd done a line of average-grade cocaine in his bathroom before they'd started. Her skin glistened and he grabbed her waist as she bounced up and down. It was bloody tough going, she thought; she'd spent twenty minutes sucking him off just to get a spark lit, and now she was getting sore. He pulled at her nipples and she pretended to enjoy it.

'Oh yes… yes…'

She felt him get a little harder and thanked God for small mercies; maybe it would be over soon. She'd seen his little blue pills beside the bed and hoped he'd taken two. She'd get two hundred quid for this evening's efforts. It was worth every penny.

That new girl was an idiot, she decided, her mind wandering. Why would you serve meals all day when one fuck could earn you ten times the money? Little Miss Perfect, they called her. Well, she'd have to get her hands dirty at some point; no one stayed clean forever.

The exertion was like a workout. Come on, old boy, she thought. He was a sweet man, and a regular. He also paid her cut to Darren. If Darren found out, he'd kill her, but she knew that Mr Day would never tell. The old man had bought her a diamond necklace and she'd got four hundred quid for it at a jeweller's in Kendal. Today he'd given her some pearl earrings, though they wouldn't be worth as much.

Her English was improving, just not in the way her mother imagined. Maybe she wouldn't go back to Poland. Darren could be aggressive, but not if she did as she was told. He'd told her that once she'd proved herself, he'd take her to a big party where loads of rich men paid to have a pretty girl on their arm, but that she had to be ready; he had a reputation to uphold.

Mr Day stopped thrusting.

Anushka looked at him. His mouth was open, gasping for air, and his hand clutched at his chest. She slipped off him and rushed to the bathroom to get a glass of water. As she came back into the bedroom, her hands were shaking and water spilled from the glass. Mr Day looked panic-stricken and she felt an urge to flee, but at the same time she knew that she should try and help him. She suddenly became aware of her nakedness, and she grabbed a jumper from a chair and threw it on. The old man was making rasping noises and trying to speak. She knelt next to him and helped him sip some water, but he began to cough and his breathing worsened. She touched his brow; it was cold and clammy. He slumped against her and she recoiled, her heart pounding in her chest. Then his eyes widened and he began convulsing, as if fighting for life itself.

He was dying. Right in front of her, of all the fucking times to do it. She pushed him away and stood up, looking around the room as if that would give her answers. 'Always clean up after yourself,' Darren had instructed her. She bent over Mr Day, who was no longer moving, removed the condom from the end of his flaccid penis and put it into her handbag. She looked at his face for a fleeting moment. His eyes were wide and staring, accusing her. The realisation only galvanised her, and she hardened her resolve once more.

She picked up the Viagra, the baby oil and the feathers she'd used to arouse him, and quickly got dressed, throwing the old jumper into her bag as well; he wouldn't need it any more. A laptop on the table caught her eye: it could be worth something, she thought, grabbing it and putting it on the floor while she continued her search. The noise of his breathing had stopped and Anushka didn't need to be a medic to work out that he was probably dead already. She rifled through his jacket and found a huge roll of cash, which she placed in her own pocket. She opened drawers and saw some car keys, which she left, and a ruby ring. Jackpot. It reminded her of the rings rich Russian ladies wore back home. Finally she leant over Mr Day's corpse and removed his Rolex.

She sprayed herself with deodorant, put on her coat and found her phone. She desperately wanted a shower, but first she called Darren.

'Nush? What's up?'

'It's Mr Day, Darren. I think he's had a heart attack.' She felt a little sick as she said the words out loud, and she wondered how quickly she could replace him with someone as generous.

'What the fuck! You rode him too hard!' Darren laughed, and Anushka felt stupid and very alone.

'Nush? Nush? You there?' He was serious now.

'Yes,' she said quietly.

'OK, I'll sort it. Fuck, this is the last thing I need tonight. I'll get over there myself to clear up.'

'Are you going to move him?' Anushka felt a wave of panic travel upwards from her abdomen.

'What the fuck else am I supposed to do? You fucked him to death, I can't have anything leading to you, because that would lead to me, and I'm not sure you would keep your pretty little mouth shut. Like I said, I'll clear up, but Nush?'

'Yes?' She knew what was coming.

'If I hear one word, I'll slit your throat.' He hung up.

He didn't mean it, she was sure. He just enjoyed scaring her.

Anushka gathered the stolen items and left the room without looking back, her mouth very dry. If Darren was planning to clear up, that meant he wanted to make it look like it had never happened, and that was a good thing because it protected her. But she'd also compromised him, and that wasn't so good. She'd just heard him say that he was going to get rid of a body, as cool as that, and that must mean he'd done it before, many times.

There was no one around as she headed towards the hotel exit; there never was in this place, except the odd girl like her. She was still wearing her whore kit under her clothes – crotchless pants and a bra with nipple holes in it, hold-up stockings that were now ripped, and stiletto heels – and she felt dirty and cheap. She stank of baby-oil-fuelled sex. She pulled her coat tighter around her, holding on to the laptop as if that would give her some comfort, and put her head down as she clacked along the pavement. Thank God it was dark.

She used the back entrance of the guest house and found her room deserted. She had no idea where Roza was. She'd had a job yesterday in the same hotel but she hadn't been back since and Nush was getting worried. She'd have to speak to Darren about it.

She quickly undressed and stuffed the dirty clothes into a laundry bag, then stepped into the shower and stood for a long time under the warm stream. Her nipples stung and she was sore between her legs. She scrubbed her nails and brushed her teeth, wanting to remove all traces of Mr Day. She couldn't help wondering what Darren would do with his body. What about his wife? He had grandchildren too; he'd spoken to her of them. She felt overwhelmed.

The reality of what she was doing assaulted her, and fear washed over her. She was playing a dangerous game, in a foreign country, with men she didn't know. She'd found herself here in pursuit of a new life, that was all. But it hadn't gone to plan. Sure, she was luckier than most in the sense that she hadn't been forced here and held against her will like so many she'd heard about. She fancied that she was in charge, she called the shots, and she alone decided who she slept with. But she was getting deeper and deeper, and she doubted if she had what it took to keep men like Darren off her case. She thought of her mother, and how far she was from the girl who'd waved goodbye seven months ago.

She stepped out of the shower and wrapped a towel around herself, sinking to the bathroom floor. She stayed there for a long time, head on her knees, wishing she was someone else, somewhere else.

—

After taking Anushka's panicked call, Darren Beckett had become engrossed in a new game he'd bought for his Xbox. He smoked more weed and looked at his watch occasionally, promising himself that after the next assassination on the screen, he'd leave for Ambleside to clear up after the girl.

When he woke, it was morning, and by then it was too late. A cleaner had entered Mr Day's room to perform her morning duties and found him dead on the bed, just where Anushka had left him. The police had been called and were on their way.

–

Anushka was working the breakfast shift in place of Roza, who still hadn't returned, when she heard the siren whizz past the hotel. It made her jump as she served kippers to a Japanese couple, and a wave of nausea overcame her. Unable to stop herself, she projectile-vomited into the woman's kippers, and again onto the floor. Guests stared aghast as the sick dripped off the table. Anushka fled the room.

The Japanese woman froze with her hands in the air and her husband began standing up and sitting down, as if part of some rhythmically challenged freak show. Gabriela ran over to their table and began apologising and trying to clear up the disgusting mess with towels. She assumed Anushka had a hangover. It was common for her roommates to spend the night out, and she suspected both of giving in to the temptation of dirty money. They'd get them all kicked out. Mrs Joliffe would be livid.

–

Out on the road, Constables Martin and Coombs used the blues for effect. The guy was already dead, but they didn't get to stop traffic often and they wanted to secure the scene. The medics were already there and had pronounced life extinct, but no one could speculate about cause until the scene had been sealed and processed by forensics.

Colin Day was well known in these parts, and the gossip would start quickly. He'd been mayor ten years ago, and had personally overseen the sponsorship that had led to the new visitors' centre and the development of the waterside promenade along part of Windermere. He was a governor at King Charles Secondary School and appeared regularly in the *Westmorland Gazette* fund-raising for various charities. On top of all that, he was a reputable hotel owner and had made a name for himself running a series of tanning salons across Cumbria – an all-round good guy.

Martin and Coombs parked on double yellows. A small crowd had gathered. They entered the Thwaite Hotel and were met by the manager, who introduced himself as Kevin Cottrell. His hands shook and his face was white; the constables doubted he'd seen a dead body before.

'How many guests are staying at the hotel at the moment?' Coombs asked.

'Mr Day was our only guest,' Cottrell replied.

The officers looked at one another. A Lakes hotel with one guest was unheard of. Coombs made a note, his suspicions roused.

'Have you any bookings due to check in today?' he asked.

'No, sir.' The manager looked decidedly uncomfortable and Coombs added to his notes.

'The cleaner is still here, yes?'

'Yes, she is. She's in the kitchen having a cigarette. I bent the rules on this occasion.' Cottrell tried a smile.

Martin turned to Coombs and nodded, understanding passing between them. They'd worked together for four years and used a series of signals that would baffle most people.

'I'll come with you to see her,' Martin told the manager.

'And I'll go to the room,' Coombs said.

Martin took out his pad so they could compare notes later and produce a comprehensive report for the crime unit; should it turn out to be a crime, of course. At this stage, their minds had to be open. Cottrell stood awkwardly between the two officers.

'You can show me the room first,' Coombs said. Cottrell was thankful for something to do, and hurried upstairs with Coombs close behind him. The hotel was a little run down, and Coombs noted that it could do with a few quid spent on it. He wondered if Mr Day was struggling for money. He also wondered why he was staying in a hotel when everyone knew he owned a luxurious pad of his own. Maybe things weren't right at home.

He sent Cottrell back downstairs before entering the room. A forensics officer greeted him. Colin Day lay on the bed; he looked as if he was asleep. Coombs had seen dead bodies before and he wasn't overly fazed. It was always a shame, no matter who they were. The guy was naked and the forensics officer walked around the bed, looking for injuries or signs of foul play, while another officer searched the room. Coombs guarded the door and watched.

After a few minutes, the second forensics officer beckoned to his colleague. He had found a small old-fashioned video camera on top of the wardrobe, pointing towards the bed. The red light indicated that it was switched on but out of battery, and Coombs wondered if it had been used recently, and why.

Chapter 6

At the Penrith and Lakes Hospital, a female police officer guarded the room of the young woman found near Greenside lead mine. The woman, who looked to be in her early twenties, had been put on intravenous fluids and had undergone a blood transfusion. The hospital had confirmed to the police that she was definitely recently post-partum, but her blood, as well as that of baby Dale, had been sent to be tested for a match.

Meanwhile Dale continued to thrive and delight the maternity ward. He had a mass of black hair and fed greedily from the bottle. In two days he'd gained four ounces already.

'I'm taking him home,' one of the nurses said.

'No you're not, I am,' another retorted.

A few reporters remained outside, hoping to move their story along. Most of them were local, but a few nationals were also interested, more in the mother than in Dale. For Carl Bradley, reporter for the *Manchester Evening Star*, the story could turn into the scoop that might get him noticed. He'd managed to get inside the hospital posing as a visiting relative and had been astounded at the lack of security. Of course, he couldn't get access to the mother, but he could work out who the female nurses were and accidentally be in the same pub after work. Carl was a player, and he'd found the perfect profession for it: give a woman the right attention and she soon opened her mouth as well as her legs.

After a few goes, he'd found Tania. Apart from having large eyes and full lips, Tania had attended the mother on several occasions, and after a few white wines in Wetherspoon's on Southend Road, where all the medical staff seemed to gather, she was only too happy to tell him what she knew. The nurses were like a tribe and obvious to spot. The girls who lived in the hospital residences were the easiest: freshly moved out of mummy and daddy's and looking for some independence, only too happy to let a stranger pay for a few drinks in turn for a cheeky kiss. Carl wagered that Tania might offer more than a kiss, and he'd chivalrously oblige, because he was that kind of guy.

The story was potentially bigger than he'd first thought. The young woman didn't appear to understand English and babbled in some foreign language that the nurses couldn't tell from Swahili. Everyone had an opinion: some said French, others Italian.

'Haven't they had a language expert in?' Carl asked casually.

'Don't ask me, I wouldn't know. There's so many different languages spoken on the ward as it is, I wouldn't notice if it was an expert or a cleaner.' It seemed to be beyond Tania's faculties to appreciate that it was foreign workers that kept the NHS afloat. 'God, they're everywhere, aren't they? Hotels, McDonald's, pubs, buses; you can't go anywhere now and hear an English voice. It's disgusting. It's not too bad in here, though,' she conceded, gesticulating to the bar staff, who were mainly British students.

'Well, I'm in modern foreign languages at Lancaster University, so I can't really say much, can I?' Carl lied easily.

Tania was instantly impressed. 'So are you a professor or something? I thought they were old and boring.' She giggled.

'I am indeed a professor. Does that put you off?' He smiled and held her gaze. Tonight was probably going to be the night, and as long as he didn't expect Shakespeare from the girl and kept his expectations low, he was confident he'd be able to perform.

'No, I'm not used to it, that's all. You speak all fancy. Can you say something in French, 'cause that's dead romantic, isn't it?' She giggled again.

'Let me see, what would you like me to say?'

'Something nice.' Her leg moved towards his and he knew that she'd already made the decision to ask him to her room tonight.

'*Vous avez beau seins mais malheureusment pas de cerveau,*' he said, with a perfect accent. His mother was half French and he'd attained an A grade at A level at the age of sixteen. They holidayed in France every year.

'What does that mean?' she asked.

'It means I'd like to get to know you better.'

'Wow, it's lovely. Will you say something else?'

'Maybe later. It's a pity, I'm sure I could help that girl.' Carl looked away.

'What do you mean?'

'Well, if they don't even know where she's from, how can they contact her family? They'll be worried sick. I bet I could work it out, if only I could hear her voice, but I'm sure no one will think of that.' He sipped his pint.

'Wait a minute!' she said excitedly. 'Listen, I could record her on my phone, she's always babbling about something.' Tania was thrilled that she'd come up with a clever idea to impress this intriguing stranger who threw his money around like he had a lot more.

'I don't know, Tania. I wouldn't want you to get into any trouble. It'd be easy enough to do, but what if you got caught?'

She rose to the challenge. 'Of course I won't get caught, no one will ever know, and then if you do recognise the language I can say that I heard something similar on a film.' She beamed.

'That would work, wouldn't it? And it can't hurt anyone, only help her. I'm writing a special paper on the common foreign languages present in the UK, and it'd be an excellent contribution,' he said, as much like a professor as he could manage.

'Would I get a special mention?' Her leg moved closer still until it was touching his, very lightly.

'I'm sure I could manage that. Now, can I get you another drink, or would you like me to walk you home?'

Tania looked at her watch and pretended to be coy, for a second.

'That's so cute of you. I don't live far. Maybe you could pop in for a drink?' she said.

Later, as Carl pretended to sleep, Tania padded to the bathroom. He hoped that his efforts would soon pay off. She wasn't shabby in bed, but she was pedestrian and very noisy. It didn't take much to feign sincerity, but he didn't want to be doing this every night. He needed a story and quickly, before someone else got it.

She slid back in behind him and her hand drifted over his side and down to his floppy penis, which she started to stroke. He was in two minds: continue to fake deep sleep or have another go. He decided that it wouldn't hurt to give the girl what she wanted, and he lazily rolled over to face her. He encouraged her to sit on top and she was hesitant at first, but she soon got the hang of it and it was a lot better than the first time.

The research for this piece might not be so bad after all.

Chapter 7

'So, you saw Mr Day yesterday afternoon?' Constable Martin asked. He was interviewing the cleaner who'd come across the unfortunate sight of Colin Day's lifeless body.

The girl nodded.

'At what time was that?'

'It was around four o'clock. I took his post to him.' She was like a frightened little bird.

'Post? He lived here?' he asked.

The girl knew she'd made a mistake but didn't know how to respond. Martin witnessed her shift in demeanour.

'He… he stayed here a lot and some of his post came here.'

Martin scribbled notes.

'Did anyone else come to the hotel yesterday?' he asked.

The girl looked at him and decided to lie.

'I didn't see anyone.'

'So, what are your hours here?' He was digging because he knew she was lying. He knew instinctively that the case would make its way to a detective at some point, and he wanted to get as much out of this girl as he could, given that it was becoming clear that she was perhaps the last person to see Colin Day alive. The guy might have simply keeled over and died, but there again, perhaps he hadn't.

The girl relaxed a little at such a trivial question, and one she could answer honestly.

'I clean in the morning from seven until ten and I'm available to work extra if I'm asked.'

'Who requests extra hours?'

'Mr Cottrell.'

'And what might those extra hours involve?'

The girl swallowed. 'More cleaning.' She thought of the ledgers in the office that she'd seen, and the envelopes of cash. She'd never asked any questions. She knew she wasn't in the employment of a clean establishment, but that wasn't her concern. Her priority was holding down a job long enough for her mother to believe that she hadn't brought a useless waste of space into this world.

'And part of that is taking Mr Day his post?'

Anna nodded.

'Why doesn't the manager take care of it?'

'Erm, I don't know, he asked me to do it,' she said.

'Thank you, Miss...' Martin checked his notes, 'Cork. I'll just take your phone number and address, please, in case you're needed in the future.'

He let her go and went upstairs to the room in which Colin Day had died.

Coombs was standing in the doorway and raised his eyebrows. 'Forensics found a camera up there on the wardrobe, pointing towards the bed. It's been bagged and tagged but they had a look first,' he said quietly.

'Anything on it?' Martin asked.

42

'Just the whole thing. He didn't die alone. Looks like he had a heart attack brought on by a great shag. She panicked and cleaned up.'

'Fucking hell!' Martin sniggered. 'Lucky bastard, what a way to go. Was she fit?'

'I didn't see it, but from their faces I'm guessing it wasn't his wife.' Coombs winked.

'Big story coming for the *Westmorland Gazette* then.'

'Yup.'

The forensics officers were busy bagging the body. A vehicle was on its way to take it for a post-mortem, to find out exactly what had killed Colin Day. Martin thought the room looked like some kind of secret lab for infectious diseases, with labelled plastic bags and technical equipment everywhere.

'We need the entrance secured, and let's get the other rooms checked. My guess is the place is a front for something else,' said Coombs.

–

Anushka stood on the opposite side of the street from the hotel, smoking a cigarette. She wore dark glasses and had her hood pulled up, concealing her mass of red hair. She saw the two police officers in the doorway and looked away. A crowd had gathered and two men who looked like reporters were asking the cops questions. She had to get away. She didn't want to go to Darren, but she had little choice. She didn't trust him but she also knew that if she disappeared, he would come looking. She was puzzled. Darren had said he was cleaning up last night, so she didn't understand what had attracted the attention of the police. If he had got rid of Mr Day's body, there would be no reason for anyone to suspect something was amiss. She toyed with the idea that there was an entirely separate explanation for the police being there, but her gut told her otherwise.

She walked quickly back to the Troutbeck. She'd already packed her bag. Panic set in and she took the stairs two at a time. Gabriela was waiting for her.

'Anushka, are you all right?'

'I'm fine. I've quit.'

'Did you tell Mrs Joliffe?'

'No, I didn't tell Mrs Joliffe, and if you know what's good for you, you'll tell her you haven't seen me since breakfast.'

Gabriela stopped breathing. Anushka was a slight girl, but her eyes were mean and Gabriela had no idea what she was capable of. Whatever she was caught up in – whatever her reasons for leaving – was none of her business. She stood aside and watched as her roommate collected the large holdall from her bed.

'Have you seen Roza?' Anushka asked aggressively.

'No,' Gabriela said. The question came as a shock to her; she'd assumed the two girls were together.

'Just say one word to Joliffe, and...' Anushka threatened. She took a step towards Gabriela, seeming to tower over her.

Gabriela nodded, her heart pounding in her chest.

'Tell Roza this if she comes back,' Anushka ordered. Gabriela waited. 'Darren.'

'Right.'

'And remember, Miss Perfect. I know you're illegal too.'

Anushka left the room and Gabriela sat heavily on her bed. She could make no sense out of anything her roommate had said, and nor did she want to. She remembered what had happened at breakfast. Maybe Anushka was pregnant. People threw up when they were pregnant, she thought. Of course, that was it. But if that was the case, why did she jump when she heard the police siren?

She needed some air, so she left the hotel and headed along the street in the direction the siren had been going. She was officially in between shifts, so she had time. A small crowd had gathered outside the Thwaite Hotel and a body bag was being loaded into a white van outside. Gabriela stared at the van, then turned and hurried back. Mrs Joliffe would want to know what had happened at breakfast, and that one of her waiting staff had disappeared. Gabriela didn't know who she was more scared of: Mrs Joliffe or Anushka. Last night, despite being offered a new role by her employer, Gabriela still felt fearful when in her presence; the woman reminded her of the armed guard at home. On the other hand, Anushka had threatened her directly. She decided to avoid her boss until she had time to clear her head. Her pace quickened as she reached the Troutbeck. She slipped in the staff entrance to the rear, and skipped up the stairs to her room.

Chapter 8

Ambleside was quiet at this time of year, with only a few tourists still strolling around its shops and walkers updating their gear. The houses in the row were identical, apart from the way the gardens were tended. Jenny Davis clearly liked to garden. Perhaps it was therapy. A blue VW Polo sat in the driveway. The area wasn't affluent, but it was clean and tidy. Birds chirped as Kelly approached the door and she kept expecting an ambulance or fire engine to burst into life at any moment. She was unaccustomed to the peace.

She was ready. She'd done it many times before. Being a woman, she was often asked to attend family notifications and tricky interviews. She had a reputation for being able to gauge the correct amount of empathy and balance it with digging. Questions whirled around her head, but they weren't questions for Mrs Davis. She'd begun the process of unravelling this case and it was leading her off on countless tangents, every one of which would need pursuing.

Lottie had been dumped when her body gave out. She'd been someone's plaything. That was why, when Kelly was reviewing the case files, she had begun to think that the girl might have been abducted to order, like the con had claimed. It was well planned. Getting a ten-year-old away from her loving family was a potentially impossible task, and very risky. A child of that age was old enough to know it was wrong, and strong enough to put up a decent scrap.

Kelly expected Mrs Davis to want to talk for a long period of time. Murder, like cancer, was a taboo, and sex crime even worse. She doubted the woman would ever be able to really let go, though she hoped she was wrong. She would let her talk for as long as she wanted and would write a report later in the car while it was fresh. She'd take some notes in front of Mrs Davis, but primarily she wanted to make her feel relaxed, encourage her to open up. Some of the most valuable information she'd ever had from witnesses had been garnered without them really thinking about their responses, because she'd disarmed them. But it was difficult to do properly. She'd have to tread carefully.

She rang the doorbell. The woman who opened the door had a soft smile. 'I'm guessing you're Kelly?' Her tone was gentle and calm.

'And you must be Mrs Davis,' Kelly said.

'Call me Jenny, please. Come in. Can I get you a cup of tea? I've made a cake, Penrith is a long way to drive; you must be peckish.'

Northern hospitality, thought Kelly. Tea and cake. Penrith wasn't actually far, but to someone unaccustomed to sitting on the M25 for hours, it might well seem a long way. Jenny Davis's warmth made Kelly sad. She should be the one being looked after, not the other way around.

She entered the house and found herself in a small, well-kept lounge. A large portrait of Lottie hung over the gas fire. It was probably two feet wide and almost three high. It dominated the room, and Kelly was drawn strongly to it. The photograph was posed, and the girl sat slightly sideways on, smiling for the photographer, who'd probably said something silly to make her laugh. She wore what looked like a school uniform: a smart grey pinafore, under a red cardigan. Her eyes were wide. She had a few teeth missing and that, along with the plumpness of her cheeks, made her innocence inescapable. Kelly felt a knot in her tummy as she remembered the autopsy report.

'That's beautiful, Jenny,' she said.

'Thank you. She was.' Jenny disappeared and Kelly stood waiting for her, mesmerised by the image. There was no doubt what this woman thought about every day as she pottered around the house, nor what anyone coming here was faced with.

She came back into the room with a tray and insisted Kelly sit down. She placed a piece of cake on a plate and put it down next to Kelly on a small table. Kelly waited for her to start.

'I'm glad the case is being looked into again. I always knew it wasn't Ian. It drained the life from him before he killed himself. We could never understand why the policeman in charge kept hounding him.' Jenny's mouth moved but her eyes didn't; she was barely living inside the cage she'd been put into by monsters desperate for sex with a minor and willing to risk everything for it. Her face became unmoving and wax-like when she spoke of her daughter.

Kelly took a bite of her cake, it was delicious. She swallowed.

'I can see from the files that the initial investigation concentrated on your husband, but there are many other

48

leads to follow and I'd really like to go back to the beginning. I want to start again.'

Jenny's eyes softened a little.

'Can you remember who knew you were going eagle-spotting at Haweswater that day?'

The question caught the woman a little off guard, and she paused to think about it. If Kelly wanted fresh information, she had to choose lines of enquiry that would be new to Mrs Davis, and this clearly was. But it shouldn't have been.

'My mother knew, I'd told her the night before on the phone. Lottie and Charlie might have told their friends.' Kelly scribbled notes.

'And who might your mother have mentioned it to? Also, can you remember who Lottie and Charlie's close friends were at the time?'

'Well, my brother, Dennis, lived with Mum then, so he'd have known because she likes to chatter. In fact, he did know because he wanted to come with us, but he couldn't because he was working. Lottie's best friend was Kiera, and Charlie is still best friends with Josh.'

'Perfect, thank you. Could you give me their addresses, please, including your mum's and your brother's?'

Jenny dictated from memory. Her mother lived three streets away, but her brother lived in Barrow-in-Furness. Kelly's heart sank. She'd be treading on South Lakes turf; it was a courtesy to tell them, but she didn't know anyone there. She'd have to spend more time digging for a contact.

'How is Charlie?' she asked. The boy would be eighteen years old now.

Jenny looked at the portrait of her dead daughter and struggled with the question. 'He's... better. He's quiet.

He… We both had a lot of help but Charlie couldn't…
You see, he was old enough to understand but not old
enough to cope…' Her voice tapered off.

'But you say he's better now?' Kelly asked.

'Yes, my mother helps a lot and he spends quite a lot of
his time there, although he's just started at York university,
studying English.' Jenny beamed: a ray of sunshine to cut
through the piles of shit.

'That's a fantastic achievement. York is an excellent
university, he'll have a great time. He must have a lot of
courage,' Kelly said.

'Yes, he has got courage, he's a strong boy.' Jenny
looked at the portrait again. 'Lottie was strong, too. I'll
never understand why she let herself be taken away from
us. She would have kicked and screamed, I know she
would… I'm sorry.' Tears emerged at the corners of
Jenny's eyes and began to fall down her face gently.

'Please don't be sorry, Jenny. I can't begin to imagine
the pain you have been through. Take your time. I get the
impression from you that she wasn't the type to wander off
or talk to strangers?' Kelly spoke softly and made another
note. She waited as Jenny composed herself and wiped her
eyes with a tissue from her pocket.

'No, never. She was a wise ten-year-old. That's why
I always knew she'd been taken by force, yet we heard
absolutely nothing.' She sniffed.

'You didn't hear a car?'

Jenny thought carefully.

'The RAF jets were practising – Ian named every one
of them. Then Charlie started calling Lottie's name. We
all laughed and thought she was hiding. They played hide-
and-seek all the time.'

'Jenny, from the moment the jets went over to the point where you became worried and started looking for Lottie – can you tell me how long you think that period was? Take as long as you need.' Kelly took a sip of tea and another bite of cake. She wanted to come across as normal as possible.

Jenny closed her eyes. When she looked up, her gaze was focused, clear and determined.

'At least twenty minutes.'

'Were you asked this question at the time?'

'No, definitely not.'

'Do you think your brother might be home, Jenny? It seems a waste of time to go all the way back to Penrith when I could carry on to Barrow.' Kelly was enjoying being out of the office, having her own paths to follow.

'I'll give him a call now.' Jenny picked up the phone. 'Den, it's Jenny... Yes. Fine, fine. Look, I've got the police here, they're looking into Lottie's case again... I know, I'm very happy too. They need to go over a few things, so could they come over to yours if you're about?... OK. All day?' She mouthed that her brother was about to leave for work; Kelly mouthed back that she could talk to him there.

'They can come to the pub... You're not working at the pub? Why, Den?... Again? All right, well where are you working now?... Right, OK Den, it'll be after that. Yes, see you later, bye.'

Jenny looked at Kelly. 'He's working on a building site on Walney Island. It's easy to find. I'll write it down, or... I could come with you?'

Kelly could see that the woman desperately wanted the distraction.

'Of course, come with me.'

Chapter 9

Chief Coroner Ted Wallis was standing over the cadaver of an old friend. He guessed this would become a more frequent occurrence as time passed and associates came to the end of their lives. Would he autopsy all of his loved ones before he himself finally died? He noticed that he was becoming closer in age to many of his dead subjects on a daily basis, and it unsettled him.

Apparently the old goat had gone happy. Only a fellow autumnal traveller would understand the joy of dying in such a manner. It didn't really matter who the girl was, just that his last thought had been one of pert breasts and smooth skin slipping over his own. Lucky bastard. But then he thought of Christine, Colin's wife.

Ted himself had recently mustered up the courage to tell his own wife that their thirty-year marriage was over. She'd wailed and smashed bottles of sherry but she'd done nothing that he hadn't expected. He'd moved out of their family home and into a flat in Carlisle. It was clean, small and very quiet. Now his usual torpor, signalled by a frequent sigh and sagging shoulders, had gone, and his gait was sprightly once more.

He adjusted his headset and examined the corpse externally. Nothing seemed out of the ordinary for a man of seventy-five. Colin had had good teeth and a full head of hair, though Ted reckoned he was fifty pounds overweight and predicted he'd find a heart clogged with atherosclerosis – a time bomb. He took samples of blood and looked under the nails. Forensics had bagged a wealth of treasure and he wondered if anything would be left for him before the cadaver was washed and presented back to the family. There was an oily substance under most of the nails and he took scrapings, being careful to bag and tag each one for analysis. From in between the third and fourth fingers on the left hand, tangled in Colin's wedding ring, he tweezed out several long red hairs. The fibres were unusually red: either hair dye or another type of fibre altogether. A small red scratch caught his eye underneath the chest hair, and he measured and photographed it. It looked to him like a wound inflicted by a human nail, but it could have been caused by any number of things. It was his job to be as thorough as possible without bias; it was up to the detectives to decide what was important.

Happy with the external examination, he made a Y incision from clavicle to clavicle and down towards the belly button. Great layers of fat sprang out around the scalpel; he'd have to get through those before revealing the organ cavity. The notes on the deceased stated that he was suffering from advanced type 2 diabetes mellitus, and there was little doubt as to its cause. In the later stages of the disease, if the patient did not modify their lifestyle and follow precise medication pathways, heart disease became more and more likely.

After sawing the ribcage open, he cracked each rib with a satisfying snap to reveal the vital organs. He noticed the liver first: it was huge, probably almost three times its normal weight; it was also an unhealthy yellow, rather than the usual copper colour. He glanced at his notes. Colin's last blood test had shown abnormal enzyme levels, indicating poor liver function. It might have been alcohol-induced; he wouldn't know that until he cut it open.

The lungs appeared fairly healthy from the outside, as did the intestines he could see. Evisceration took a long time, and he noticed the unusual weight of the organ sac. He weighed it and left it on the side for his assistant to photograph while he examined the cavity left behind. All seemed normal there, so he turned his attention to the organs, one by one.

It didn't take long to find the cause of death: myocardial infarction caused by a sudden lack of blood to the heart. Now he had to investigate whether the lack of blood was caused by a gradual closing of a blood vessel or a sudden clot of plaque breaking away and preventing blood flow. As he sliced through the coronary artery, which would normally be the diameter of a pencil, he saw that it was completely occluded. Bingo. Without doubt, the cause of Colin Day's demise was coronary heart disease. Of course, heart attacks were survivable, but not this one. Ted wondered who Colin's GP was, and if the old man had taken any notice of the warnings he'd doubtless been given.

He left part two of the autopsy report blank until he heard back from toxicology and histology, because there were no obvious secondary findings. His assistant helped him rearrange the organs inside the cavity – minus the bits and pieces for further investigation under a microscope – and then Ted stitched the cadaver back up. When he had finished, it looked like Colin Day again: an overweight but extremely happy man.

He didn't blame the girl, whoever she was. His notes said that the heart attack had happened during coitus, but he couldn't help wondering what her side of the story was. It was human nature to ponder such things. One thing was for sure: whoever it was, it wasn't Colin's wife. Christine was in a wheelchair and had been for ten years. The local press were going to have a field day.

Chapter 10

Tania unlocked the front door of the nurses' block and Carl followed her in. She giggled as he squeezed her bottom.

'Stop it!' she squealed, unconvincingly.

'How can I stop it? You can't see what I can, but it's begging to be squeezed, like the rest of you.' He stopped her in the corridor and pinned her against the wall. His hands travelled quickly to her breasts and he lifted up her blouse.

'Carl! Wait!' She ran towards her flat and he followed. She'd made the recording and it was on her phone. He was about to get an exclusive.

Once they were inside, she dropped her bag and began taking her clothes off, moving just far enough away so he couldn't touch her.

'Tease,' he said, and smiled. 'OK, I'll just watch.' He sat on the sofa and lay back, she'd grown in confidence and he was genuinely turned on. Her coat fell to the floor and she started unbuttoning her blouse. Her skin was smooth and his erection struggled against his pants. She slid off her jeans, then came to him and unzipped his trousers, tugging them down along with his boxers.

She knelt down and kissed his balls, then slid her tongue all the way up until he was fully inside her mouth.

She was good. No teeth. He felt as though his balls would explode but tried to keep it going. He stopped breathing and all he could feel was the purest pleasure from what she was doing with her mouth. She went a little faster and his head throbbed. He had to come, it was too good an opportunity; he'd make it up to her later.

'I'm going to come, Tania.' It was her last chance. She didn't stop. Good girl, he thought.

He came into her mouth, pulsating over and over again. He only realised he was sweating when he began to breathe again. She swallowed.

'That was amazing,' he said, and she smiled, pleased with herself.

'Come here.' It was a command, and she lay down with her back to him. He held her with one arm and undid her bra with his free hand. Her tits were perfectly hand-sized and he cupped them and played with her nipples with his thumbs. She began to moan. He slid her pants off and expertly teased her clitoris until it tightened. He felt himself go hard again; he was most impressed with himself. He positioned her so he could enter her easily and held onto her hips from the back, pushing deeply. Her tits bounced and her arse wobbled satisfyingly. Soon enough, she went off like the fourth of July and he came for a second time.

'Do you want a drink?' she asked after he'd given her the obligatory cuddle.

'Sure.'

She got off the sofa, pulled on a sweater, and returned with two cold beers.

'So, like I said, I recorded the foreign woman: she was babbling all shift.'

58

Carl feigned nonchalance, and pulled on his pants. 'She's getting better then?' he asked.

'Yes, she's making a good recovery. I feel sorry for the baby, though; he'd be better off if she died.'

'What do you mean? That's a bit harsh, isn't it?'

'Not really. She clearly doesn't want him, so what kind of a start is that? He's fucked anyway. He'll probably spend his life in and out of foster homes and set fire to something when he's ten; another drain on the state.'

'But if she wasn't supposed to be here in the first place, he might be sent back to where they came from and perhaps be looked after properly.'

'Doubt it. They're never sent home, are they? Violation of human rights or some other bullshit.' She jumped up to get her phone from her bag. 'Here,' she said, tapping in her password and handing it to him. 'It's in camera because voice memo is too short.'

'You filmed her?' Carl was incredulous but excited. Tania giggled. 'A bit. She's weird, watch them.'

'Them?' he asked.

'Yeah, there's a few on there.'

Carl opened Tania's photos and scrolled backwards. There were seven video recordings in all. He clicked on the first. What struck him immediately was that the woman was very young – more of a girl, in fact. She was tossing and turning and pulling at her IV, which was when the first video stopped; Tania had obviously realised that to look after her patient she'd have to put the phone down. The second video was a close-up of the girl asleep. She could barely be twenty one years old, Carl thought.

Tania grew bolder with each recording, and by the last one, she was asking the girl questions in English

59

and recording the replies. The girl was shaking her head, clearly baffled but also very afraid. She had the look of someone being held captive, and it was clear that no one had bothered to explain to her where she was.

Something else was clear in Carl's mind. She was speaking Serbo-Croat, and he'd heard her accent a thousand times before; he'd bet his life she was from Bosnia. Reports from the war there had been used daily as part of his journalism degree because so many of them went on to win awards, and the language as well as the images had stuck in his brain. He knew just who to take the videos to for confirmation.

'Can I send them to my phone? I want to be sure. I think I know where she's from but I need to check. There's a guy in our faculty who's Russian; he'll know for sure.'

'You think she's Russian?'

'She might be.'

'She could be a spy!'

'Maybe the baby is Putin's.'

'Who's Putin?'

'Never mind, it was a joke. Here, let me do it.' The last thing he needed was Tania gaining access to his personal mobile.

'That's fine. I'll delete them anyway, I'm not interested in them. Should we go out?'

Carl completed his task and put his phone into his jacket.

'How about a takeaway? I'll go and get it, you make yourself comfortable.' He kissed her.

'Deal. I'll have a shower.'

She disappeared and Carl rolled his eyes, gathering his clothes. He looked around for the last time, making sure he had all of his personal items, and left the flat. He had no more use for Tania. As soon as the story hit, she'd know it was him, so he couldn't use her any more anyway.

She'd get over it.

Chapter 11

Mrs Joliffe was seething. She'd offered the Japanese couple a night's free accommodation with breakfast included, but they'd packed their bags and left anyway. She could do without the negative attention. Every time the front door opened, she jumped up to see if Anushka had returned, but there was no sign of her, or Roza.

'You must know where they are, Gabriela, you girls gossip about everything. They must have gone somewhere together, and I can only assume they're not coming back. Typical. You give people a chance and they throw it in your face.'

Mrs Joliffe had come to her room to find her, and now she was hoovering her office, trying to avoid eye contact. Gabriela let her boss rant on. She had no idea where either girl had gone but she knew it had something to do with someone called Darren. She'd keep that to herself, though. Mrs Joliffe didn't need to know, and besides, it wouldn't help. She said as little as possible.

With all the fuss happening around her, Gabriela had considered going home. She wanted to see Nikita, to buy him ice cream and tell him stories about these rich people who ate too much and wore too much make-up. It was either that or accept Mrs Joliffe's offer. It paid more money, but what really attracted her was that it promised to be very quiet.

Night manager. It sounded grand. It would mean she'd have to sleep all day and she'd hardly see a soul, but that was just what she needed to keep away from people like Anushka. It was a lot of responsibility, and she was flattered that Mrs Joliffe trusted her.

Her boss was still chuntering under her breath. Anushka and Roza had left her short-staffed.

Gabriela's mind wandered. Everyone knew about the man who'd died in the hotel down the road, and the presence of the police was making a lot of people jumpy. Would they want to interview staff from other hotels in the area? No one knew, but if they did, would they also want to see ID and work permits?

Gabriela had followed the story in the newspaper. The article said that Mr Day was an important man and his passing was a great loss. There'd been a picture of him and his wife, who was in a wheelchair, at an important event. She felt sorry for the woman and her three children. The paper said he'd had a heart attack. What she couldn't understand was what he was doing in a hotel if he was a loving family man with a home a stone's throw away from Lake Windermere. Maybe he and his wife had fought and he'd checked in to cool off.

Mrs Joliffe interrupted her thoughts.

'Gabriela, turn that thing off.' Gabriela did so and stood to attention, still managing to avoid Mrs Joliffe's gaze.

'Things are getting tricky, shall we say. I've managed to get hold of a work permit and I've filled out your details. It's for your own protection, you understand?'

'Yes, Mrs Joliffe.'

'And I'll need your passport.'

'Now?'

'Yes please. Have you thought about my offer?'

'Yes, Mrs Joliffe, I'd like to accept if it remains available.'

'Excellent. You'll need to get some sleep so you can start tonight at ten.'

'Thank you, Mrs Joliffe... Will I be receiving any training for the post?' she asked, unsure of her new role.

'You won't need any. Just use your wits. You know your way around and I'll tell you tonight what to expect.'

'You'll be here?'

'For your first evening, of course. Now, off you go.'

Gabriela went to her room to fetch her passport. She wondered if she might be so bold as to ask if she could have the room to herself with the girls gone, as she'd be sleeping through the day when the hotel was at its busiest.

She took the passport to Mrs Joliffe's office and handed it over.

'Thank you, Gabriela. It's what you might call my insurance, if you know what I mean,' her boss said. A sinking feeling formed inside Gabriela's tummy, and the corners of her mouth dipped ever so slightly.

'Yes, Mrs Joliffe,' she said. She knew that she had just made her first mistake.

Her shoulders sagged as she climbed the stairs to her room and sat heavily on her bed. She decided to write to her mother. Emails and Skype were all well and good, but she enjoyed writing real letters, and her mother loved to receive them. She described everything she saw – the clothes, the cars, the food, the freedom with which people came and went – and even included little sketches. Now, as she put pen to paper, she tried to be buoyant and entertaining. She didn't want to mention anything that would worry her mother, so she said nothing about Anushka, Roza or Darren. Neither did she mention her new position.

After she had finished, she folded the sheets of paper and laid them on her bed. She knew she was supposed to be resting for the long night shift ahead, but she felt wide awake. Anushka's bed was bare, but Roza's was still littered with her belongings. She obviously intended to return at some point. Gabriela's curiosity got the better of her and she walked over to Roza's bed. She knew it was wrong, but she had an urge to look at the other girl's belongings. Perhaps it was to understand her better – because she herself was so different – or perhaps she just wanted to know what Anushka and Roza got up to when they stayed away for days at a time.

A photograph on Roza's bedside cabinet caught her attention; Gabriela assumed it was either her mother or her sister. She carefully opened the top drawer. It contained underwear. The next one held a large packet of condoms. Gabriela had never had sex and she wondered what it was like. She was quite baffled by girls who did it all the time with different people. She took one of the condoms out of its packet and opened it up. It was silky soft and very long. She imagined a man's penis filling it; it was an ugly vision and it didn't excite her at all. She knew about erections and orgasms but had never felt that close to a boy, ever. She wondered how many different men Anushka and Roza had slept with since arriving in Ambleside.

The next drawer contained a fat envelope. She peeked inside. It was full of cash. She threw it back into the drawer and closed it, her heart pounding. She didn't want to think about how Roza had earned it. Next she turned to the wardrobe. Anushka's shelves were empty, except for a laptop, but Gabriela had seen her put something into Roza's before she'd left earlier.

It was still there – a small drawstring bag. Did Anushka intend to come and collect it, or was it Roza's in the first place and she'd been returning it? Gabriela wanted to know the answer. She put her hand inside and pulled out a watch; it was a Rolex. There was also a ring wrapped in a piece of toilet paper. It was a beautiful shade of rose gold and it clasped a large red stone that she was sure was a ruby. The final item in the bag was a roll of notes held together with an elastic band. More money. Dirty money.

Gabriela returned everything as she'd found it and knew that she hadn't seen the last of the two girls. It was out of the question that they'd leave their hard-won earnings behind. But the watch hadn't been earned. It was a man's watch, and Gabriela was pretty sure it had been stolen.

Chapter 12

The drive from Ambleside to Walney Island was long and drab, with none of the dramatic scenery that had accompanied the first leg of her journey this morning, though now and again the coast could be glimpsed from the car. But Jenny Davis wasn't bored at all. Not only was she getting out of the house for the day, she was travelling in a very smart car.

'What is it?' she'd asked Kelly as they approached the sleek vehicle.

'A BMW 1 Series,' Kelly said, embarrassed. She would look at getting a replacement as soon as she had time, something inconspicuous.

'Gosh, it's fun!' Jenny said.

'Shall I put the roof down?' Kelly asked, thankful that she'd brought some delight to the woman's life, if only very small.

Jenny grinned. The woman was incredibly endearing, and it made Kelly like her even more. Despite her horrific circumstances, Jenny had survived, and Kelly presumed it was because she had to, for Charlie. The two women chatted easily over the rushing wind, and only occasionally would Jenny fall silent and stare into the distance. During these moments, Kelly didn't interrupt her.

'My brother is a little slow. I thought I'd better tell you. I think they call it special needs these days.' Jenny smiled.

'Is that why he moves jobs frequently?' Kelly asked.

Jenny nodded. 'He forgets to turn up, or turns up late; he doesn't think like the rest of us. He can only cope with one thing at a time, so if he's thinking about lunch, he'll forget he has a shift starting afterwards, and by the time he does remember, it'll be too late.'

'So do I need to ask him questions in a certain way, so he doesn't panic?' Kelly asked.

'Just try to stick to one thing at a time and give him time to answer before moving on to the next question. His memory is good, so he should be all right if you keep things simple and direct.'

'And he'll have you there to help. Thank you for coming and making the drive more interesting,' Kelly said.

They were approaching Barrow-in-Furness, the ship-yard dominating the skyline like some gigantic power station. It could be seen from every street and ruined the view of the bay beyond it. After the charm of Ambleside, Barrow felt like a sprawling metropolis. Once a jewel in the British Empire's crown, the place had seen happier times. If the iron industry had endured, that might still be the case.

The streets were largely deserted, reminding Kelly of the East End of London early in the morning, when the illegals had gone to bed but the rest of humanity had yet to rise. As they crossed Walney Bridge, the tide was on its way back in and some boats had begun to catch the water, while others still lay lopsided and waiting. With Devon-shire Dock behind them now, the view was beautiful and they could see all the way to Black Coomb.

Jenny guided them to a quiet street and Kelly spotted the renovation straight away. Two men were climbing scaffolding and another two stood beneath, chatting and gesticulating. They stopped talking at the sight of unfamiliar faces and, more importantly, a smart expensive car driven by a woman. Kelly clicked the roof back into place with her key fob. The men continued to stare.

'Can I help you?' one of them asked eventually.

'My brother Dennis is working here. I was wondering if we could speak to him; it'll only take a minute,' Jenny said.

'Working's one way of putting it,' the man replied rudely. Jenny's face went red.

Kelly decided to show her badge and his demeanour changed dramatically.

'Is he in trouble?'

'No, not at all. I just need to ask him some routine questions.'

'He's round the back, mixing cement.' The man moved aside as Jenny walked past him.

'How's he getting on?' Kelly asked him. 'It means a lot to his sister.'

'Sure, I understand. I've had worse. I'll keep him on for the time being, for her sake, you know? I guess she's the mother of the little girl who was murdered. Everyone knows she was Dennis's niece.' His face reddened.

So, the guy knew about Lottie, and had a heart.

'Thanks,' said Kelly, and waited. She was aware that both men were studying her, clocking her suit; there weren't many women on Walney who dressed like that. She didn't move, or look away; just returned their stares with a smile.

Eventually they both dropped their gaze, and one made an excuse to disappear round the back just as Jenny emerged with her brother.

Dennis was a big man, vast and lumbering, and he looked agitated; Jenny was speaking to him soothingly to calm him down. He didn't take much notice of Kelly, who glanced at her car and wondered how they'd fit in. Jenny had suggested they drive to Biggar Bank; she said her brother loved the sea and it would encourage him to talk.

'I think you'll have to get in the back, Jenny. I'm afraid there's not much room.'

Jenny nodded and bent down to climb into the tiny space. When Dennis got into the passenger seat, the car dipped visibly to his side. Kelly slipped in behind the wheel and started the car, and Jenny gave her directions.

Biggar Bank was a bleak spot that could have been in the Outer Hebrides, it was so windswept and desolate. As she parked, Kelly looked out to the Irish Sea and saw huge wind turbines far out on the horizon. She could feel the wind moving the car – even with Dennis in it – and after the engine was switched off she could hear it raging around them.

Jenny took the lead and leant forward to explain to Dennis why they were here. At first, the man's eyes darted about and he wrung his hands together, but gradually her voice seemed to calm him down.

'Den, this woman is a police officer – a detective – and she's going to look at Lottie's case again, like I told you on the phone. It's great news. They want to ask you about the day Lottie was taken. I've already told them what I remember. Now it's your turn.' Kelly noticed that Jenny took her time over her words and spoke very clearly.

'Lottie...' The huge man began to cry. Jenny put her hand on his shoulder she looked like a doll soothing a giant. The windows began to steam up.

'I know, Den, but it's all right. She's on our side, I promise.' She nodded to Kelly; that was her signal.

'Hi, Dennis, my name's Kelly. Pleased to meet you.' She held out her hand. Dennis stopped crying and took it. He sniffed, and Jenny found a tissue for him from her handbag.

'Dennis, Jenny told us that she invited you to go eagle-spotting with Lottie and Charlie. Did you want to go?'

Dennis nodded emphatically.

'Can you remember why you didn't go?'

He looked up to the ceiling of the car, thinking. No one said a word.

'I had a new job,' he said eventually.

'You must have been disappointed that you didn't get to go,' Kelly said.

Dennis nodded.

'And did you tell anyone that you were disappointed?' she asked.

He looked her straight in the eye and froze. He seemed to zone out, and she wondered if he suffered seizures.

'Dennis?' said Jenny. He began moving again. Kelly's pulse quickened.

'I can't remember,' he said finally.

'OK, Dennis. Did you tell anyone where your sister's family was going? Did you share the information with a friend or a work colleague perhaps?' asked Kelly.

'I can't remember,' he said again.

Jenny shook her head: it was too many questions for him to process. Kelly needed to slow down. She decided to change tack.

'Was Lottie excited about the trip, Dennis?'

'Oh yes! She wore her red dress.' He beamed. The car fell silent. Jenny looked at her hands.

'Did you tell a friend that she looked pretty in her red dress?' asked Kelly.

'Oh yes, I told Wade.' Dennis turned to his sister, his smile dropping when he saw her face. Jenny looked cross and Kelly didn't know why.

'Who's Wade, Dennis?' she asked.

The big man's brow furrowed and his eyes darted about. It was difficult enough maintaining eye contact with him, but when he became agitated, it was impossible.

'A school friend,' he said eventually.

'Wade Maddox is no good, that's what he is. I told Den he shouldn't see him,' Jenny said.

'Are you still friends, Dennis? Did Wade work with you? Was he working with you that day?'

Damn, too many questions. Dennis began to wring his hands again.

'Sorry, just tell me if you're still friends, Dennis.'

'No.'

'OK, was Wade working with you the day you couldn't go eagle-spotting?'

'No.'

'When did you tell him about how pretty Lottie looked in her red dress, Dennis?' Jenny swallowed, and a vein in her neck began to swell. She fully understood where Kelly was going with her line of questioning. Her brother looked out of the window.

72

'I need to get back to work now,' he said.

'I know, Dennis, but if you could remember where you were when you spoke to Wade, that would be helpful for us and your sister.'

'It was at his place. He let me play on his Nintendo.'

'So was he a good friend?' asked Kelly.

Dennis nodded.

'But not now?'

'No.'

'Can you remember his address, Dennis?'

'Can I go back to work?' he asked, pleadingly.

'Sure, you tell me the address and we'll get going now.' Kelly turned to the wheel and started the engine nonchalantly, getting out her notepad and scribbling down the address as Dennis blurted it out. He looked at Jenny for confirmation and his sister nodded.

'Well done, Den. I think you've been really helpful. Let's get you back to work.'

Kelly drove back to the renovation and stopped outside. Dennis got out of the car and walked away without looking back. The two men who seemed to be in charge had gone. The air in the car lightened and she flicked the roof down once more; they needed a breeze.

'It's a Barrow address,' said Jenny, biting her nails. 'Can we go?'

'I don't think it's a good idea for you to come with me,' Kelly replied. 'You introduced me to your brother, and that was really helpful, but this is going to be an interview with someone you've already stated you don't like, someone who is potentially connected to the case. I'm sorry.'

Jenny nodded and looked down at her hands.

'Do you think he had something to do with Lottie going missing? I've been over it a thousand times, and it's always the same. She chose the red dress herself; she was very independent.'

'I can't possibly know that yet. All I can do is follow leads as they come up. I'm so grateful that you're allowing me to gain an insight into your daughter's life. I'll do my best to find you some answers.'

Kelly started the engine. She would let the office know her movements when she had an opportunity. It looked like she'd be spending the best part of the day in Barrow-in-Furness.

Chapter 13

Darren Beckett paced up and down the living room of the one-bedroom flat on Barrow Island. He'd fucked up big time.

He needed to think about how to save his skin.

He sucked hard on a cigarette but it did nothing to deliver clarity. The guys he was facing made Barrow boys look like fairies, and they wouldn't hesitate to erase someone as small-town as him. For the time being, he had no desire to go back to Ambleside, but he'd have to sooner or later. Marko wanted to see him, and Darren wasn't fucking stupid; he'd seen what happened when these guys didn't get what they wanted.

He should've studied harder at school. His maths was good, he could've been an accountant or something for BAE, but he'd had to chase the fucking weed instead, and girls, and vodka... The list went on. His teachers told his mother that it was a waste seeing such talent thrown away. How was he supposed to know that one day he might need a legitimate job? No one had told him. One thing led to another, and before he knew it, he was involved in all sorts of scams, staying one step ahead of the coppers. It was negligible stuff: the odd burglary, roughing someone up, driving a van, delivering packages. But he had a feeling that was about to change. He owed Marko a debt because he'd made a mistake; he knew how they operated. He'd have to prove himself. Or get away.

Darren had met Marko in a club in Bowness. That had been six years ago, and now his neck was on the line, as he'd always known it would be. No one worked for a man like Marko and stayed clean. Marko was smooth and knew how far he could push people before they had to be forced, and he'd played it perfectly with Darren, knowing that his bag was dealing. Dealing in the Lakes was easy; always was. But Darren was in trouble and he knew it. Branching out on his own was a mistake, and he'd pay for it; he just hoped he could convince Marko to give him a second chance. It wasn't about the money; it was about the risk. He should've stuck to what he knew, but he couldn't resist the opportunity to make a few extra quid on the side with the girls.

He couldn't think straight. His brain was fuddled, stuffed full of drugs and booze. He considered his options and, for one of the very few times in his life, decided to face the issue head on. He had no alternative. He was broke, and Nush didn't have a penny on her, though he knew she'd stashed it somewhere.

He had one thing in his favour. The night before Nush had fucked the old guy to death, he'd been cleaning up for someone else. He wasn't even supposed to be the binman that night; Tony was. But Tony had been high into the stratosphere, or at the bottom of a bottle as usual. Marko should've got rid of him months ago. For whatever reason, it was Darren who got shafted with the housekeeping.

Roza was a mess by the time he got there, and the guy was jabbering on about how sorry he was. Sorry. Sorry! Sorry for breaking her neck and carrying on anyway?

Necro. It never ceased to amaze Darren how sick these perverts were with the girls. Roza had shat herself and Darren thought he would throw up with the smell. The guy left him three hundred quid and that encouraged Darren to tolerate the stench and clean up. Funny how money did that. So that was his trump card. Somebody else had fucked up and that was why he'd made a mistake. It was totally someone else's fault.

Nush's moans interrupted his pathway to self-congratulatory justification, and he went to the bathroom. He'd plied her with booze and she was paralytic, collapsed over the bath. He helped her to the bed and she slumped onto it, face up. She wore only her underwear and he moved the cup of her bra to expose part of her left breast. He was horny, but he'd let her get too drunk. She knew she'd have to pay for what she'd done, and Darren looked forward to making her work off some of the debt before he got rid of her.

She slept on as he moved her pants to one side. She didn't move. She really was out of it. He slid her pants down her legs and threw them onto the floor, then pulled her bra up. Still she didn't move. His head was fuzzy and he wasn't sure if he was actually climbing on top of her or not, but whatever he was doing felt good. He doubted he'd be able to actually complete the task, but he was enjoying being in control. He managed to get his own pants down and opened her legs wide and actually managed to get it in. It felt fucking fantastic.

Until she woke up. There was panic on her face as she struggled beneath him, trying to work out in her confusion what was happening. Her eyes were wide in

77

fear, but Darren ignored that. There was no stopping now. He grabbed a pillow and held it over her face.

She stopped moving, but he carried on, taken by the pure waves of pleasure. He forgot where he was and who was under him and ploughed on until he'd finished. Then, sweaty, buzzing with satisfaction and drugs, he flopped over onto his back and lay there labouring for breath. Christ, he was out of shape. That was intense, but it had been just what he needed. Nush owed it to him anyway.

He turned towards her, but she hadn't moved. The pillow was still half over her face and she lay with her hands above her head. He pulled it away. Her eyes stared sightlessly towards the ceiling and she wasn't breathing.

Darren jumped off the bed and jerked and hopped about as he pulled up his pants and jeans. No, no, no, no… He was no better than the fucking pervert who'd killed Roza. He felt hot and his body shook, and he knew he was about to be sick. He ran to the small bathroom and vomited into the pan. He retched again and spat the vile liquid out, then went to the sink and rinsed his face with cold water.

As he looked into the mirror, a thought came to him. Marko wanted him to prove himself, wanted him to display his loyalty and show that he could be relied upon. He'd just done that by removing a loose end: a key witness who at some point the police would get round to tracking down. He'd done Marko a favour. This was an opportunity.

He went back to the bedroom to reassure himself that Nush really was dead, then looked around for something to wrap her in. She wouldn't be heavy; they were all the same, these young girls, they'd rather starve and buy fags than eat. Now she could join Roza in the back of his car, and he could tell Marko that he'd tidied up not one problem, but two. He stripped a couple of pillowcases and put one over Nush's head down to her shoulders, and another over her feet. He fetched a sheet, then wrapped her up and taped her, just like he had Roza, and went to get bin bags from the kitchen. By the time he was finished, it was totally dark outside.

The flats had no gardens, just yards, and the alley-ways were dark and deserted. He carried Anushka's body outside and heaved it into his boot alongside Roza's. He was surprised that there was still no smell, but it didn't matter anyway because they'd be gone soon enough.

He returned to the flat and decided to have a vodka to celebrate. One led to another and he drifted off listening to music through headphones. His sleep was shallow and he darted between images. It happened a lot; it was his brain's way of processing all the shit he'd done. Faces, mainly of girls, came to him and pleaded with him. There were hundreds of them. Sometimes he dreamt of them as slabs of meat in a factory, all hooked up ready for the client to choose their favourite cut. They writhed and moaned and looked silly; they were just pieces of meat, right?

Sometimes they had names.

By the time he woke from his stupor, it was an hour or so before dawn. The birds hadn't yet started to sing and the moon was still out. Traffic had ceased, apart from the odd taxi, and it was a good time to drive to Ambleside.

He showered to sober up. He felt ill and couldn't remember the last time he'd eaten. Thoughts whirred in his head. He'd shown he had balls, and now it was time to tell Marko. Roza and Nush were pretty busy girls and they must've racked up a fair amount of cash. All he had to do was find it, and he had a pretty good hunch that he should start with their room at the Troutbeck Guest House. If he could find it and give it to Marko – well, most of it anyway – then he could make even more of an impression on his boss.

He took a last look around the flat and wondered if he'd be back. It was rented for cash and the owner would come and reclaim it if the payments stopped. He was going to disappear into Marko's world, of that he was sure. He thought of the way his mum shook her head whenever she saw him.

'When's the last time you had a shower? Are you taking drugs? When was your last proper meal?' she'd admonish. He didn't want to hurt her, but he had no choice. She should never have had him in the first place. Besides, he'd inherited his love of the booze from her.

He threw his few things into a bag, then locked the flat and went to the car. It was non-descript and low-spec, but it did the job. The streets were empty and the lamps shone on damp roads. It was a good time to leave.

He didn't look back. He drove past the turning to his mum's house on his way through Dalton and on to the A590, stopping for petrol in Ulverston and buying a sandwich, though he wasn't hungry. He was through Newby Bridge in twenty minutes. Ambleside would take him another twenty. Beyond that, he didn't know where he would end up, only that he needed to find the cash.

Chapter 14

Kelly was parked outside Caffè Nero, waiting for Jenny to bring them coffee. She'd called the office and told them she'd be away for the rest of the day. It was gone three o'clock and she still had to pay Alan Bell a visit: the fell runner who'd found Lottie's body. She was chilly, and looked in the boot for a jacket. It didn't help that she was wearing a skirt and thin tights; yet again, she wished she could wear more casual clothes to work. In reality she could wear what she liked, but a lot of the job involved extracting information from people unwilling to give it, and she had to project some kind of authority.

The office had informed her that the hospital had called to say the unknown woman was making progress and they should be able to visit her tomorrow. That was good news, although they hadn't yet been able to pin down a language expert. Kelly had the name of some professor at Lancaster University, and she made a note to call him later. She also had a phone call to make to DI Craig Lockwood at Barrow's Serious Crime Unit. If the Lottie Davis case were to take her to Barrow again, she really ought to inform them. At some point down the line she might need their aid, and she wanted to introduce herself before they got wind that a copper from North Lakes was snooping around asking questions. News travelled fast here – Kelly hadn't forgotten that in the time she'd been away – and she didn't want to tread on anyone's toes.

Her thoughts turned to Jenny Davis's brother. He was more than a little odd but that didn't necessarily mean he had anything to do with Lottie's disappearance. But she was keen to speak to Wade Maddox.

She rang her mother.

'Hi, Mum, I'll be really late. I'm in Barrow.'

'What are you doing there?' her mother asked. It sounded like a challenge rather than an enquiry, and Kelly was fifteen again. The details didn't matter; the distrust remained the same. As far as her mother was concerned, she must be doing something she wasn't supposed to.

She sighed and watched Jenny carry two coffees to the car. She had dropped Jenny in town while she went to the address Dennis had given her for Wade Maddox. His mother had answered the door and informed her that Wade no longer lived with her, and that wherever he was it probably wasn't good. Kelly established that Mrs Maddox wasn't her son's biggest fan; she was quickly piecing together a picture of Wade Maddox as somebody who perhaps wasn't that popular.

'I've just got to make one more phone call, Jenny, then we'll get off,' she said. 'I've got someone else I need to see in Ambleside, so I want to get back there before five if I can. I'll drop you at home first.' Jenny didn't need to know that she was going to see the man who'd discovered her daughter's body.

'Thank you, Kelly. I've got a friend in Dean Street if you have to do something else in Barrow before we head back,' Jenny replied.

'Perfect,' Kelly said. That would give her time to pay DI Lockwood a visit.

Jenny directed her to Dean Street and got out of the car. Kelly promised that she wouldn't be long. She watched Jenny walk away, then called the Barrow DI.

'Detective Inspector Craig Lockwood speaking.' The voice was sharp, formal and clear. Kelly explained her situation briefly. He'd heard of the case and, like everyone, glad it was being reinvestigated. She told him of her desire to track down Wade Maddox and why, and it piqued his interest. He invited her to his office. The man didn't mess around. From his direct manner it was clear that he could be an asset to her.

She found the station easily and was led to the correct department. The place was smaller than Penrith but had a similar atmosphere. Officers worked at their desks or shared information over coffee. The room was amicable and people smiled at her.

DI Lockwood was in his mid-forties. He stood well over six feet tall and his forearm was the width of Kelly's calf. He had an open face but eyes that drilled holes in their beholder. Barrow had its fair share of crime and she'd bet he'd seen a bit. She was intrigued by him and his smile disarmed her. She put out her hand and he took it. He had a solid handshake, just as she'd expected.

'So you're looking for Wade Maddox? I knew his dad. He started off as a petty criminal, you know, nicking stuff, drunk and disorderly. Job turned nasty and he ended up in jail. The lad never stood a chance. One of those you could pick out from the pram and predict he'd end up banged up or beaten up.'

83

'Yes, I know the sort,' Kelly replied. 'Have you always worked Barrow?' she asked.

'Nah, I was in Manchester for fifteen years until I got too old and fancied a break.' They both laughed, and Lockwood winked. Burnout. It was lethal. Now she *knew* he'd seen plenty of shit if he'd worked Manchester for fifteen years.

'So do you know Wade as well?'

'Course I do. He's a scrote. What's he got to do with the Lottie Davis case?'

'I'm not sure. I need to ask him some questions.' Kelly filled him in on their conversation in her car at Biggar Bank. Lockwood raised his eyebrows.

'I remember that case well. It sticks in everyone's throat that it wasn't solved. You said you tried Wade's mum?'

'Yes.'

'I know where some of his mates hang out.' Lockwood looked at his watch. 'Can you come back tomorrow? If you've got to see someone in Ambleside tonight, you could go and do that and I'll track down Wade.'

'Are you sure?'

'Of course, no problem.'

Kelly smiled. 'Thanks.' She was glad she'd dropped by. She was building leads and she had an ally.

She walked back to her car and returned to Dean Street. Jenny was ready to leave and Kelly was reminded of the woman's obliging nature. They set off and straight away hit traffic on the A590. There was a good reason why North and South Lakes forces were separate, thought Kelly. There weren't many options when trying to navigate around Cumbria. There was pretty much one route to everywhere, and only fells in between. Not given to

84

patience, she had to fight her irritation, but Jenny was pleasant company. The traffic eased towards Coniston and soon they were heading under the shadows of Coniston Old Man and a clear drive to Ambleside.

'Thank you, Kelly,' Jenny said when they pulled up outside her house. 'And thank you for looking into Lottie's case again.'

Kelly smiled. 'I'll be in touch,' she said. She watched Jenny go into her house, then checked the address she had for Alan Bell.

Chapter 15

Alan Bell seemed nervous when he answered the door. Kelly showed him her badge and was eventually invited in.

'Like I said on the phone, Alan, it's about Lottie Davis. I'm looking into the case again.'

Alan nodded. He ushered her into his lounge and they stood uneasily opposite one another. Kelly was used to witnesses being tense. She looked around the sparse little room and guessed that he lived alone. The only decorative features were paintings of peaks and Lake District scenes hung badly on the walls.

'You're a fell runner?' she asked him. He relaxed a little and even smiled.

'Yes, I used to compete,' he said. 'Would you like a drink?'

Kelly didn't want to break the moment, and anyway she was full of coffee.

'No, I'm fine, thank you,' she said.

He sat down and she followed his lead. He ran his fingers through his hair and sighed.

'I was running that day. I was training for the Wastwater scree race, which was the following week. Dobbin Wood is a good place to do it because of the gradients round there. I was hill training.'

Kelly nodded; he'd get round to it in his own good time. Her back ached and she wanted to stretch. She longed to get out of her tights and go for a run herself. She waited.

'I slipped. I was pushing too hard. I slid down a dip and fell into a hole covered in loose leaves and earth and stuff. It stank.' He put his hand over his mouth. Kelly knew what rotting flesh smelled like; it never left you. 'I thought it was a deer or something, you know? Then I saw the red cloth and an arm and I knew it was a person, and then it hit me that it was a child.' He put his hand over his mouth again.

'The police told me a few days later that it was the missing girl, and I felt terrible for the parents.' He spread his hands and looked at Kelly. She waited. He said nothing else.

'So you went straight to the police?'

'I dialled 999 right then.'

'Do you know Dennis Hill, Alan?'

'No,' he replied without hesitation.

'Wade Maddox?'

'No.'

'Did you know Ian Davis? Lottie's father?' Kelly already knew the answer.

Alan paused. 'We played squash together now and again, but I didn't know the family,' he added nervously.

'I've got a bit of a problem there, Alan,' Kelly said. Alan shifted in his seat. She carried on. 'Jenny Davis told me that Charlie and Lottie regularly watched their dad play squash and sometimes went to McDonald's afterwards with Daddy's friend called Alan. Am I wrong to presume that's you? Are there any other members of the squash club called Alan?'

He shook his head.

'So if they remembered you, why don't you remember them?'

Alan swallowed, and his hands went back to his face. Kelly watched him. She had nothing on him, but he'd lied to a police inquiry and she wanted to know why. She had no warrant, no evidence and no right to keep him talking, but she'd fired a warning shot and he'd remain a person of interest until she was convinced otherwise. He was holding something back; in effect, denying that he knew the victim.

'We only went to McDonald's once,' he said. 'Kids are kids, you know? If you haven't got them yourself, you don't really take any notice of them.'

Kelly accepted that this was a legitimate explanation. The same thing happened to her: friends would introduce her to their little darlings and she would instantly forget their names. But Alan had played squash with Ian, and Ian must have talked about his kids all the time.

'Did Ian continue to play squash after Lottie was killed?' she asked.

'No, I never saw him again.'

'Didn't you call him? Surely you'd become friends?'

Alan looked away. 'I didn't know what to say. I never knew if they were told who found her.' His face crumpled and he wiped his eyes.

Kelly got up and handed him a card.

'Please, Alan, if you remember anything else at all, call me.'

He took the card and nodded.

After the detective had gone, Alan made himself a cup of coffee and went back over what he'd told the police all those years ago. What a mess. He'd only taken the kids to McDonald's once, for God's sake. Usually they waited in the car after squash, when Ian came in with him to pick up a new racquet or a packet of balls, or for a quick coffee. No one could ever know that he never actually left with any of those things. Their sex was quick but immensely enjoyable because of the illicit risks involved. Neither man was ready to be outed, though.

Ian wasn't Lottie's killer, but he might as well have been in his own mind. Losing his little girl had crushed him, and Alan could only guess at what he'd gone through. They only had one conversation after her body was found. It was their last. Ian told him that he was convinced that Lottie's death was some kind of fucked-up punishment for being gay and that he would pay for it with his own life. Alan had thought him dramatic and put it down to grief. A few weeks later, he heard that he had killed himself.

He couldn't change his story now. Truth was like a sand dune, and once you slid off the top, there was no way back until it had carried you all the way to the bottom. In any case, Ian's wife had been through too much already. Alan wasn't sure how much shitty news one person could withstand, but he was pretty sure that having your daughter murdered, your husband hang himself and then finding out he'd been gay all along would be high up there on the list of stuff guaranteed to send you over the edge. No, he'd take Ian's secret to his own grave.

Chapter 16

Kelly's late drive back to Ambleside meant that by the time she reached the Kirkstone Pass, it was dark. It looked entirely different from earlier in the day. As she drove, she mulled over all the things she'd learned today, and for the first time since moving back, she felt as though she had her teeth into something. It only took her forty minutes to write up her reports back at Eden House, after which she left for home.

Her mood dipped as she pulled up outside her mother's house. She had no idea when she'd make the time to look at houses for sale, but every time she parked up here, she knew she had to. She let herself in and shouted down the hallway as brightly as she could.

'Hi, Mum!'

Wendy Porter looked around the kitchen door.

'Hi, love. Gosh, it's really late. It reminds me of when your dad worked silly hours. I was on my own with you and your sister, trying to feed you and bathe you and get you off to bed, and he'd come in and start singing to you just as I got you settled. It drove me mad.'

'I bet it did,' Kelly said. 'I'm starving, but I need to get out for a run first. It's been a really long day.'

'But it's dark,' her mother said.

Kelly could hear the TV on in the lounge. It was a soap. Dad had never allowed them.

'I'm a big girl now, Mum.'

'Well be careful,' warned her mother.

'I will be.' Kelly laughed at the irony and was glad her mother hadn't seen where she used to run in London.

This morning's argument seemed to be forgotten, but Kelly still felt a little guilty and wished she didn't play into her sister's hands so often. At least Nikki had gone home.

'I'm sorry about this morning,' she said.

'You've already said that. You've got a temper like your father, but your sister knows what she's doing too. I should just bang your heads together.'

Kelly wondered what it must be like for a parent to raise two kids only for them to end up disliking one another so openly. She didn't hate Nikki; she just had nothing in common with her. Every word and every action revealed their differences. She was sure that Nikki felt the same about her, judging by the looks of disapproval she got from her sibling. They'd chosen different paths, that was all. Kelly would never have been able to live Nikki's life; it was too straight, too safe.

She went upstairs to change and savoured the moment she slipped her tights off to be replaced by running shorts. She connected her phone to her headphones and selected her favourite playlist, giving her mum a quick kiss on the way out. The hairs on her arms stood up when the beat started. She made her way up the hill round the back of their house, and towards Beacon Hill. It wasn't overly taxing but it was challenge enough. The dark enveloped her, with only sparse street lighting showing the way, and she fell into a rhythm. Her thoughts turned to her day and she tried to process all the information she'd collected.

She'd created a bundle of leads from not very much at all, and in only a day. She knew to seize momentum when it came, because this time next week it might be gone. She was looking forward to the rest of her week with something she hadn't felt for a long time: passion.

Kelly saw investigations as giant jigsaw puzzles. Both things required patience, memory, order and time, all of which she possessed. Matt the twat had taught her well; she wasn't so proud that she couldn't admit that. He'd taught her about the golden hour, and about how to stay impartial, as much as one could. He'd taught her how to create balance in an inquiry and never to let anything go uncovered. The tiniest nugget of information could break a case wide open. A shoeprint, a shard of glass, a fag end, a type of mud; they could all decode a case, but equally they could all get forgotten. Most of all, he had taught her to be thorough. Working with him had been exhilarating. Which was why, when he didn't stick up for her, she felt so betrayed. But her anger was subsiding, and now when she thought of him, her blood didn't boil. Her thoughts turned instead to Johnny, and she wondered if she might see him again.

As Tinie Tempah got her to the top of the hill, Kelly remembered the Coryn Boulder case: her last in London.

It had tested them all. Coryn was a pretty student at the London School of Economics, but to raise money, she also worked as a hooker. One night things apparently went a bit too far and she was strangled and dumped in a waste bin behind Tesco in Whitechapel. It took them a year to find the killer, and in the end it hadn't been a client. It was the boyfriend who'd originally reported her missing; he'd found out about her extracurricular activities and killed her in a fit of rage.

The problem for Kelly was that somewhere along the way, a young suspect had jumped off the top of a building, and she was the last person he'd spoken to. Matt told her DCI, then the story got out and the press ran with the whole ugly question of police rough-handling. Morale dipped and Kelly kicked Matt out of her bed. During their blazing rows about why he hadn't fought her corner, all he could come up with was that he hadn't known what to say when asked about the incident. That was bullshit.

It emerged later that the boy had jumped off the roof because he was being mercilessly bullied at college – a fact that only emerged after his death. In fact during Kelly's last conversation with him, she had assured him that he was no longer a suspect. But none of that mattered. She'd made the unit look bad and someone needed to be held accountable. Matt made DCI a month later for solving the case, after she'd spent hundreds of hours chasing leads, trawling data, harassing labs and driving round the M25.

She didn't have to leave, but she'd lost her hunger. Now, though, it was back.

As she planned the coming days in her head and listed all the things she had to do, her music was interrupted by an incoming call. It was a duty sergeant from HQ.

'Yes, that's my case,' she confirmed. 'What's happened?'

She was floored. Some jumped-up journalist had written an exclusive in the *Manchester Evening Star* claiming that the mother of baby Dale, still seriously ill in the Penrith and Lakes Hospital, was a Serb-Croat refugee. The story had made national TV and the Home Secretary was pushing for answers. There had clearly been a leak inside the hospital and someone's head would roll, but Kelly doubted it would be anyone senior; it would be some poor sod who actually needed a job. She was livid that some journo could access her witness before she could.

She was at the top of Beacon Hill now and she looked west to the mountains as she listened to the sergeant. After she'd hung up, she googled the article and read it quickly. She was getting cold and she'd have to get moving again soon. The journalist, Carl Bradley, quoted an 'inside source' and that meant one thing: a nurse. No one else had been given access to the woman. It wouldn't take much to find out who'd been on shift the last couple of days, and exactly who had access to the room.

She made a call and spoke to a night clerk at the *Manchester Evening Star*, who searched for Carl Bradley's private number but couldn't find it. Funny, that. Then she called DI Lockwood. It was a long shot. He was probably putting his gorgeous kids to bed or having dinner with his perfect wife.

'Hello.'

'Lockwood, it's Kelly Porter, we met today.'

'I remember. Is there a problem?'

'I'm after a favour. I hope I'm not interrupting anything.'

'No, not at all, I'm watching my son play football and they're getting thrashed, so please distract me.'

'How old is your son?'

'Fifteen going on twenty. Thinks he knows it all like they all do at that age.'

Kelly figured she herself had been a bit younger when she knew it all.

'When you worked for Greater Manchester, who was your media contact? I need to get hold of a reporter for the *Manchester Evening Star* and it's pretty urgent.'

Lockwood thought and came up with a couple of names for her to try. He couldn't guarantee they'd still be in post, but he remembered their extension numbers at the paper.

'Thank you, I owe you one,' she said.

'Two, actually, I think I've found Wade Maddox,' he said.

'Really? Nice job. Tomorrow is looking tricky – someone has thrown a spanner into a live case – so this might have to wait a while, but I'll try and make it by Friday.'

'I'll go and rattle his cage for you in the meantime. What do you want to know?'

'That'll be three I owe you then. I want to know his relationship with Dennis Hill and whether he knows anything about the Lottie Davis case, I'll send you an email. I hope your son's team picks up.'

'No chance. Goodnight, Porter.'

Her run back down the hill was unyielding and she pounded the ground furiously. It was time to pay the hospital a visit.

Chapter 17

Gabriela slept fitfully but felt refreshed after a shower. Mrs Joliffe had offered her one hundred pounds in cash per night shift. She'd been told to wear her usual black skirt and white blouse but she'd also been given twenty-five pounds to buy a pair of nice black heels. She wanted to look as smart as she could and so she blow-dried her hair and put on a little make-up. She might have made a mistake, but there was no going back now if she was to have any chance of retrieving her passport.

There was no sign of her roommates. She wasn't sure if they still had their keys. She thought about mentioning her unease to Mrs Joliffe, but a feeling in her gut told her to wait. She checked her appearance again and left the room, locking the door behind her.

The hotel was quiet and Gabriela was unaccustomed to it. There was no bar, so if guests wanted a drink they had to go elsewhere. Ambleside was full of great places, though Gabriela herself didn't go out much – not because she didn't want to, but because she wanted to save her money. She tried to reassure herself that Anushka and Roza were probably in one of those bars right now, dancing and drinking, but a knot formed in her stomach and she knew it wasn't true.

Mrs Joliffe was already waiting for her in reception, looking smarter than normal. She was tall and always dressed in black, and to Gabriela she seemed glamorous. She wore a lot of expensive-looking jewellery and came across more like a sophisticated businesswoman than simply a hotel manager. Gabriela felt out of her depth. She wondered how many other passports Mrs Joliffe kept in her safe.

'Good evening, Gabriela. You look very nice, well done. Let's get started, shall we?'

Gabriela nodded and followed her employer into the office behind the reception area. Mrs Joliffe also had a private office, which was always locked. They started with housekeeping. Gabriela would be the only member of staff on duty from the hours of ten p.m. through till five a.m., so she needed to know where everything was. She also needed to know emergency procedures and what to do in certain situations. She was learning a lot.

Then Mrs Joliffe showed her the night manager's log. It was separate from the usual register, and Gabriela was impressed by Mrs Joliffe's organisation. There was a long list of names inside, and Mrs Joliffe explained that the vast majority of her evening guests were business clients, coming back after long meetings and leaving before breakfast. It made sense, because Gabriela recognised no names from the breakfast list.

'This is where the money is, Gabriela. I've built a reputation amongst certain companies from London and Manchester, and Scotland too, for providing simple comfort and uncomplicated service. These clients like to be left in peace.'

'Of course, Mrs Joliffe.' She was proud that she'd been given this responsibility; she wouldn't let her boss down. Perhaps holding her passport was just a precaution on Mrs Joliffe's part, with no other intent apart from protecting her business.

'Good. Now your job is to make sure that their every comfort is taken care of. After a long day guests may request extra bubble bath, or a snack, or perhaps clean sheets or towels. I know I shouldn't, but I have on occasion nipped out to get the odd bottle of champagne. They tip well, Gabriela.'

Gabriela took in all the information. These were important clients; she was slightly nervous but determined to get it right.

The reception bell rang. Gabriela followed Mrs Joliffe and watched as she greeted a man in a suit.

'Ah, Mr Fellows, how lovely to see you. May I introduce our new night manager? Gabriela, this is Mr Fellows, he comes to us once or twice a month.'

'Hello, Mr Fellows,' said Gabriela. The man extended his hand and she took it. His smile was broad and he nodded to Mrs Joliffe. Gabriela thought he looked pretty chirpy after a long day of meetings, but maybe he was just happy to be relaxing for the evening.

Mrs Joliffe handed him a key, then turned to Gabriela. 'I'll stay for a while in case you have any questions, though I'm sure everything will go smoothly. I'll pay you weekly, but I'll give you an advance of two nights now so you can treat yourself.' She went to the cash drawer and counted out two hundred pounds, her gold bracelets jangling together. Gabriela was astounded but took the money gratefully.

Mrs Joliffe was still with her at midnight, by which time three more men had checked in. Gabriela had also noticed a couple of girls walking through reception, and had looked at Mrs Joliffe to see her reaction. When a third girl arrived without approaching the desk, she couldn't keep quiet any longer.

'Do I stop guests I don't recognise, Mrs Joliffe? I'm sure I haven't seen her before. She might be lost or she might be a thief.'

'Oh, don't worry, Gabriela, I'm sure you can spot someone with bad intentions. I know that girl. Some of the guests like to have friends over from time to time; it helps them relax.' Mrs Joliffe smiled and crossed her arms, looking at Gabriela mischievously. It was a test, she realised. And Mrs Joliffe had her passport.

'Right. I understand,' she said. Her pulse quickened and she clasped her hands behind her back.

'Good. Like I said, my evening clients have been coming here for a long time. They are trusted and loyal, and they pay very good money. Discretion is everything, Gabriela. Any problems, you call me direct, do you understand?'

'Yes, Mrs Joliffe.' Gabriela knew that the chances of getting her passport back any time soon were very poor. 'Mrs Joliffe?'

'Yes.'

'Who had this job before me?'

'Ah, just a young girl like yourself, looking for work and willing to put in the hours. She left. It didn't suit her. And if it doesn't suit you, you can just leave too.'

Gabriela wasn't sure she entirely believed that, but she willed herself to calm down. There was nothing

99

wrong with men renting hotel rooms to entertain female partners, though something told her that these were business arrangements rather than romantic ones. Was this where Anushka and Roza had earned their money? she wondered.

Mrs Joliffe left at twelve thirty, and by five a.m. Gabriela had counted seven men and six girls entering the guest house, all of whom had now left. She put the night ledger away in the safe, at the same time checking to see if her passport was there, but the only other item was an envelope containing a bundle of cash; another test from her employer, she suspected.

George, the day manager, arrived shortly after five and greeted her. They'd got to know one another quite well, and he had a soft spot for her.

'What are you doing here so early?' he asked.

'I'm the new night manager,' she replied.

He raised his eyebrows. 'Just be careful, Gabriela.'

She was exhausted and didn't push him for an explanation.

Back in her room, she undressed and fell onto her bed. She could shower later; now she needed to sleep. The evening had passed without incident and the guests had all been quiet and polite. There'd been no drama or anything that concerned her. Her apprehension had been for nothing.

Chapter 18

Kelly had been at her desk for less than five minutes when a call came from HQ. A new case had come in; did she want it? She was on a roll with her other cases, but this new one sounded interesting and would take her back to Ambleside. She was also very bad at saying no.

She opened the email. The video tape taken from the crime scene was being sent over this morning, as well as various papers and ledgers from the hotel office. The two uniforms who'd been first on the scene – PCs Martin and Coombs – had done an excellent job. The notes were very detailed. She read their report and noted with interest that they questioned the integrity of both the manager and the cleaner who'd found the body.

When she opened the autopsy report, the coroner's name struck her. Ted Wallis had autopsied Lottie Davis five years earlier. Of course: this was Cumbria, there was one chief coroner and he'd perform all important post-mortems. The deceased in this case, Colin Day, had been a prominent civic figure in the area. Kelly had never heard of him, but there were photos of him with his wife at various fund-raisers. She googled him and he came up as the owner of six tanning salons and several hotels, including the one he'd died in. Looking at the notes, neither the manager nor the cleaner had bothered to mention this fact.

It could be a high-profile case, and the baby Dale case was looking the same. She was allowing herself to be vulnerable by juggling three big investigations, and she wondered whether she should have taken on this latest one. The wobble of confidence shook her and she chastised herself. Of course she was up for it. Her eagerness was coming back and she wasn't about to get wound up over a fear of what might happen.

Apparently the old guy had died in the middle of intercourse with a young woman in his own hotel. It wasn't the first time a hotel owner had been serviced by his staff, and it wouldn't be the last, but there was something odd about this case in that the woman hadn't hung around. Of course she would have been scared, but she hadn't reported the incident, which could mean she had something to hide.

A uniform entered Kelly's office and handed her an envelope: it contained the recording from the hotel room, on a USB. Phillips and Hide came in behind her and put four boxes of papers on the floor next to her desk.

'From the hotel office, guv,' said Hide.

Kelly nodded. The PCs had noted that the hotel had no guests, and hadn't for a while, and so she wanted to look through the books.

'I'll need some help going through this lot after I've seen the tape, then I'll hold a preliminary meeting in the incident room,' she said.

She inserted the USB into her computer and pressed run. The quality of the film was good but the room was dark. She wondered if Mr Day had recorded the meeting because he would get off on it later, or because he was worried about something and this was his insurance. She focused on the screen and watched as he walked away from the camera and sat on a chair. After a short while, he got up, apparently to go to the door, and a woman walked in. Mr Day gave her something, and Kelly could make out enough to see that she was pleased. She embraced him, then he walked to his jacket slung over a chair and took a roll of cash out of the pocket. He counted out several notes and gave them to the woman, who put them into her handbag. Then he reclined on the bed and the woman undressed. The colours merged into a dark brown mass at this point and it was impossible to see her face, though her hair looked to be a shade of red and possibly a wig.

Kelly took notes as she watched the recording, pausing often to scribble and circle questions that came to her, rewinding and fast-forwarding where necessary.

Seven minutes in, the woman was down to knickers and a bra and was playing with feathers. She removed Mr Day's clothes, then got on top of him, his hands all over her. She let him play with her and arched her back a lot; she looked like a pro, Kelly thought. This meeting wasn't one between two lovers. Yet it was clear that they knew each other, an easy familiarity between them. This wasn't their first time, she decided. It all set off warning bells.

She paused the recording again so she could take in more details. The woman was younger than she'd first thought – not much more than a girl. She noticed that there were little blue pills on the bedside table; she guessed Viagra. The young woman's handbag was large and not expensive; her coat was long – a dark-coloured mac perhaps. She looked at Mr Day's jacket on the easy chair, the pocket from which he'd pulled the cash still bulging:

there was a lot of money in there, she thought. But with no paying guests in a hotel with large overheads, how rich did one need to be not to care?

She checked her notes and scanned the inventory of what forensics had found in the room when they arrived: cash wasn't listed. There was also a laptop on the table, and when Kelly checked the list again, that hadn't been recovered either.

She pressed play again. The girl was really going for it now and Kelly couldn't help thinking that Colin Day must have been one happy boy when he carked it.

She stopped the recording and rewound slightly. Mr Day had stopped moving, although the girl hadn't. Kelly noted that it was eight forty-five p.m. She restarted the tape. About five seconds later, the girl stopped moving too, then climbed off him and rushed out of view. When she came back, she was carrying a glass of water, which she spilled slightly in her haste. She put on a discarded jumper – also not recovered; Kelly reckoned she was covering her shame now that things had gone wrong. Then she knelt down beside him and tried to get him to drink, touching his forehead tenderly.

A thrill of excitement shot through Kelly and she rushed to pause again. She rewound a few times and finally got the frame she needed. There it was. She noted the time: eight forty-nine p.m. It wasn't great quality, but for that split second, she could make out the girl's face. She made a note to contact media forensics. She would need enhancement, authentication, reproduction, colour and brightness – the whole works. Her adrenalin was pumping.

She finished watching the recording as the girl cleaned up and got dressed. She gathered various bits and pieces from around the bed and at one point took something from Colin Day's groin area that Kelly reckoned must have been a condom. Nice. The old man stopped moving at eight fifty-three p.m., after which the girl went through his jacket and took out the large wad of remaining cash. She also removed something else from his jacket and stopped to look at it. Whatever it was gave off a spark of light and illuminated her face a little, giving a clearer view than the previous one. Kelly recorded the time. Finally she leant over the corpse and removed Colin Day's watch before making what appeared to be a heated phone call at eight fifty-seven p.m.

'Third party,' Kelly said, out loud.

The young woman left the room at eight fifty-nine p.m. Kelly fast-forwarded the recording but saw nothing else before the camera ran out of battery at just gone midnight.

Her mind raced. She needed to talk to Anna Cork, the cleaner who had found Colin Day, and anyone else who worked at the hotel, but she also needed help with the baby Dale case. Now she'd really have to earn her badge. She wondered if Lockwood had seen Wade Maddox yet. She would deal with the mother of baby Dale first, who'd had protection since the breach of security. She needed to verify the woman's nationality and then she'd have to find a translator. She also wanted to check staff records at the hospital to narrow down who might have access to her – this process had already been started. She wondered how much Carl Bradley had paid his source, or if they'd allowed themselves to be set up.

She went back to Colin Day's autopsy report and saw that there was sildenafil citrate in his blood – the drug used to treat erectile dysfunction – and several red hairs had been found around his wedding ring. The coroner had stated that they looked human but the unusual colour cast doubt. Kelly wrote 'Hair dye or wig?' on her pad and circled it. Then she turned her attention to the four boxes of papers by her desk. There was a lot to get through and she called Hide and Phillips back into her office.

'I need help with this lot,' she said. 'I think it's worth going through just to figure out why a hotel in the middle of one of the busiest tourist spots in the country had no guests.'

The DCs looked at one another and pulled up two chairs, and the three of them began to read in silence. Occasionally one of them would get up and add a paper to one of the piles forming on the desk. They were running out of space. Hide was the first to speak.

'Guv, I'm no accountant, but these aren't the accounts of a struggling business with no clients.'

'I know, I'm seeing it too. Have you come across payments from an offshore company called Tomb Day?'

'Yes, I've seen several.'

'Let's google it.'

The result was a shell company registered in the Isle of Man. It didn't say who owned it.

'It doesn't have to, guv. That's why they're sometimes used to hide stuff.'

Kelly shuffled through her papers.

'I've got a payment here to HCCD Art Handling for twenty-five thousand US dollars. And here's a deposit from the Westmorland Estate Agency in Ambleside for seven hundred and fifty grand.' She looked at Phillips.

'I've got payments to the personal bank accounts of Colin and Christine Day, guv. As well as the Thwaite Hotel.'

'So he made money from art and property to prop up a failing hotel where he just so happened to be entertaining prostitutes? Are you buying it?'

Hide and Phillips looked at one another.

'I think it's worth checking the companies out.' Kelly stood up. 'Selling sex isn't illegal, but arranged prostitution and owning or running brothels is. Something is bugging me, and it's not just the girl robbing him; it's the sheer wealth of Colin Day. These are huge amounts of money. We need to know exactly who he was connected with. If the hotel was failing, why not sell it? It doesn't seem like he needed the money; it looks like he wanted to keep it as a shell – but literally. I wonder what his tanning salons are worth; can we find out?'

'We'd have to find out who his accountant is. Maybe it's in his will,' Hide suggested.

'Let's start a list of transactions coming in and out of the offshore company. Anything about Tomb Day, put it here.' Kelly indicated a pile of papers.

By the time they had gone through all four boxes, the Tomb Day pile was by far the largest on the desk. Kelly skimmed through a few bank statements from Colin Day's personal account and saw that in three months alone he'd been paid over seventy thousand pounds from the company.

'Emma, I want you to come to Ambleside with me and start making enquiries in the immediate area of the

Thwaite Hotel about a young woman, about five foot seven inches tall, slim, and with bright red hair. We'll pay the Westmorland Estate Agency a visit too. Will, I want you to set up a meeting with the Serb-Croat expert to interview the mother of baby Dale at the hospital, then try and find Colin Day's accountant or at least get one of our own to start on this lot. It's mumbo-jumbo to me. Great work, guys, we're getting somewhere,' she added.

According to the coroner, Colin Day's death wasn't homicide, but it was a robbery. In addition Kelly had clear evidence of payment in cash for sex, so there was suspected prostitution as well, and prostitutes almost always worked for someone. The young woman might have re-dyed her hair by now, or taken off her wig, but she might also be completely unaware of the tape, and Kelly had to make sure it didn't leak to the press. She'd be keeping the information strictly within Eden House. A plan was forming and she turned her attention to her next immediate task. If she and DC Hide set off for Ambleside now, they'd be back in time for a five o'clock briefing, when she would play the tape to the team.

Colin Day's widow was available to talk, and Kelly grabbed her jacket and handbag. They could stop for coffee on the way.

Chapter 19

Christine Day answered the door herself, her expression remaining unchanged when Kelly greeted her. Unsurprising, given the news she'd had. The house was a generous detached property made of local stone. A large ramp led up to the front door and another round to the back. Two new-looking BMWs sat on the driveway. Mrs Day wheeled herself backwards in a gesture that beckoned Kelly inside.

'Please close the door behind you.' Her voice was monotone. No one had told her about the tape yet; that treat had been left to Kelly.

She led the way into a large reception room at the front of the house that allowed in a beautiful stream of sunshine. It was light and airy, and had been decorated to a high standard. Mrs Day appeared to favour large, bold prints, and fresh flowers wafted an aroma around the room. She seemed like a woman who had achieved just what she'd wanted in life. Kelly calculated that she was in her seventies, but reckoned she'd had some work done. It was the way her smooth skin disappeared effortlessly into her hairline, as if gravity had passed her by. Kelly knew enough to spot a face lift, and it shaved years off the woman. She also noticed that Mrs Day wore a lot of jewellery, and it wasn't costume jewellery either; rather a collection of hefty items sporting gold and jewels. The woman stank of money.

But her face was etched with sadness and all the material wealth seemed insignificant now.

'Can I get you a drink?' she asked.

'I'm fine, thank you,' said Kelly.

'I don't know you. We... Colin and I... know our fair share of police and I don't recognise you.' The woman waited for a suitable response.

'I'm new, Mrs Day. I worked in the Met in London for ten years, but I grew up here.'

'Please call me Christine. London, how exciting. But not as beautiful as here. I'm not surprised you came back.'

With the pleasantries over, Christine got down to business.

'So why has my husband's death been passed to a detective? He had a heart attack.' She was clearly no pushover.

'Christine, there was a video tape.' Kelly let the information sink in. Colin Day's death had been captured on camera. It was an unusual detail; not everyone was privileged enough to watch their loved ones pass.

Christine looked perplexed. 'What tape? Why would there be a tape?'

'It was set up to record a meeting.'

'What kind of meeting?'

Here we go, thought Kelly.

'With a woman. A woman we have evidence to suggest was being paid or looked after by your husband. The whole encounter was recorded and your husband's heart attack occurred during the, erm... appointment.' She allowed the news to sink in; she'd say no more until Christine responded.

'Encounter? Can you be more specific?' Christine asked.

'They were having sexual intercourse, Christine. I'm sorry.'

'Don't be ridiculous!' said Christine, but it was half-hearted.

Kelly felt for her; it was a shocking legacy to have to deal with. She stayed silent.

'Why...' Christine's mouth opened and closed and finally she looked away. 'Who is she?'

'We don't know.'

'What do you mean, you don't know?' It was scathing. Christine Day was in pain and needed to lash out.

'She disappeared after your husband's death; she panicked and left. The video is dark and we haven't been able to identify her yet,' said Kelly.

'You've watched it?' Christine swallowed hard.

'Yes.'

Christine wheeled herself to a large window and looked out to the garden beyond. Her mouth was pursed tightly, holding back a deluge of emotion desperate to get out.

'Christine, what kind of watch did Mr Day wear? We believe it was taken, along with a large amount of money and perhaps a valuable ring.'

Christine shot round. 'A ring? The bastard, he said he'd taken it to fix a claw. It was meant for her, wasn't it? Other bits have gone missing too. Perhaps he had a different girl each week.' She looked away again; her cheeks burning.

'Did he make a habit of staying at the hotel?'

'Oh yes. So she took his Rolex as well, did she? Good. Good luck to her, she deserves everything she can lay her hands on. I hope she gets away with it.'

Christine was becoming angrier. Kelly had to get as much from her as she could before the woman lost focus.

'Could you describe the ring?' she asked.

'Rose gold, worth a fortune, a ruby the size of my thumbnail. It was my mother's. Bastard.'

'Do you have a joint bank account, Christine?'

'No, don't be stupid. He knew better than that, didn't he? We have separate accounts and now I know why. I wonder how much he paid them.'

'Do you think you could give us a descriptive list of the valuable items you think he might have taken?'

'Of course I can, I'll do it right now.' She wheeled herself towards the door.

'May I take a look around? Did Mr Day have a study, perhaps?'

'I'll show you. You can take what you want. The press have been on the phone already. What do I tell them?'

'I can't tell you what to say, but we would certainly like as little as possible to get out until we find the girl.'

'Done. My husband being serviced by a whore isn't something I'd like my daughters to watch. With the internet how it is, it would only take five minutes for it to get out. Follow me.'

They entered a large study that boasted a beautiful oak desk with a red leather top. Christine wheeled herself up to it and found a sheet of paper, then began scribbling furiously. After a minute she stopped and turned round.

'Help yourself,' she said, and went back to her list.

Kelly began opening drawers and cupboards. She found a file calling itself 'Bank Accounts' and another titled 'Hotels'. There were more, all labelled neatly with different names. She scanned through them: 'Connor Temple', 'HCCD Art Handling', 'Real Estate'... It looked as though Colin Day ran a tight ship. From her cursory glance at his background, she had him down as making his wealth from tanning salons, so whatever she was looking at here could possibly be further investments. Christine had told her to help herself, so she did, flicking through the files and taking out pages that contained addresses, codes, transactions and anything else that caught her eye.

'Did he have more than one phone?' she asked.

Christine looked tired. 'Yes, he had two: one he called his work phone, although he didn't work anymore, or maybe he did, what would I know? Then he had a personal one. He carried them both at all times. Were they taken too?'

'No, two phones were recovered. We'll let you know if we find anything on them.'

Kelly came to a drawer that was locked, and the noise of her pulling it caught Christine's attention. She turned around.

'He called that his private drawer. Said he needed somewhere to keep surprises from me. The key was on his key fob. I'll get it; it was among the things given back to me after...' She tailed off and left the room.

She was back in under five minutes.

'Here you go.'

The drawer clicked as Kelly turned the key. Inside were three USB sticks and a large envelope marked 'Onchan Island Bank'.

'Christine, have you heard of the Onchan Island Bank?'

'No, I haven't. What have you got there?' Christine looked nervous, as if she wished she hadn't been so hasty in giving Kelly the key. But Kelly could see that she was angry with her husband and had perhaps had a lapse of judgement because of it. She showed her the USB sticks.

'Do I have your permission to take these, Christine?'

'I want to see what's on them first.'

'Are you sure? I could check them first if you'd prefer.' Kelly couldn't stop Christine watching them: they were on her private property, and she had no authority to remove them.

'I'm made of strong stuff, Detective. I want to know.'

Half an hour later, they'd both seen enough to know that Colin Day was meeting prostitutes regularly, and he wasn't the only one. Christine looked pale and Kelly felt for her. She wondered what else they were going to find out to torture this woman.

'I want them destroyed.' She was shaking with renewed anger.

'I'm sorry, Christine, they contain evidence and I have to add them to the inquiry. I do have one more question. Have you ever heard of a company called Tomb Day?'

'No, never.'

'Thank you, I'll see myself out.'

–

With the door closed, Christine Day made an urgent phone call to the only person she could trust. She couldn't stand the woman, but she had no choice.

Chapter 20

Darren waited outside the door. It was non-descript except for the graffiti: a peace sign sprayed in blue and a few messages scrawled in ink. One said, 'Fly me to the moon', another 'No way back'. Darren had already read them a dozen times. He leant against a ladder that stood up against the cement wall. The small balcony smelled of piss, and dogs barked incessantly from within the building. His stomach was in knots and he'd needed to take a dump twice as his guts churned and liquefied the contents of his bowels. He bit his nails, even though his mother always told him not to. She said he'd get worms.

He looked at his watch; it was five thirty-five p.m. Marko would keep him waiting for as long as he felt like. Darren had received a message while he'd been driving around deciding what to do with the bodies in his boot. It had been to the point and uncompromising; an answer wasn't required, just his presence, and he was out of alternative ideas. So here he was. He hadn't even had a chance to check Nush's room for the cash. But he had got rid of the bodies.

The door opened and a large man appeared. Curtis, one of Marko's thugs. He wore a dark shirt tucked into jeans and his long hair was scraped back into a ponytail. If he'd been one of Darren's mates, he'd have had the piss ripped out of him for looking like a girl, but no one would dare suggest such a thing to Curtis. His hands were the size of Darren's head and his eyes saw everything, so much so that Darren thought he could even see that he needed another shit.

Curtis nodded and beckoned for Darren to follow him inside. The barking was louder here, and Darren knew that the dogs were being wound up and baited to kill, ready for a big fight tonight. He had seen a couple of the fights – he thought they were awesome – but he wasn't invited often because he couldn't afford to bet. His mother still thought their Jack Russell had just wandered off out of the garden one day, but Darren had brought her here for training purposes. He'd watched as she'd had her paws tied together and her muzzle taped so she couldn't fight back. She'd hung in the air, whining, as two fighters, one an Irish Staff bull and the other an American Staff bull, tore her apart. It was mind-blowing to watch. Marko had once told Darren that if he ever screwed up, he'd tie him up too and throw him to his favourite bulls. Darren believed him.

Marko now sat with his feet up on a table, smoking. He was a quiet man, and rarely spoke, but when he did, it sent tingles down Darren's spine. His voice had a foreign lilt, one that Darren didn't recognise, though it sounded as though it belonged in a movie. His eyes were dark and merciless, and his thick black eyebrows made them even more sinister.

'Darren. I have a problem.' He exhaled smoke. Darren watched him. Underneath Marko's black jumper, he could see ink all over his arms and he guessed the guy was covered in tattoos.

'Marko—'

'Shut up. Now, you need to tell me that those girls are taken care of and you also need to tell me that the manager and cleaner are going to disappear. I don't need this kind of bullshit. Why was one of my girls screwing Colin Day?'

'She arranged it on her own, Marko, I swear. She must have met him when she was seeing another client.'

Marko banged his fist on the table and sat up.

'Don't tell me bullshit! You arranged it and you were taking a cut. A cut of my money, Beckett. I should fucking kill you now.'

Darren felt as though he wanted to piss in his pants.

'Where is she? And the one she was inseparable from? If you tell me you don't know, you're not walking out of here.'

'Both of them are dead,' Darren said with confidence. He'd take the credit for Roza too.

After dumping the bodies, Darren had driven around, buzzing, as if he were in *Goodfellas* or something. But now, as he stood in the dark flat, he realised that he was anything but Marko's hit man. He was shit scared, and unsure about his next move. Curtis hovered behind him like some kind of menacing troll, and Marko nodded to him. Darren felt a hand on his shoulder, and he swallowed. Any minute now, he'd piss himself and it'd go all over the guy's shoes.

'They were both fucking around, Marko, but I know where they left their cash.'

'Are you telling me you killed Nush and Roza for me?' Marko spread his mouth wide and chuckled.

'Yes,' Darren replied, too quickly and too enthusiastically.

'I could have sold them, you stupid bastard.'

Darren's heart sank. He hadn't thought of that.

'But they still might have talked,' Marko added. 'And my little problem could have turned into a very big problem indeed.' Darren breathed a little easier: there was hope yet. 'But I'm impressed, Beckett. You shouldn't have any problem with the manager and the cleaner then. I knew I couldn't trust Tony to clean up.'

Darren knew that Tony had been Colin Day's choice as binman. Apparently he was a friend of Day's son and Day felt protective towards him. Fucking idiot, no one gave alcoholics jobs. Marko had predicted trouble, and now he'd been proved right.

Marko shook his head and stroked his chin, putting his cigarette out with his other hand. Darren noticed that he wore two rings, one made from thick gold with a diamond, and the other a silver piece with black, purple and green stuff set into it. Rings on Darren would have made him look like a pansy. They made Marko look meaner.

'What do I do with the manager and the cleaner, Marko?'

'Use your imagination, Beckett. Do you want me to send you on a training course?'

Darren thought about confirming that that would be a good idea, but decided not to.

'No, Marko.'

'Good. Find out if they said anything to the police first. I'm sending Sasha with you.'

This was interesting. Interesting and terrifying. It meant that Marko wanted the job done well and he was throwing Darren a bone; an opportunity to learn from the best. But it was also a warning. Sasha was Marko's son and his best asset, and he wouldn't consider *whether* to kill Darren – only when and how. Darren tried to tell himself that he was a long way down the food chain where Marko was concerned, but that wasn't the point. Marko was taking this whole Thwaite Hotel thing seriously. Day must have been up to something bigger than just shagging illegal girls. There was always supposed to be a night manager with access to an untraceable mobile phone and there was always supposed to be a binman. Both jobs on the night in question were supposed to be covered by Tony. But no one knew where he was. It was a knee-jerk reaction to tidy up the dead girl first; after all, the old guy had only had a heart attack. No crime had been committed. But now Marko didn't seem so sure.

'The place has been crawling with detectives, Beckett, and it seems that the old bastard was filming the whole thing.'

Darren's mouth opened and closed. Fucking hell. No wonder Marko was worried.

'I'll get the tape,' he said.

Marko laughed. 'You idiot. The police have it, it's long gone. What did you do with the girls' bodies? I'm intrigued.'

'They're taken care of.'

'Where?'

'Barrow Dock.'

Marko folded his arms and stared at him.

'Did you do as I asked?'

'Yes, I left the flat without telling anyone.'

'Good, here's an address where you can stay.' He handed Darren a slip of paper and a wad of cash. 'And buy yourself some decent clothes and take a fucking shower. Sasha will pick you up at eight.'

'Thank you, Marko.'

'Don't grovel. It's not necessary and it makes you look weak. If you're going to be working for me properly, you need to grow a backbone.'

Darren didn't say a word.

'That's better,' said Marko.

Chapter 21

'What did you tell them, Anna?' Kevin Cottrell asked.

'Nothing!' the cleaner replied.

'I can't believe you called 999 before speaking to me.'

Kevin paced up and down the reception of the Thwaite Hotel. Detective Inspector Porter would be there any moment and they had to have their story straight.

'You repeat what you said to the police last time: I'm just a day manager so I don't know anything about the night shift. The hotel hadn't had bookings for a while, we don't know why. We think they had financial difficulties and we were both looking for new jobs. Mr Day liked his room and stayed a lot; we had no idea he had guests. Are you getting all of this, Anna?'

'Where was Tony?' she asked.

'Pissed, in bed as always. He probably slept through the whole thing.'

'Do we mention him?'

'I think we do, then it takes the attention away from us. He's supposed to be the night manager after all. Then I'm out of here. I've found a new job.'

'Where?'

'I'm not telling you. You're on your own after tonight.'

'Do we really think it's a brothel, Kevin?'

He laughed. 'Of course it is, you stupid cow! I wish I'd never taken the job, I was desperate. The place is a shit hole.'

–

Kelly approached the hotel with DC Hide. The enhanced photo had come through on her iPad and she had it with her. DC Hide had done a fantastic job and had several sightings of a red-headed girl who had worked in hotels in Ambleside over the past few months.

A man and a woman were waiting for them in the hotel lobby. The man looked as though he was about to make a run for it, and the young woman appeared terrified. Kelly thought it unlikely that, after seeing the papers this morning, anyone could work here and not know what was going on. She decided to start with the girl.

'Anna Cork? I'm DI Kelly Porter, the detective assigned to look into the death of Colin Day. Thank you for waiting for me. I just need to ask a few questions. Shall we sit down?'

Anna stood back, wide-eyed, the man hovering behind her.

'Kevin Cottrell?' Kelly asked, and he nodded and held out his hand. 'Good, shall we make a start then? I won't keep you long.' She wanted to make them comfortable; to break down their guard.

Anna led them to a small table just off the reception area and the three of them sat down. Hide stood nearby, watching. A uniform guarded the door. Kelly got out a notepad. She'd interview them together initially to keep things fairly relaxed. She could gauge their relationship by how they reacted and interacted.

'So, Anna, you found Mr Day on the morning of Friday the twenty-first, is that correct?' she began.

Anna nodded.

'Can you tell me exactly how you found him?'

'Well, the door was unlocked and I went in to start cleaning. I could see straight away that something was wrong. I went to him, but I soon realised he wasn't breathing. He was very cold.' She looked distraught.

'How well did you know Mr Day, Anna?'

'Er… we chatted a bit when I took him his post, but he wasn't usually there in the morning, so I only saw him a few times. He was nice, he left good tips,' she added.

Kelly was aware that Cottrell was watching her, but she concentrated on Anna.

'I read in the notes that he had post delivered here. Was it personal stuff, or was it addressed to the hotel? After all, he was the owner.'

'I can't remember.' She looked at Kevin, wondering if he knew that the hotel belonged to Mr Day. He was staring at the detective.

'Did you know he had regular guests, Anna?'

'No,' she said, too quickly.

'Do you recognise this woman?' Kelly showed Anna her iPad. Kevin swallowed.

'Er…' Anna squinted at the screen for a long time, colour mounting in her cheeks. 'No, I'm sure I don't.'

'Kevin, what about you?' asked Kelly.

'No, definitely not,' he replied, though he'd barely looked at the picture.

'And how long is it since there have been other guests at the hotel?' Kelly glanced down at the notes made by Martin and Coombs.

Anna and Kevin looked at one another.

'OK, let me put it another way. According to the log book in the office here, several men rented rooms on a long-term basis, but there have been no short-term visitors – holidaymakers – for at least as far back as I looked.'

'I don't think many people stayed here. I haven't seen guests for about four weeks. I was looking for a new job.' Kevin sounded defensive.

'And who was the last guest you saw?'

'I can't remember.'

Kelly knew that the interview wasn't going anywhere. It was obvious that they were both lying and she had to find out why.

'There's not a lot of work to do round here, is there? With no guests. Who interviewed you for the jobs?'

'My mum got me the job,' said Anna, and finally Kelly believed her.

'I know the night manager,' said Kevin, and she almost believed him.

'So, where was the night manager when Mr Day was having his heart attack?'

'He has a drinking problem. When I came in in the morning, he was in bed.'

'And where is he now?'

'I don't know. He left and I don't know where he went.'

'The hotel will remain closed for the time being at Mrs Day's request, so it looks like you will both need to find new jobs. Maybe next time you should find out a bit more about your employers,' said Kelly, raising her eyebrows. 'I'll need the master key, please, and I'd also like you to show me the night manager's room. I don't suppose you have any employment details for him? A photo?'

'They'd be in the office,' Kevin replied.

She couldn't recall coming across any details about a night manager.

'And his name?'

'We only knew him as Tony.'

Kelly decided she wasn't going to get anything more out of them.

'If either of you do suffer a moment of lucidity or conscience, then please call me.' She handed both of them cards. 'You can show me the room now.'

Kelly and DC Hide followed as Kevin Cottrell showed them upstairs, along a corridor and into the room occupied by Tony. Anna accompanied meekly behind, not knowing if she was required or not.

'Thank you, you can go now,' said Kelly, accepting the master key from Cottrell.

'Christ, guv, that was like pulling teeth,' said Hide, once the pair had left.

'Impressions?'

'Bullshit. They both recognised the photo. She's not exactly inconspicuous, is she?'

'Quite. The lab confirmed it's real hair and not a wig, but she could have dyed it by now. Did you get a name for her?'

'Nush. Short for Anushka. None of the people I spoke to could give me any more details, though apparently she worked at the Troutbeck Guest House from time to time. I took a walk down there and a waitress confirmed she'd been working there and that her surname is Ivanov. I ran it through the Home Office and there's no work permit in that name. There's also no trace of her at the Passport Office.'

'Isn't the Troutbeck another of Day's hotels? Who runs it?'

'A woman called Mrs Joliffe, unavailable. I've left messages.'

'Well done, Emma. Let's have a look around here.' Kelly accepted a pair of latex gloves from DC Hide, and they went in.

The room was dark and smelled of stale body odour. Kelly flicked on a light and they began looking around for hints of the man who lived there. It was sparse, and littered with the detritus of an alcoholic: bottles were strewn all over the surfaces as well as the floor, and boxes of headache pills lay ready for use. A wallet sat on the side and a cursory glance showed that there was cash and ID inside. The driving licence gave the owner the name Tony Proctor. The man clearly hadn't gone to buy alcohol; he would need cash and the black jacket which was discarded over a chair. With the hotel closed, Tony Proctor had nowhere to sleep, so where was he?

'Come on,' Kelly said. She used the master key to open other doors. They went from room to room, finding messy beds, filthy bathrooms and discarded personal items, including plenty of condoms, used and otherwise. They lifted and looked under objects, looking for anything that might help with the investigation. Kelly knew that she'd need to get a photographer here to compile a file for her records. No-one would be allowed in the place from now on, except herself and anyone she sent.

They went back downstairs and walked in and out of the reception rooms and Kelly ran her hand over cupboards that hadn't been cleaned for months. It would appear that Anna Cork was only told to keep the functional areas clean – in other words, the bedrooms.

They found a small basic kitchen and opened the fridge. It was empty apart from some in-date milk. It didn't give the impression of a working area: dust was gathered in every corner and there was no aroma of recent cooking. Next they went into the small office behind reception, the one that had yielded the piles of paperwork. They would have to go over the rest of it as soon as possible, and Kelly realised that it was going to be a long night. They needed evidence of any money changing hands, and where it went to, as well as the personal details of other 'guests'. Christine Day wouldn't be the only betrayed spouse here, of that she was certain.

She thought for a moment about sex. She'd worked dozens of cases that revolved around either illicit or secret sex, and she'd come to the conclusion that she herself was quite ordinary. She'd only ever slept with one man at a time, she didn't pay for it or charge for it, she stayed away from other people's husbands (she hoped) and she didn't use equipment. She felt terribly boring facing this parallel world of desire and toxicity that tore people apart. She wasn't sure what she thought of Colin Day. He'd betrayed his wife and hurt her, but was Christine more worried about the public shame or the fact that he had a sex drive she couldn't satisfy?

And then there was Lottie Davis, who'd been subjected to unimaginable pain and terror because of some man's perverted desires. Kelly would have to control her feelings if she stood any chance of catching Lottie's killer, but it was tough. Detective work was liable to put one off people generally; it was the nature of the job. She shook her head. Getting results was all that mattered; the weirdos could spend all the time they liked telling their prison psychologists why they did what they did. But first she had to catch them.

Kelly's phone rang. Nikki. She toyed with ignoring it, but her conscience got the better of her.

'It's Mum, Kelly. She's in hospital.'

Chapter 22

Marko wouldn't watch the dog fight tonight; he had other things to attend to. A new batch of girls was scheduled to arrive and he was always keen to be there at the beginning. Only he decided who went where. Most of them were only good for sticking a needle in and fucking, but occasionally a little gem would surface that he could use for his more select contacts. A young, fresh one with big tits could sell for two thousand to the right people, and he knew the right people. Then there were the ones with attitude and intelligence who came over under different circumstances, with longer-term potential; girls like Nush, although that had gone badly wrong, one of Teresa's rare failures.

Teresa was an elegant woman in her forties with the moral compass of a snake. They'd worked together for over ten years. She added to the flavour of authenticity, especially when dealing with the higher-end customers, and was a genius at matching girls to clients, and also breaking their will. She'd only failed a handful of times, but it hadn't mattered, because he could always find other ways of making money from the girls. Like ivory, diamonds and meth, the market for women was constantly buoyant.

It had been the right move leaving Liverpool; it hadn't interrupted business much at all. Everyone was moving out of the cities and into the country, where there were more places to hide and fewer police. Besides, he'd expanded his business since moving to the Lakes, branching out into the leisure industry. Diversification: it was the lifeblood of good business.

When he'd first come to the UK from Serbia over twenty years ago, he was broke, spoke little English and lived in a bedsit in Speke. It hadn't taken him long to work out who was in charge when the lights went out and the good tax-paying citizens were tucked up in bed. That was when the underbelly came to life, and he soon wormed his way in. There had been ups and downs, but now business was good. He'd learned who to trust and who to get rid of. He left competitors alone and showed respect to those in the industry who'd been around longer, although nowadays they were few.

He'd made enough money to retire, but he wasn't ready to go yet. He enjoyed staying at grass roots; that way he had more control. Start giving responsibility to those who couldn't handle it and that was when cracks appeared. He ensured he was at every meeting, every shipment, every tasting and every decision. One day he would hand over to Sasha, but not yet.

The drive was short; he rented several warehouses in and around Penrith. The town was small enough to lack resources but big enough to stay anonymous, and he kicked himself for not moving sooner. Merseyside was crowded with people doing the same thing, and the drugs had got out of hand. Here, he could smooth off rough edges, polish his services and take advantage of the huge untapped potential of the place.

Darren had compromised him, but Marko always gave second chances; never third, but always second. The boy had potential, and had already got rid of a couple of mistakes for him. That was the other thing about this area: dozens of deep lakes and dark fells to dispose of waste. There'd only ever been one mistake in cleaning up, and the guy responsible had been punished for a good couple of hours before being weighted and thrown into a disused mine shaft full of water.

Marko had known Curtis for fifteen years and trusted him with his life. Curtis had gone ahead to check the delivery. The girls had all paid for passage to the UK; some of their families had contributed too, though Marko cared not how they got the money. The average was three thousand sterling. That got them the whole voyage. What they didn't know was that they were paying to belong to Marko. Their passports were destroyed on arrival, along with their hopes, and replaced with the realisation that they'd been tricked.

He stopped short of the warehouse and looked around. The streets were deserted. He flashed his lights and Curtis stepped out of a metal side door. If there was trouble, Curtis wouldn't appear. Marko left his car and walked to the building.

Curtis had three brothers and they'd all proved themselves to Marko. All four men looked the same: over six foot tall, dark shaggy hair and huge hands; only Curtis wore his in a ponytail. They stood when Marko came in and Marko saw that there were around ten girls sitting on the floor. They huddled together, terrified and cold as the four brothers circled them, fondling baseball bats to heighten their terror. It worked. Each one was gagged for now, but they made little noise anyway, believing they'd be saved should they behave. Marko could tell that Curtis was pumped, as he always was on nights like this, though he knew that the girls were off limits for now. They had to be delivered unmarked and still possessing some form of hope; it was more attractive that way.

The girls came from all over Europe, and further afield, and so the men didn't bother speaking, using gestures instead. It was made clear that Curtis wanted them to stand up. Two of the girls were crying. Marko nodded to Curtis, who walked over to one of them and slapped her face. It wasn't hard – not enough to leave a mark – but it was vicious enough to shut her up. Now a hush descended, and Marko approached the group and began to examine the girls individually, lifting their chins, assessing their bodies and calculating what each might be good for; which would earn him the most money. He was attracted to one in particular who hadn't made a sound; her eyes were defiant, and she'd be difficult to crack. He couldn't decide whether to send her straight to a holding house or to trust Teresa again. She'd go for a decent price, and he decided to give Teresa another chance.

He approached another who looked perfect for entertainment, though not to his own taste. She tightened her jaw as he stared into her eyes. Too much of a loose cannon, he decided with regret; she'd only be good for a holding house. He gestured to Curtis, who came to stand beside him, then began pointing at the girls, indicating where he wanted them taken. There were two options at this stage. The girls deemed to be low grade would be taken directly to one of numerous holding houses he owned in the Lakes. Those he thought suitable for his elite clients would be taken to an old farmhouse near the A66, where they'd be 'developed'. Either way, they'd soon begin their path towards drug dependency and demise. The longer they lasted, the better. The ones destined for the holding houses would be good for around ten appointments per day for as long as their bodies held out.

Once the girls had been separated into two groups – one of seven and one of three – the larger group was instructed to follow Curtis and one of his brothers. There were the usual attempts to resist and Curtis had to use his brutishness again: that was what he was employed to do. The remaining three followed the other two men without much fuss. Vans waited outside for them, and they'd be strapped together for the journey.

With business concluded, Marko thought about the evening ahead. He had a gathering to go to where he was showing off some girls who'd been recently broken in. There was a lot of money at stake.

He'd rented a fifteen-bedroom mansion near Ullswater from a discreet company that never asked questions, and he was excited as he drove there. It was secluded, legitimate and quiet. The house had been stocked with booze and drugs, and clients could please themselves: they could remain with the main group or go off to their own rooms. The girls would do as they were told. The clever ones learned that if they behaved, they were rewarded and the abuse subsided. If they broke the rules, they got a beating – or worse. There really was no way out.

The main road skirting Ullswater's northern shore was quiet, and the moon bounced happily off the water.

Marko preferred it out here in the sticks; it was like his own little kingdom. He negotiated the tight bends and felt the power of the engine, heightening his anticipation. After a while, he turned off onto a single-lane road, with barely enough room for cars to pass each other, and slowed down. There was little ambient light, and he flicked his headlights to full beam. The house sat at the end of a long driveway, and Marko parked on the gravel outside the front door. His guests would be comfortable in their rooms, preparing themselves for the night ahead. He checked his hair in the rear-view mirror and got out of the car.

Teresa was at the house already, making sure that everything ran smoothly. She watched over every event like a wolf tracking a flock of sheep. She could tell if a girl had had enough and needed a break, or if someone needed to be escorted to their room, and she kept the booze flowing. She was Marko's right-hand man, and he paid her well.

Marko never drank or touched drugs when he hosted, and he never touched the girls either, though he did watch. He also filmed. That was his insurance. Mr Day was a wise man to do the same. But recently the old fool had grown sloppy and arrogant. He should've handed over the business to Marko years ago but he just couldn't let go.

As Marko stepped through the front door, Teresa was there to greet him. She wore a long black dress that showed off her figure, very high heels and lots of diamonds. Her blonde hair was recently styled and her make-up well done. She wasn't Marko's type, but she impressed his clients and gave him the whiff of legitimacy. There were several important guests staying with them over the next couple of days, and he was charging wildly different prices depending on how wealthy they were. Tonight he had a Canadian, a Texan, two Italians, five Russians and three Englishmen. The richest was the Texan, who was paying twenty thousand for three nights. Marko had paired him with Sofia, a fine bitch from the Ukraine, but he could take whoever he liked, of course.

Teresa lined up the girls as the first guests arrived and they served the clients drinks. Marko introduced each pairing, as well as the spares. Some of the men took an instant liking to their bitch and others fancied someone else, but it all worked out in the end. They had seventy-two hours to try everything on the menu.

As conversation started to flow, Marko noted with satisfaction that everybody seemed to be relaxing nicely. The girls had been given enough drugs to keep them calm but not so much that they'd be no good. They knew that they needed to perform or face the consequences.

'Sofia,' he called.

Sofia nodded to show that she knew what to do. Teresa turned the music up, and the bitch began to dance. The men fell silent and turned to watch. Marko was a man of his word.

Chapter 23

The sky was dark and the wind had picked up. Darren smoked and blew it out of the window. Sasha was silent. There was no need for conversation. They'd both looked at the photos. Darren's pulse quickened. The nicotine helped his nerves, but it also stimulated his bowels, and he wondered if he had a problem.

They had agreed to do Cottrell first; he was in charge and knew the most, they assumed. The day manager lived alone, and a light shone through his first-floor window. Sasha fiddled with the radio, and when he couldn't find what he was looking for, he switched it off angrily and turned off the engine. They hadn't discussed a plan and Darren was beginning to regret his involvement. He felt like an idiot. He had no idea what he would do if Sasha intimated that he wanted him to execute the deed; he had brought no weapon and neither Sasha nor his father had given him one.

They didn't have long to wait. Kevin Cottrell left his apartment building and walked towards the car park. Sasha got out of the car and Darren followed his lead. Kevin stopped, immediately suspicious, and looked at the two men; they were perhaps five metres away. The exit from the car park lay beyond them and Kevin knew he was cornered. He approached them slowly.

'Get in,' Sasha ordered, and nodded to the car.

'Look, whatever it is you want, I don't have it. I'm going to my car now and I won't hesitate to call the police,' Cottrell said.

He started to move, but Sasha took two steps and hammered his fist into the other man's gut. Cottrell bent double and collapsed. His phone fell to the ground and Sasha picked it up and put it into his pocket. Darren helped Sasha bundle Cottrell into the back seat of the car and they jumped in and drove away with their captive groaning behind them. Darren's heart pumped.

'Get in the back and shut him up, I'm sick of his fucking noise. And put this round his wrists,' Sasha demanded, handing him a plastic cable tie.

Darren undid his seat belt and climbed over into the back, putting his hands around Cottrell's throat until his face went red, his eyes wide and frantic. The man was terrified, and a thrill burned in Darren's veins: someone was scared of him and it felt good. He wondered where Sasha was heading and wished he knew what was expected of him. He hoped they'd be alone for whatever was to come.

He went over Marko's words in his head. He hadn't exactly used the word 'kill', and even now, spinning into the darkness, Darren wondered if they would just scare the guy. The anticipation churned his guts and he farted.

'For fuck's sake!' said Sasha, and pressed a button to let his window down. Fresh night air filled the car.

After a while, they slowed and turned off the main road. Darren recognised the abandoned Kirkstone slate quarry. The car stopped and Sasha jumped out and opened the back door. He grabbed Cottrell, who looked petrified, and started to drag him to a building, calling to Darren to get a torch out of the boot. Darren's eyes darted around. He couldn't work out if they were alone; anyone could be waiting for them. He concentrated on following Sasha, but couldn't help looking back several times.

The building was a ramshackle tin shed. It stank. Something had died in here, Darren thought.

Cottrell pissed himself and started to beg.

'Please... I don't know what you—'

Thump. Sasha hammered his fist into the guy's face and his nose spewed blood. He fell to the floor and rolled around, groaning. Sasha looked around and found a piece of old iron machinery that looked heavy. He passed it to Darren, who looked at the torch.

'Give it to me.'

Darren knew what was expected now. I can do this, he thought. He'd got rid of Nush, hadn't he? But she was less messy. Come on, Darren, he willed.

He thought of his mother. He thought of Marko. He thought of his old English teacher, who'd said he had potential.

Cottrell put his arms above his head and started to whimper. 'Please... please...'

Darren stood over him, lifted the hunk of metal, and brought it down, crunching through soft flesh and bone. He did it again and again until the thwacking simply thumped soft meat. There was blood everywhere, together with pieces of human being; his hands were slick from it and he looked at Sasha, who stood smiling at him.

'Good job,' was all he said.

Sasha went to the wall and unhooked a hosepipe, and began washing the mess off to one side. The bloody water ran into a drain.

'Show me your hands,' he commanded. Darren did so and Sasha rinsed them off too. He then emptied Cottrell's pockets and dragged his lifeless body over to the wall of the shed, where he manhandled it onto a tarpaulin. The stench was worse here, and Darren thought it might be coming from a rolled-up carpet that was lying nearby.

'Come on, I don't want to be at this all night,' said Sasha. He indicated for Darren to help him wrap the body.

Cottrell was still warm, and Darren held back bile. As he was bending down to secure the tarpaulin, he caught sight of a head inside the rolled-up carpet and shot upright. It was badly beaten, but he could still tell that it was Tony's. Proctor wore a large gold hoop through his left ear and Darren spotted it clearly, and that, along with the white hair, left no doubt in his mind. So, he'd been taken care of too. They finished wrapping Cottrell and pushed his body next to that of Proctor, and left them there.

In the car, they both smoked as Sasha drove. He was a handsome bastard, thought Darren, like his father; he had a straight jawline and a strong brow, his hands were muscular and his shoulders filled his jacket.

Sasha laughed.

'What?' asked Darren, nervous.

'Did you see the way his head came apart? You were an animal. I'll tell my father.'

As they drove back the way they had come, Sasha's phone rang. He nodded several times, then hung up.

'The girl is waiting for us. My father told them to wait; he wants you to do it. Well, my friend, after that, I don't think you'll have a problem.' Sasha was smiling.

Darren did have a problem: it sounded like there would be more people there – a fucking audience. They'd expect a show. He guessed that Sasha would have thought it through, so he decided to simply follow his lead.

He looked at his hands. He hadn't cleaned away all the blood, and dark brown stains had formed on his jeans and shoes. He marvelled at Sasha's coolness; he didn't seem to think there was the remotest possibility that they'd be pulled over by the police. His mind whirred.

They were just outside Ambleside when Sasha stopped the car. He jumped out and again Darren followed. Sasha obviously knew the place. They entered a barn that was attached to a stone house. Darren wished he'd had a shot of something. Marko's man Curtis was here, and that always meant someone wasn't getting out alive.

The girl was tied up and gagged and the arrival of two more men made her thrash about. Darren swallowed hard. She was tied to a chair, and underneath it was spread plastic sheeting. He guessed it could get messy.

The girl was trying to scream but the gag was too tight. Curtis unfolded his arms and kicked the chair; it fell sideways with a loud clatter and the girl writhed on the floor. Sasha nodded and Curtis handed Darren a large knife.

Oh Christ, he thought. Sasha passed him a hip flask and Darren drained it. It made him feel slightly better, though his hands shook and the girl was still flailing about on the floor. Curtis went to her and held her by the arms, picking up the chair with her in it as if it were a handbag.

He sat her upright, then went behind her and jerked her chin up, exposing her neck.

'I can't do it,' Darren said. Sasha looked at Curtis.

'If you don't do it quick, I'll do it slow,' said Curtis, whose hold on the girl was vicelike. Darren told himself that it wouldn't take long, and that he didn't, after all, have a choice. It was the girl or him.

He had bragged to Nush on several occasions that he'd slit her throat. Well now was his chance to actually do it to someone. He tightened his grip on the knife and walked to one side of the chair. Curtis bent the girl's neck the other way, offering him plenty of space. It also meant that Darren didn't have to look into her eyes.

He blocked the girl's face out of his mind, holding onto her hair with one hand and placing the knife under her left ear with his other. The blade went in easily but the sound was sickening and the blood spurted like a hosepipe.

She stopped struggling and Darren stood back. His body began to shake and he forgot where he was. There was so much blood. Curtis asked him to move off the sheet as the girl was untied from the chair. He dropped the knife and it was wrapped up along with the body. Another man emerged from the shadows and helped Curtis tidy up, rolling the girl in the sheet. The floor was clear; they'd contained it. The men looked as though they were packing up camping equipment.

'Come on, there's showers through here, and I have spare clothes,' Sasha said from behind him. 'We need to get rid of these.' He indicated their stained outfits.

The adrenalin began to leave Darren's body and he fought vomit back down his throat. He followed Sasha and found a shower room next door with fresh towels on a chair. He stripped and piled his stained clothes into a bundle, then stepped under the hot water. He scrubbed his body, lathered his hair and used a brush under his nails. The dried blood from earlier liquefied and slipped off him. He held his hand over his mouth.

After he'd dried and dressed, choosing from the clean pile of garments on offer, he took his soiled bundle of rags out to where Sasha was waiting. Sasha beckoned him outside to their waiting car, where he opened the boot and threw the clothes in next to the girl's body.

'One more job before bedtime,' he said, handing Darren a bottle. Darren threw back his head and gulped. At least the liquor eased the noises in his head. He wondered what kind of report Sasha would give to his father. Maybe he'd say he showed potential.

The drive to a desolate stretch of the shores of Rydal Water didn't take long, and there was a small boat waiting for them. They loaded the girl into it, and Darren rowed as Sasha attached the chains.

Darren looked to the sky, and in a tiny moment of lucidity, he appreciated the quietness and the stars. He felt different. The boat broke the smooth surface of the lake, and the moon's reflection rippled black and white.

Sasha motioned him to stop, and the two men heaved the chained package over the side. The boat swayed and tipped and Darren sat down. Soon the swirl of bubbles stopped, and Sasha was satisfied.

Darren Beckett knew that his life now belonged to Marko.

Chapter 24

Kelly stood in front of the whiteboard in the incident room at Eden House. The photo of Anushka Ivanov stared down at her, alongside several other images of girls taken from the USBs found in Colin Day's office. Presumably they'd all been recorded by him. From various tell-tale signs such as the writing paper on the table, the uniform furniture and the twee artwork, it had been ascertained that they'd all been filmed in hotel rooms.

Kelly had left her mother in hospital, stable and comfortable. Her sister had overreacted, as always. Elevated blood pressure, alongside palpitations, was being investigated and there was little she could do. Perhaps she should suggest her mother move in with Nikki for a while, as she herself was so wrapped up in cases. Of course, Nikki would see it as an excuse not to pull her weight, but Kelly had gone beyond caring what her sister thought of her.

'We need names for these faces. We also need to find out if they're legal or not. I want every member of staff in all seven of Colin Day's hotels interviewed. Have we managed to get hold of Mrs Joliffe yet?'

The answer was negative, and it was becoming suspicious.

'We also found the addresses of various lodges and holiday homes that we need to look at. What were they

144

being used for? Are we just scratching the surface here? DS Umshaw, did you contact other forces to see if any investigation like this one is ongoing?'

'Yes, guv. It's a no. There are similar investigations at any given time, but no links to hotels or addresses on our turf.'

'Thanks. DC Phillips, how's the paper trail going?'

'The bank accounts show large amounts of money moving between various personal accounts and offshore businesses. We have the Tomb Day transactions, plus income from his other hotel interests. It seems at first glance – I've spent only two days on it with two accountants – that Colin Day was bringing in around half a million a year on top of his legitimate salary and pension from the tanning salons, but there's another thing: the salons are making around double what you'd expect from businesses that size in those locations. The sums don't add up.'

'Which is his main bank account?'

'We haven't worked that out yet, guv. But a lot of money goes through the Onchan Island Bank in the Isle of Man. Some of it gets ploughed into his personal expenditure and some gets shifted on to other accounts in the names of his various hotels and businesses, but one of the accountants pointed out that, so far, his calculations on income and expenditure don't match. There's extra cash coming from an unknown source.'

'What about his property dealing? Or the art? That can involve huge sums. Westmorland confirmed that he sold a house in Windermere through them recently. Do we know what Connor Temple is?'

'It's a speedboat company, based in Workington Port. But even with the art and property deals, the figures don't work. We're missing something.'

'And most of it goes through Tomb Day,' Kelly concluded. 'It's only the tanning salon money that goes straight in and out of UK bank accounts.'

'Why can't we trace Tomb Day?'

'Day's accounts are frankly erratic, and the accountants reckon he must either be financially ignorant or doing it on purpose to create confusion. There was one thing that stuck in my mind, though, that I think you should know. There are large payments from Tomb Day to a local haulage company here in Penrith. Crawley Haulage.'

The name struck a chord with Kelly, and she paused. Surely not. She fiddled with her ponytail.

'DC Hide, mobile phones? Any attempt to contact?'

'We're due a list of contacts from both phones this afternoon, guv.'

'What about Mr Day's will?'

'Everything left to the wife.'

'Did we get an accountant's name?'

'Yes, guv. Chase and Chase, Workington.'

'Chase? That's funny. Has it been traced?'

'Yes, guv. It was sold back in 1998 to the current firm by Harry Chase.'

'Harry Chase from Merseyside? *My* Harry Chase from the Lottie Davis case?'

The room fell silent.

'Who owns the accountancy firm now?'

'We haven't found that out yet, guv.'

Kelly tapped her lip with her pen.

'So, we have groups of girls appearing to be on the game. We have large payments to and from an offshore company, and a haulage company is somehow involved. Can we check out the possibility of smuggling – perhaps money-laundering of some kind? Keep ploughing on. The answer is in those accounts. My immediate concern, though, is the other girls. Where are they? Are they being held against their will? Anushka Ivanov was working at a local guest house, so you'd think that if she was in that situation, she'd have mentioned it to someone there.'

'Unless she was too scared to.'

'Exactly. I want to know who she was working for, and we need to find out where she was living when she disappeared. I need boots on the ground in Ambleside talking to anyone in and around those hotels. Someone somewhere has to know what's really going on. If anything illegal is happening, I want to get warrants to shut them down, but you know what it's like – I need solid evidence. We haven't got enough yet. I think it's time the press saw a photo of Anushka Ivanov. Hide, can you follow the Chase transaction, I want to know why he sold it, if he really sold it, and his involvement. I never knew he had an accountancy firm in Workington.'

'Yes, guv.'

Kelly wrapped up the meeting and called HQ at Carleton Hall to see if her boss, DCI Cane, would give her any more resources. She didn't want to come across as the cowboy from the big smoke who suddenly unearthed a massive operation in the Lakes that no one else had picked up on, but equally, she couldn't ignore the facts. The Home Office knew that operations like this were more prevalent in the provinces, thanks to the abundance of places to hide. And sleepy villages like Ambleside in the heart of the Lakes were perfect. Cane agreed to transfer some resources from South Lakes, as Ambleside nestled in between the two areas, and Kelly was thankful that she'd already introduced herself to Lockwood. A quick phone call to him reassured her that South Lakes would be happy to help. He also informed her that he was due to chase down Wade Maddox later on.

After a long afternoon of paperwork, dead ends and phone calls, Kelly completed her update of HOLMES and decided to pluck up the courage to ask Johnny out for a pint. His phone went to voicemail and she casually left a message saying she'd be in the Red Lion at Pooley Bridge. She felt herself unwind as she drove towards the shores of Ullswater and parked up outside the pub.

The town was fairly quiet, with only a few tourists wandering around the gift shops or having a well-earned pint after a day of sightseeing or walking. Kelly didn't like to drink in Penrith, and came here whenever she sought peace and quiet. It was where she'd met Johnny the other night. Maybe she'd look at property here.

She was standing outside smoking a cigarette when her phone buzzed. It was Johnny: he could make it by eight p.m. A gang of young men walked towards her and one asked for a light. She offered her lighter, reflecting on the fact that so few young people smoked these days. When she'd been at uni, everyone had smoked; in bars, clubs, restaurants, and even outside lectures. But now it was like a curse. The younger generation seemed much more sensible, and when she sneaked a very rare fag nowadays, she felt guilty.

'Thanks. You all on your own, love?' he asked, lighting up and sucking hard.

Kelly was taken aback by his bravado. Funny, a young man addressing her as 'love'; it was so dated and reminded her how far away from London she was. She found it amusing, though, and decided to play along.

'And what if I am? Are you going to rescue me?' she teased. He must have been only twenty, twenty-one at a pinch.

His mates prodded one another and sniggered. Kelly straightened and smiled, holding his gaze. He faltered.

'So where shall we go, because I don't know about you, but I could do with a man, you know?' She winked and blew smoke seductively. The boy swallowed hard and his mates fell about laughing, in turns taunting him and whistling at Kelly. She stubbed out her cigarette and ran her fingers through her hair.

'Kelly Porter!'

The boy swung around to where the voice had come from. Kelly's eyes lit up.

'Flash! What the hell! You scared these poor boys,' she said, nodding at the gang, who by now were reconsidering their options.

Paul 'Flash' Gordon approached the boy who'd fancied his chances with Kelly, and the lad laughed nervously.

'All right, Flash, don't scare him. I see you're still throwing your weight around,' Kelly said.

The boys retreated quietly and made their way up the main road, and Kelly turned her attention to her old school pal.

'God, Kel, you've looked after yourself, girl. Look at you!' said Flash. He stood back to admire the view and

Kelly rolled her eyes. He was with a mate and it took her a moment to recognise him.

'Dave?' Surely it couldn't be.

'Hi, Kelly, you look fantastic. I thought you went to London?'

'I did; it didn't work out. I'm working in Penrith now and it's good to be back,' she lied, wondering if she sounded convincing.

'So how are you?' Dave asked.

She studied him. When he'd been the love of her life, he'd been athletic, square-jawed, quick-witted and smouldering, or so she remembered. The man standing in front of her now was quiet, shy almost, apologetic and earnest. He'd shrunk; not in stature, but in personality. His eyes lacked life and his belly pushed against his shirt. He blushed, and Kelly felt sympathy, an emotion not usually associated with lust. Flash stood back and gave them a moment.

'So what are you up to now?' she asked, not quite wanting to know the answer. A cherished and pleasant memory was crumbling before her eyes.

'Oh, I still work for Dad.'

Kelly's gut tensed. 'Right. Married?' She already knew the answer. Nikki had enjoyed informing her sister that Dave had shacked up with one of her friends.

'Er, yes, Katy Paterson.' He looked down.

'Kids?' Kelly felt sorry for Dave: Katy was a first-class bitch, and it was clear that she had sucked the life out of him.

'Yeah.' His face lit up. 'Josh is ten and Courtney is seven.' He searched his phone and showed her pictures. The children were cute. Like Dave had once been.

'What about you, Kelly?'

'No, I'm not married, and no kids either. I, er…' She struggled for anything else to say.

'Are you going in here, Kel?' asked Flash.

'I am, yes. I'm meeting a friend,' she said.

'Come on then, we'll buy you a drink to say welcome home,' Flash insisted.

After a few minutes chatting with her old friends, Kelly realised that it felt good to be with familiar faces. There was something safe about stepping back in time rather than having to constantly forge ahead. Flash hadn't changed and fooled around like he always had, but Dave was quiet. He'd just begun to open up when Johnny walked in, and Kelly beckoned him over.

'Johnny! These are some of the reprobates I went to school with. Flash and Dave, meet Johnny.'

Johnny held out his hand and the three men exchanged pleasantries. Dave retreated back into himself and Flash downed his pint and suggested it was time to move on. They said their goodbyes and Kelly watched them go. She wondered if Dave had wanted to leave because of Johnny's presence, but he had his own life now; surely he didn't still have feelings for her.

Johnny wore a baggy red jumper that hung off his broad shoulders, rolled-up cargo pants and flip-flops. His manner was as unfazed as his dress. His hair was too long for an ex-army officer and tinged with the sun. Something stirred inside Kelly and she wondered why it had taken her so long to pick up the phone.

'So, I can't leave you alone for a minute, Kelly Porter. I need to be more careful,' he said.

Kelly smiled at him, 'I can look after myself.'

'I know you can, I've no doubt about that.'

'It's good to see you. Have you been busy?' she asked.

'Manic at work, but I also went down to Manchester to see my daughter.'

Kelly didn't say anything.

'Josie's almost twelve.'

'So you were married?'

'Yup. I wouldn't recommend it. Can I get you another drink?'

Kelly was relieved at the change of subject. They took their drinks to a table and sat down.

'You look gorgeous, by the way,' he said.

'Thank you. It's actually been a shit day.'

'Really? Why?'

'Work. I'm stuck on a few things. Also my mum went into hospital.'

'Is she OK?'

'Yes, she's fine. My sister rang an ambulance because she was having a massive panic attack. Her blood pressure is sky high, and they did an ECG and it's abnormal, so they're monitoring her. Sorry, I'm just knackered.'

'It's good to moan, it puts everything into perspective. And it's also good to relax. Shall we order some food?' he suggested. 'Or we could get a takeaway and take it to mine.'

Kelly had planned to get a cab home, but now she realised that she wanted nothing more than to fall into this man's bed, and this time know where she was when she woke up.

'Let's go.' Johnny took her hand and led her out of the crowded bar.

As they walked towards one of the few takeaway joints in the tiny village, he put his arm around her shoulders. It felt good. She tried to clear her mind and enjoy the moment, but it was always hard for her to unwind. It was especially hard after seeing Dave. She was glad to have bumped into him and Flash, but it also brought back painful memories of the boy she'd once adored. And there was something else, too. Something Phillips had said this afternoon. Dave had told her he still worked for his dad, and Kelly had been thrown. Not just by the fact that he had never moved on, but also because Dave Crawley, of Crawley Haulage, had just been thrust back onto her radar for more than a catch-up.

Chapter 25

DI Lockwood drove along Dalton Road and turned off towards Barrow Island, passing identical rows of run-down flats that had been built for Scottish and Irish immigrant workers during the nineteenth century.

Lockwood had spent a lot of time on Barrow Island. It was bullshit what the government said about crime; they tried to insinuate that initiatives and handouts could change the culture of criminality in these places, but that was just politics. The fact was that economic status was directly proportionate to felony, and that was true the world over.

Wade Maddox was a twenty-five-year-old pain in the arse. Lockwood had gone to school with his dad; Bagger Maddox had been the sort of boy who started fights, picked on the remedial kids and put frogs and beetles in the girls' bags. He was no bright spark and had been caught in the wrong place at the wrong time during a robbery that had turned into manslaughter. It didn't matter that his previous record had always been minor stuff; he'd chosen the wrong job and been sent down for fifteen years. Of course a middle-class kid with good lawyers would have gone down for two, but Bagger Maddox wasn't that kid. He came from Barrow Island.

Wade never stood a chance with a dad like that. He got into trouble at school, in the pub, and pretty much everywhere he went. Lockwood had escorted him home on many occasions, but he hadn't seen him around for a few years. Now he'd turned up with a group of young men who'd made their home in a flat on Barrow Island. Lockwood didn't really care what went on in the flat, just as long as they didn't hurt anyone. Sometimes gangs of lads could be hounded by the police until they were driven further and further into serious crime. Lockwood believed in cutting them some slack if they were doing no harm.

He parked his vehicle outside the flats. He was here to find out if Wade Maddox knew anything about the disappearance of young Lottie Davis, and if he did, he'd wring his neck. He wanted answers for DI Kelly Porter. He had respect for a fellow officer who'd done time on a force in one of the UK's major cities, and Kelly Porter had balls, he could see that. It hadn't gone completely unnoticed that she was also easy on the eye, but he could forget about that: those days were over. Besides, she was too young. She probably had some guy at home ten years his junior who could keep up with her.

He straightened his tie and knocked on the door of the flat. After a long wait, it was opened slowly by a kid whose face was covered in spots typical of substance abuse, though that wasn't Lockwood's concern today.

'Afternoon, pal. I'm looking for Wade Maddox. I've got nothing to say to the rest of you. It's just Wade I need to see.' He waited.

'Who are you?' The lad wasn't stupid. Just wasted.

'Detective Inspector Lockwood. He knows me.'

The boy's eyes widened, as Lockwood knew they would.

'Like I said, I'm not interested in anybody else, lad, just Wade. I need to speak to him.'

Lockwood's demeanour was open; he showed no signs of impatience or superiority, and it worked. The lad opened the door and beckoned him in. He saw Wade straight away, slouched in a chair playing on an Xbox with three other boys. They were all in animated game mode and didn't notice the detective come in.

'Wade. How are you, lad?'

Wade's eyes darted from the DI to the boy who'd let him in, and back again.

'I just want to talk. Can you spare ten minutes to walk with me? It's nothing to worry about, you're not in trouble. I need to ask some questions. That's all.'

Wade knew he had no option. He turned to his mates, who simply shrugged and resumed their game, now one player down. Lockwood went to the door and Wade followed meekly.

'How're you doing, Wade?' Lockwood said as they stepped out into the street. 'I haven't seen you for a while.'

Maddox shrugged.

'I heard your old fella's inside again. I'm sorry. Not planning to follow in the family tradition, I hope.'

'He's a wanker,' said Wade.

Lockwood couldn't disagree. He had a soft spot for kids who found themselves born into shit, it being no fault of their own. It was Darwin's theory right here, living and breathing. He decided to get down to business.

'Five years ago, you were mates with Dennis Hill.' He let the statement sink in and watched as Wade's demeanour shifted. 'Why'd the friendship come to an end, Wade? I was told you two were close.'

'Nah, we wasn't close.' Wade intimated that closeness to Dennis Hill would be repugnant and embarrassing.

'Not what I heard. Why don't you tell me your side of the story?'

Wade was silent for a moment. He seemed to be trying to work out what Lockwood was digging for.

'Nothing to tell. He kind of hung around, you know? He was kind of a baby. I went away to work. Is he all right?' Some long-forgotten sense of decency prompted Wade to ask after the man with the slow brain and the big hands.

'He's fine, lad. I just want to know if you were mates when his niece turned up dead or had you parted company by then?'

Wade coughed and put his hands in his pockets.

'He said he told you that his niece looked pretty in her new dress, and where they were going eagle-spotting. Ring any bells?'

'Nope.'

'So you never told anyone about their little outing to Haweswater?'

'Nope.'

'Not a soul?'

'Nope.'

'But you do remember Dennis's niece?'

'He was cut up about it, I remember that.'

'So apart from you, who else do you think might have known about their trip?'

'Dennis told anyone who'd listen about her. He had this sick obsession with her. It gave me the creeps. He could have told anyone where she was going.'

'But he told you. And who might you have mentioned it to, Wade?'

Wade's hands were firmly out of sight now, and he looked away from Lockwood.

'Were you questioned about her disappearance at the time?'

'No! Why should I've been? I don't know nothing! What did he say? It's lies! It's—'

'Calm down, Wade. I didn't say he said anything. I just want to know who you told about her dress. So I can rule you out, you understand?'

'I didn't mention no fucking red dress.'

'I never said it was red, Wade.'

They stopped. Lockwood waited while Wade groped for an answer. He looked up at the detective, then away again, as if working out a way to get past him.

'I thought you said it was red. Dennis must have told me.'

'Let's walk back.' They turned round and went back the way they'd come. 'The case has been reopened, Wade, and your name came up. Now, you know how this goes. If you were the only person Dennis told, then that puts you in a very awkward position.'

'Darren Beckett! I told Darren Beckett. Fuck, will you leave me alone now?'

Craig paused and raked his memory. He thought he'd heard the name somewhere.

'What exactly did you tell him?'

'Just that Dennis wouldn't shut up about the eagles and her dress.'

'Address?'

'Oh, Jesus. I don't know. He doesn't live round here now. I haven't seen him in weeks.'

'So where did he live?'

'Over there.' Wade pointed across the road.

'Number?'

'5B.'

'Thank you, Wade. I'll be in touch. Now keep this safe and stay out of trouble.' He handed Wade his card and crossed the road. There was no answer at 5B.

When he returned to his desk, Lockwood punched Darren Beckett's name into the database, not expecting any luck, but a result came up straight away. His mother had filed a missing persons this morning. Apparently Darren always visited her on a Thursday and brought her cigarettes and brandy. The woman was more concerned about her booze than her son, but the file had to be typed up anyway.

According to his mother, Darren Beckett worked in the hotel industry and regularly travelled out of the area for long periods of time. A tip-off from a fellow petty criminal wasn't enough to secure a search warrant, but Lockwood knew the landlord of the block of flats containing 5B.

First, though, he called DI Porter.

Chapter 26

One positive of Kelly's mother being in hospital was that she wasn't home to give Kelly that look when she opened the door the next day.

Kelly could fit in an hour with her mother before she started work, and at the same time visit baby Dale's mother. A language professor had agreed to meet her at the hospital at nine fifteen. She'd managed to track down Carl Bradley, who knew full well that he hadn't committed an offence, but at least she'd got out of him confirmation that the woman did indeed speak Serbo-Croat, and she could work with that.

Nikki was at her mother's bedside when Kelly arrived, and she wondered if she'd been there all night.

'She's very tired,' said Nikki in a saintly whisper. Kelly ignored her and walked to her mother and took her hand.

'Mum?'

Her mother's eyes opened and she smiled. 'Kelly!' She tried to sit up.

'It's all right, Mum. Just lie still. You need to rest until they've done more tests.'

'It's all a fuss about nothing,' her mother said.

'That's right, Mum, you'll be home soon.' Kelly felt her sister's eyes on her back and wished she'd leave her on her own with Mum for a bit. It would be nice if for once they could be in the same room without playing the competition game.

Their mother drifted off again and Kelly looked at the dials and switches next to her bed. They all seemed normal, but what would she know?

'So, you're still after Dave Crawley, Kelly? Katy knows everything. She's livid.' Nikki savoured every word.

Kelly looked at her sister with incredulous eyes. She contemplated punching her, but she knew the pleasure it would bring would be short-lived, nor would it make any difference to the disproportionate size of her sibling's mouth compared to her brain.

'What the hell are you talking about?' she asked instead. Their voices had subsided to whispers.

'You. Chasing Dave around Pooley Bridge. She knows everything.' Nikki gave a self-satisfied grin.

'Oh Jesus, Nikki. Get your facts right before you go hurling accusations. I bumped into him with Flash Gordon in a bar and said hello.' Kelly's blood was boiling.

'No one calls him Flash any more, Kelly. We've all grown up.' Her sister looked at her defiantly, and Kelly burst out laughing.

'That doesn't even deserve a response. Not one that you would understand anyway,' she said, and Nikki's cheeks smouldered.

'Stay away from him,' she ordered.

Kelly laughed again. She knew she was the least of Katy's worries. By the looks of it, Dave was already a broken man, and although Kelly wasn't interested, it still made her sad.

'Oh polish your fucking halo, Nikki.' Kelly walked out. Their mother appeared to sleep on.

It didn't matter how little Kelly saw of her, her sister was still able to get under her skin, but this morning she had more important things to worry about. She had time to grab a coffee before she went to reception to meet Professor Cole. They shook hands, then walked to the ward together. The professor had managed to find out that the woman's name was Jovana. She'd been reunited with her son, and according to the nurses, over the last couple of days she'd seemed to perk up.

DC Phillips had arranged for twenty-four-hour cover outside Jovana's private room, and after introducing themselves to the ward sister, they were shown inside. The girl was understandably uncomfortable with the presence of more strangers, but Cole spoke quickly and Jovana relaxed. Kelly went to her and looked at the baby.

'Tell her he's beautiful,' she said to Cole. He spoke in a strange language that Kelly thought sounded like a cross between German and Russian. She'd never heard anything like it. Jovana smiled and said something in reply. Kelly looked at Cole.

'She says thank you. She would like very much to go home.'

'Where is home?'

'Sarajevo.'

'And what is she doing here?'

The professor translated all of Kelly's questions and Jovana answered them. Kelly didn't know if the answers were honest or not, and with the language barrier, it was difficult to tell, but at least they had something to go on.

'She came with her husband looking for a better life.'

'How did she get here, and where is her husband now?'

'They came in a lorry. She doesn't know where her husband is; all she knows is that he paid for them to be brought here, but something went wrong. She's saying that horrible people have got him.'

'Did she come all the way from Sarajevo in the same lorry?'

'No, she's saying that they drove to Budapest where the lorry picked them up. It dropped them somewhere in England – her husband told her they were in England – and then she was transferred to a van without her husband.'

'Ask her why she is not with him.'

'She says that she was able to get a lift from someone – the man in the van – her husband paid. Her husband was very scared, and left her with the driver for her safety, and she hasn't seen him since. The man said he dropped her off in Patterdale, and wouldn't take her further, and she's sure her husband wouldn't have paid for her to be left in the middle of nowhere. She wandered round until she found some shelter. She gave birth on her own and wrapped the baby in some of her clothes, then in a fit of confusion and fear thought he'd be safer without her.'

Kelly listened as Professor Cole conversed fluently with the woman and she tried to pronounce Patterdale.

'Sounds like she's been done over pretty badly. What sort of person drops a heavily pregnant woman off miles from anywhere? Christ. Ask her if she can give a description of both the drivers and the vehicles.'

'She said she can. She wants to know if the men who took her husband are coming to get her.'

'What's her husband's name?'

'Nedzad Galic.'

'Does she know who her husband paid to bring them here?'

'No. She says he was going to meet them to hand over some money, but he never came back. He'd given the van driver money before he left. She's saying maybe it was a trap.'

'Can you check if I've got this right? She and her husband paid to come to England from Budapest. Once in England, they stop somewhere to hand over more money; she changes vehicles, and he gets taken?'

The professor relayed this to Jovana, and she nodded. 'She doesn't know where the exchange took place.'

Of course she doesn't, thought Kelly. The poor girl had probably never been outside Bosnia.

'So there were two vehicles involved in the journey? Can she remember both of them?'

The professor said she could: one was a large lorry and the second a smaller van.

'Can she describe the large lorry first?'

The girl moved her mouth slowly around an alien word, as if practising something she had been thinking about for some time.

'Crawley,' she said, in a near-perfect English accent.

Kelly's arm hair stood up and she remained very still for what felt like minutes, without making a sound.

'DI Porter?' It was the professor.

'Sorry, yes. Right. Can you get her to write down her address in Sarajevo, and anyone there who might be missing her. I'll call the embassy.'

After thanking Professor Cole, Kelly went to the canteen and ordered another coffee. She sat nursing it for a long time, figuring out what to do next. She felt dazed by what Jovana had told her. Eventually she looked up a number in her phone and dialled. It was a long shot, but the family might still live there. It was answered on the third ring.

Yes, this was Mrs Crawley speaking. No, Dave wasn't there. Yes, Dave lived near Penrith. Yes, how lovely, he would be thrilled to hook up with an old friend. Yes, she had the number right there.

Kelly thanked her and hung up. She dialled the number and Dave answered.

'Dave, it's Kelly. I need to speak to you.'

Chapter 27

Gabriela looked at the poster and a knot formed in her stomach. The police photo showed a girl's face and a flash of red hair; she knew that it was Anushka. Roza still hadn't returned, and every morning, after her shift, Gabriela checked to see that the money, watch and ring were still in the wardrobe.

She toyed with the idea of approaching the police solely on the basis that she was worried about her room-mates. They would've run out of money by now: they had no jobs, and they'd left valuables behind. Not just any valuables, but stacks of cash, and in the world of the illegal, cash was everything.

Mrs Joliffe rarely checked on her at night anymore; she seemed pleased with Gabriela's discretion, as she called it. Every morning she wafted in on a cloud of perfume and make-up, shaking her perfectly curled hair, and asked the same question.

'Any problems, Gabriela?'

'No, Mrs Joliffe,' she'd reply.

'Super.' Then she would smile and straighten her suit in front of the mirror.

Gabriela was becoming confident in her new role, and figured that if she carried on the way she was going, she'd soon be much richer than if she'd stayed serving breakfast. But would she get her passport back? That was the burning question.

She'd met women like Mrs Joliffe before, all business and no pleasure. They seemed empty of a story and came across as terribly sad. Since taking the job as night manager, she'd had more time to think about such things, and more time to watch. When things were quiet, she made sketches of the people she'd seen coming and going at the hotel in the middle of the night. She also gathered her own insurance. She didn't know exactly which ledgers and documents were important, but she began photo-copying them. If Mrs Joliffe, for whatever reason, chose to withhold her passport, Gabriela would need to be able to negotiate. She also suspected that Mrs Joliffe was avoiding the police, who'd been into the hotel asking questions. She'd watched with her own eyes as Mrs Joliffe slipped out of the back of the hotel as two policemen had come in the front, and Gabriela was sure it wasn't a coincidence. The receptionists had all been told to say that Anushka had been sacked, which was a further untruth. Gabriela was young, but she knew that if someone lied to the police, the chances were that something else, something bigger, was at stake. Mrs Joliffe had become more edgy after that, spending less and less time at the hotel. Thankfully, so far, Gabriela hadn't encountered any police on her night shift.

She couldn't sleep and she tossed around in her small bed. The sunshine pierced her windows despite the hand towels she'd tacked over the gaps; she saw daylight every-where, and she couldn't stop staring at Anushka and Roza's beds.

She looked at her watch. It was only midday. She sat up and sighed, running everything over in her mind to check and double-check her tracks. The photocopies of clients' details were safe under her mattress, along with the drawings and her wages, which totalled over five hundred pounds so far. She had made it clear that she was happy to work seven nights a week.

She was gaining the trust of Mrs Joliffe, who regularly tested her. One night her boss hid a diamond ring in the office, under some paperwork; another night she left a heavy gold bracelet on the desk. Gabriela had simply tidied around them.

Suddenly she froze.

Someone was turning the handle of her door. They hadn't knocked; clearly they had no intention of announcing their visit. She stared at the handle, hardly daring to breathe but needing to as her lungs screamed. She began to shake. Something was being inserted into the lock, and she ran to the door and flipped the bolt. The fumbling stopped and Gabriela waited.

Sunlight shone under the door, and she dropped to the floor to peer through the gap. She made out a shadow, but it didn't move. She tried to focus and thought she could see a pair of shoes; men's shoes, she was certain – in fact they looked like boots. The handle turned again and Gabriela held her breath, but the bolt held. The man rattled the door but he couldn't get in. He punched it hard and Gabriela jumped back towards her bed, almost falling onto it. The feet paced up and down, boots clumping on the thin carpet. He wasn't going away.

After a few minutes, her breathing slowed a little, but she was too scared to open the door. She smelled cigarette smoke. She took a towel from the bathroom, rolled it up and placed it along the gap under the door. Then she pressed her ear against the wood but couldn't hear anything. Whoever it was, she knew what they wanted. She thought about the cash. The watch. The ring. The laptop at the bottom of the wardrobe.

She went to the wardrobe and took out the draw-string bag. Then she removed the envelope full of photocopies, drawings and cash from under the mattress and got dressed. There would be no sleep today. She phoned reception and asked George, the day receptionist, to investigate the second floor for anyone who shouldn't be there. Then she waited. She had no idea if the figure beyond her door had gone.

From her room, she could make out a little of the street below, where the traffic rumbled steadily. It was a tiny hatch window and so she couldn't climb out onto the roof to go looking for a fire escape. As far as she could work out, whoever was on the other side of the door hadn't expected the room to be occupied and therefore did not know her identity; this was her trump card and she needed to keep it that way. She also needed to move rooms.

She began packing the large rucksack that had travelled all the way with her from Lodz. She had no doubt that the person on the other side of her door knew what had happened to Anushka and Roza, and might even have harmed them. She realised now that her roommates might never come back. She packed the envelope and the drawstring bag, then got the laptop out of the wardrobe, and squeezed it in too. Still, she waited.

A man's voice wafted up the stairs; it was George. There was an exchange, and for the first time, Gabriela heard the voice of the man who wished to get into her room. It sounded local.

'Sorry, mate, I was looking for my girlfriend. She used to work here and I haven't seen her for a while, you know?'

'What's her name?' asked George.

'Nush. I'm pretty sure she said she stayed in this room here.'

'She left. She used to work dinner and the occasional breakfast – red hair, right? I haven't seen her in a while.'

'So who's in here now?'

Gabriela's heart stopped.

'I've no idea, mate. I'll see you downstairs.' There was a silence. George was five foot nothing tall but also five foot wide, and his night job was bouncing in some of the roughest nightclubs in Bowness. He sported tattooed sleeves depicting animals and war, and his biceps were the size of Gabriela's thighs. Gabriela hoped this was enough to put off the man with no name and no face.

It was.

'Gabriela? It's George. He's gone.'

Hands shaking, Gabriela tentatively unbolted the door. George stood before her, smiling. She couldn't imagine him violent, but she was sure that he could be.

'Thank you, George. I think he was looking for the girls who used to stay in this room. I don't suppose there are any other staff rooms free? I get the feeling he'll be back and I didn't like the sound of him. He tried to pick the lock.'

'Let me see what I can do. Go back in and bolt the door.'

Half an hour later, he was back. He'd found a room on the third floor, in the attic, that was free. Gabriela said she'd take anything.

'George, will you come with me?' She was terrified and didn't want to be alone.

Deciding that any enquiry downstairs could wait, he helped her carry her things up to her new room. It was musty and hadn't been lived in for a while, but she could deal with that. She checked the door: it had a bolt. She threw open the window for some air.

'Thank you, George.'

'If he bothers you again, just you tell me.'

Once George had gone back downstairs, Gabriela closed the door and bolted it. She put her bag by the wardrobe but didn't unpack. She was extremely tired suddenly, and wanted to lie down and forget everything. She climbed into the small bed, even though it wasn't made properly, and slept until her alarm woke her at nine p.m. It was time to go back to work.

Chapter 28

Kelly had a few names for some of the faces of the girls servicing men for cash in Colin Day's hotels. The names they did have weren't English, and they hadn't applied for work permits. But it was taking time ploughing through all the data they'd collated so far. A picture was forming, but as yet, it didn't make sense. Kelly knew that money was at the centre of it all, and somehow, Colin Day was producing lots of it and making it legitimate. He owned tanning salons in Penrith, Ambleside, Keswick, Barrow, Ulverston and Kendal and every one of them turned over a staggering profit every year. It was a cash-intensive service business – perfect for placing dirty money and hiding it.

The names of the clients at the Thwaite Hotel were more than likely fictitious. They were classic clichés such as Mr Jones, and Mr White; there was even a Mr Trump. Kelly's guess that they'd be dead ends turned out to be right. The extent of Colin Day's dealings was overwhelming and the investigation took over their lives.

'I'm going to visit the Crawleys myself. They're a well-known Penrith family, and need handling with tact.' Kelly sipped coffee. Her team had grown, thanks to DCI Cane, and they watched and listened intently as she spoke; it was testimony to how far she'd proved herself up to now. DI Richie Park had left her to it, and gone on leave, and when he returned it would be to Lancaster. She was firmly in charge.

'The centre of our investigation is Colin Day. His wife didn't think he'd be running this rig on his own – her words: "he'd enjoy the trappings but not the hard work". Now we can't base our assumptions on one witness – a hostile, bitter one at that – but if we pursue the lead, it points to an accomplice: Tomb Day. How are the accountants getting on, Will?' Kelly knew she'd given Phillips the dullest job, but that was because he was diligent and could handle it; besides, she was monitoring how he handled the lower-profile leads. So far, he'd impressed her.

'They think they might have something, guv. In the paperwork from Day's personal office at home, we found details of what at first glance appears to be a holiday, though it's clearly something else entirely – something he stood to make a lot of money out of. This was found amongst the papers.' Phillips approached the whiteboard and used his laptop. Documents appeared on the screen that did indeed look like a holiday itinerary. There were photos of a beautiful stone mansion hidden away in the Borrowdale valley sleeping thirty people, as well as details for helicopter landing sites. The company renting the property was called Elite Escapes. Prices were circled and a quick profit sheet had been sketched out. It summarised that if revenue was around a hundred thousand pounds, and costs around twenty thousand, it would make a handsome profit. But what was on sale? Also interesting, written in red alongside the accommodation details, was a note to self. It read: *Trust Marko with cash?*

'Clearly not a holiday, then. He's selling something,' Kelly said.

'We don't know who this Marko is, but there are certainly a few shady characters about who flag up when entered in HOLMES. One of them is Marko Popovic, known to have operated for some years out of Merseyside. He hasn't been on their radar for a while, though.'

'Does he have a record?' asked Kelly.

'No, never could pin anything on him.'

'So he was never charged with anything? Why is he on HOLMES?'

'He was interviewed regarding an ABH in a club he owned.'

Kelly considered the Merseyside lead.

'What's Harry Chase up to at the minute?' As part of her investigation into Lottie Davis's murder, she had spoken to an officer at Merseyside Police who had a personal interest in Chase: his cousin's son had been groomed by a paedophile ring linked to him, but the CPS had decided to go after someone else because they didn't have enough on Chase.

'Low profile, since his time inside.'

'We'd need a warrant to look into his financial affairs.' It was frustrating. Kelly decided to keep it as something to follow up. It didn't matter where in the UK they lived: criminals all knew each other. They might not be best pals, but they were aware of each other and didn't step on toes. She wondered why Marko Popovic had left the area, and whether he'd moved to Cumbria.

'Hide, did we find out if Chase and Chase was owned by our man?'

'Yes, guv, it was. It's the same Chase, it was bought by another local firm which doesn't appear – yet – to have any links to its former owner, but I'm still working on it.

'A coincidence perhaps. I'm not convinced. OK, it's another lead. I'm guessing that Marko Popovic is of eastern European origin with a name like that? Did Merseyside Police say?'

'Yes, he's from Sarajevo.'

'Same as our young friend in the hospital.' Kelly shifted in her seat. 'Interesting. DC Hide, anything on Colin Day's two mobile phones?'

'Yes, guv. The personal mobile has several numbers in the log, all so far turning out to be legitimate, but the phone that his wife said was his work mobile only has three numbers, which appear over and over again. None of them are traceable, so all three must be pay-as-you-go.'

'Keep trying them.'

'Forensics have come back about the red hair tangled in Colin Day's wedding band, confirmed to be human: they told us that one had a follicle attached and are trying to get a DNA profile.'

'Have we had any more sightings of Anushka?'

The answer was negative. Enquiries at local pawn shops indicated that no one had tried to pawn the ring or the Rolex.

'I've got a photograph of Mrs Day wearing the ring.' Kelly brought it up on screen; it was stunning, and she was surprised that the young prostitute hadn't tried to sell it. She had also been given a photograph of the 2005 Rolex Oyster Perpetual, found on a vintage Rolex site by Christine; that appeared on screen alongside the ring.

'The substance under Mr Day's nails comes as no surprise: perfumed mineral oil, a distillate of petroleum – in other words, bog-standard baby oil. So apart from proving that Colin Day liked to oil his ladies up, it's a dead end. Every house in the country has a bottle of baby oil tucked in the cupboard.'

Kelly turned to DC Phillips. 'What about the codes from Mr Day's home office?'

'They could be passwords or safe combinations, guv. Some are six digits and some are eight – those could be bank accounts or phone numbers.'

Kelly rubbed her eyes. 'I don't need to tell you all that this investigation is growing at an alarming rate. Any hits on for Anushka Ivanov in and out of air and sea ports? Trains?'

'No, guv.'

'Not surprising. If Jovana Galic's story turns out to have legs, we're unlikely to get any joy there, as Anushka will have other means to travel illegally. This is certainly more than a local operation. It's slick and organised. Phillips, I'm reassigning you to look into this Marko Popovic. Could I have a volunteer to take over the accounts?'

A hand flew up and Kelly thanked the young female DC from South Lakes.

'I'm going to Barrow to follow a lead in the Lottie Davis case. It'll give me an opportunity to brief DI Lockwood on how we're using his resources too. I have my iPad and phone – don't hesitate to contact me about anything at all. That's all for now, thank you. Keep up the great work.' She grabbed her coat and closed her computer down. Dave had rearranged their meeting giving her some excuse about work, she'd have to wait another day. He'd only meet her at Junction 40 services, and nowhere else. He was terrified of being caught with his old girlfriend anywhere near Penrith. Kelly didn't mind either way. The last thing on her mind was the insecurities of a friend of her sister's. This was pure business.

As she was about to leave, her phone rang and she swore. She recognised the number and answered it hoping that Constable Coombs had something interesting to say. She was recommending him for detective work; he had an eye.

'Constable.'

'Ma'am. I thought you'd like to know that we've just had a missing person's report logged. It's Anna Cork's mother: she hasn't seen her daughter in three days.'

Chapter 29

Kelly's drive to Barrow was uneventful. She took the M6 to miss the Lakes traffic, and was there in under an hour. On the way, she reflected that for once she was grateful to her sister. Their mother had been released from hospital with a flimsy excuse and no diagnosis, and Nikki had taken her in for the time being. Stress had been mentioned, and that gave Nikki the green light to point the finger at her wayward sister, rocking the boat and sending Mum's blood pressure even higher. Kelly ignored her. At least with her mother at Nikki's, she wouldn't feel so torn when she worked such long hours.

DI Lockwood made them coffee and they chatted about the two cases that seemed to be involving the DI's patch more each day.

'So you found Wade Maddox?' Kelly said. 'What was he like?'

'Just as I expected: wasting his life playing computer games, drawing dole and hanging out with the wrong crowd. He remembered Lottie's red dress, Kelly. I didn't mention it; he did.'

'Christ.'

'I know.'

Lockwood told her what Wade had said about Darren Beckett's knowledge of the Davis's trip out, as well as Lottie's dress.

'And Beckett's landlord was more than happy to hand over the keys?' Kelly asked.

'Beckett's behind on the rent so he wants the place cleared out. He figures if he can get someone else to foot the bill – the police in this case – that's better than him having to do it himself.'

'Have you been in?' Kelly asked.

'No, I was waiting for you.'

They left the office and walked to Lockwood's car.

'How did the football match go?' asked Kelly.

'Terrible. When they win – which is rare – he's up in the clouds; when they lose, God, he's a grumpy little shit.'

Kelly laughed.

'You got kids?' Lockwood asked her.

'Nope. Sounds like the hardest job in the world to me.'

'And that would put you off?'

'I've never thought about it like that. Anyway, I'm too old now.'

Lockwood laughed. 'Christ, you can't be a day over thirty!'

'I'll take that as a compliment. I'm thirty-six.'

Lockwood parked outside flat 5B. Kelly noted how grim the area was compared to the place she'd returned to live. It was a concrete mass of flats, with little light and no greenery to speak of. The place was deserted. It must be a bleak place to live, but perfect to be anonymous.

They approached the flat, and Lockwood took out a key and opened the door.

The place stank. It was a smell that took Kelly back to her student days: unwashed bodies mixed with cigarette smoke and something else – poverty. It was a hovel. They put on gloves.

The living room consisted of one sofa and a TV. They moved the sofa and looked underneath, then turned the TV upside down and replaced it.

There were only four rooms in total. They entered the bathroom next, and Kelly gagged. The toilet hadn't been flushed by whoever had last used it, and the stench of faeces and strong urine hit them. They covered their mouths. Lockwood shone a torch into the bathtub; it too was appalling. On closer inspection he noticed hairs around the scum line, and took out a bag to collect them. They were long, but in the poor light from the cheap bulb, it was impossible to tell what colour they were. Kelly turned her attention to the sink. It was surrounded by a whole array of drug paraphernalia – a syringe, used foil, three teaspoons and a spilled bottle of diazepam – which she bagged. She scraped residue from the enamel and bagged that too. Lockwood said he'd check with Darren's GP about a prescription. Kelly thought it strange that someone would leave a drug such as diazepam behind; users usually suffered if they missed their downers. Maybe they belonged to someone else.

The next room had a double bed, on top of which lay screwed-up dirty sheets. Apart from that, the only other item in the room was a wardrobe with a few pieces of clothing thrown inside. Kelly rooted through them and noticed that they included some women's garments: a bra, stockings and a tailored jacket, as well as some dirty jeans and some tissues. In the corner of the wardrobe, at the back, there was a handbag. Kelly thought it looked familiar. She picked it up and glanced inside. There was a phone, a wallet, and a folded piece of paper with a number written on it in pencil. There was also a name badge like those worn by hotel workers. It read: *Anushka, Waitress.* She turned it over, not quite believing what she was seeing. On the back was a sticker with the address of the Troutbeck Guest House. She flicked through the wallet. Anushka's Polish driving licence was in there, with a clear photo. She showed the bag to Lockwood.

'The Colin Day case, the one I'm stealing all your officers for – this bag belongs to a major witness. We haven't been able to trace her at all, and now she turns up here, in a flat on Barrow Island. Who is this Darren Beckett, Lockwood? And what's he been up to?'

'According to his mother, he works in the hotel industry, and travels out of the area regularly.'

'Wait a minute. She called someone.' Kelly spoke quickly and Lockwood was lost.

'What?' he asked.

'Colin Day died during an encounter with a prostitute – Anushka, the owner of this bag. He taped the whole thing. After she'd robbed him, she called someone. When you were talking to Darren's mother about the missing person report, did she give you a phone number for him?'

'Of course. I've tried it several times,' Lockwood said.

Kelly held up the phone from Anushka's bag. 'If she called Beckett, it'll be on here. If we find Beckett, we find Anushka. That hair you found in the bath – let's have a look at it outside.'

Lockwood followed her out. In daylight, she could see that the hairs were bright red.

'Shit, where do we stand getting a warrant for this place now we've found this?'

'We don't need one,' Lockwood said. 'The landlord is the owner, and he let us in.'

'OK. I need a forensic team here to establish whether these things were stolen, or whether Anushka Ivanov was here in Darren Beckett's flat.'

Chapter 30

Darren vomited for the fourth time into the grubby sink that had once been white. Marko was kindly allowing him to doss in one of his more unsavoury apartment blocks in Penrith. It was a dump, and it rained here even more than it did in Barrow. His twenty-eight-year-old body was letting him down prematurely. He was losing weight fast but he had no stomach for food. His last bowl of cereal was now being stirred into the plughole in an attempt to unblock it.

The appeal for the young woman with red hair was becoming more prominent in the news, and it made him nervous. He racked his brains for reassurance that he'd cleaned up properly. Nobody swam in Barrow Dock anymore; only the odd fishing boat went anywhere near the shallows on its way in to unpack a few mackerel or bass caught off Walney. Like most of Britain's docks, the place had died long ago.

In the middle of the night, though, when irrational fears took hold, he wasn't so sure. The bodies might move; they might come loose, away from the belts he'd strapped around them, or they might come alive and fucking swim up to the surface. After he'd sweated his way through another nightmare, he believed anything was possible. He also knew that at some point he'd have to go back to his old flat. He'd thought he'd tidied up before he left, but a thought kept niggling away at him: Nush had kept a small stash of clothes at the bottom of his wardrobe that he'd completely forgotten about.

He was needed for another job tonight, but he felt like death. Curtis would pick him up at nine p.m. apparently. He had no idea what was expected of him, but judging by the last time, it wouldn't be good. He laughed at the irony: he'd slit a woman's throat, and yet here he was wondering if Marko and his men had limits.

He knew the answer already.

He questioned whether he had his own limits and what it would take for him to say no to Marko, but that hurt his head and he went to the cupboard and got out a bottle of vodka. It would anaesthetise him a little; take the edge off, in his mother's words.

He lay on the small, uncomfortable sofa, and flicked around the TV, desperate for distraction; something to make the image of blood spurting forcefully onto the plastic sheeting go away. The images mingled with the meaty pulp that was all that was left of Kevin Cottrell after he'd pummelled him with the piece of rusty iron.

MasterChef Australia did the trick. There were two chicks in particular who caught his eye, and he became engaged in their struggle not to be eliminated. The food looked good too, but he wished the girls wore skimpier tops. After the programme finished, he searched around to see if he could get more on playback. He found what he was looking for and settled back to follow Tania from Queensland and Laura from Tasmania battle it out to the final.

Five hours later, he was asleep on the sofa when the door buzzed. He woke with a start and looked at his watch: just after nine p.m. He stood up and realised that his trousers were undone: Laura from Tasmania needed a good seeing-to, and she'd been the focus of a rather gratifying dream. The pleasure didn't last long before another wave of nausea gripped him.

The door buzzed again. He fastened his flies, put the vodka away and went to the door. It was Curtis. He always made Darren uncomfortably nervous. The guy was huge – over six foot five, with hands that resembled bunches of bananas. But it wasn't just his size; it was also his composure. Darren had witnessed how much damage he could cause.

They didn't shake hands.

'You'll need a coat, it's fucking freezing,' said the big man. The advice was a rare occurrence.

Between Curtis and Sasha, Darren thought it highly unlikely that he'd ever refuse to do anything Marko asked of him, and that thought depressed him. He was no longer in charge of his own destiny, but then he guessed he never really had been anyway. At least this way he had some sort of protection from the meanest bastard in Cumbria – if he didn't screw up, of course.

He grabbed his coat and went to the bathroom to splash cold water over his face. His guts were still churning. As he went to turn off the TV, an item on the news caught his attention. He stopped, frozen. Facing him on the screen was a photo of himself. The cops wanted to talk to him. Darren couldn't move and Curtis walked over to see what the problem was.

'Oops. Looks like you need to impress Marko even more now,' was all he said.

Darren closed his eyes. Curtis was right.

They left the flat and Darren followed Curtis to a dark van. It was a Ford and suitably anonymous. His pulse quickened and he wondered when he'd be let into the plan for the evening.

'You been working for Marko long?' he asked as they drove, trying to make simple conversation to calm his nerves and get rid of the sinking feeling in his tumultuous gut. In reply he received a long stare. He watched the road anxiously for what seemed like minutes as Curtis continued to look at him.

'The road...' he said eventually, pointing through the windscreen.

Curtis smiled and looked back to the dark lane ahead. There was no one else about.

They travelled south and hit traffic on the A6. After ten minutes, they turned off onto a minor road. Not for the first time, working for Marko, Darren wondered whether he was being taken somewhere remote because he'd come to the end of his usefulness. His hands were clammy. Now that the cops were after him, surely Marko wouldn't want the hassle.

Curtis turned into a long driveway and stopped outside what looked like an old farmhouse. Light shone behind the windows. Questions raced through Darren's head and he couldn't help himself asking Curtis what they were doing there.

'Simple job tonight, pal. You've seen a dog fight before?'

Darren calmed a little. 'Yes,' he said.

'Well tonight it's not dogs, just people, and our job is to make sure the lads stay in the ring.'

'Lads?'

'The guys fighting, you fucking idiot.'

'How do we do that?' Darren asked.

Curtis looked at him as if he was educationally challenged, but it was a genuine question. Darren wanted to make sure he didn't make a mistake. It could be a simple case of asking them to stay in, or, if force was needed, how much to impose. He was excited about the prospect of watching illegal fighting; it would be messy but breathtaking. He was a big fan of *Thrill Kill*, Sony's unreleased video game depicting so much sexual violence that even an 18 certificate didn't cut it. Copies had leaked anyway, and made their way onto the illegal market. Darren had always wondered if people fought like that for real; he figured that if someone had dreamt it up in a game, then it must exist somewhere, because humans were sick like that.

'Why do they need our help? Don't they want to win?' he asked.

Curtis smiled at him, but it wasn't a pleasant or jovial smile; it was piercing, challenging and disarming all at the same time. Darren wondered how many people the big man had hurt on Marko's behalf.

'They don't want to be here,' Curtis said.

'Oh.' Now Darren understood.

Curtis jumped out of the van and Darren followed suit. The big man went to the back and took out a bag. 'Come on then, Marko said you'd be a virgin.'

Darren didn't care for the term, but it was true: he'd never seen men forced to fight one another, and he guessed they'd need to use a fair amount of force to keep them at it.

They went around the back of the building, where two of Curtis's brothers were guarding the door. They moved aside and Darren followed Curtis into a kitchen. Curtis slammed the bag onto the table and unzipped it. Inside was the sort of stash of weapons that might be hauled in by Mexican police after a drugs shootout. There were knives, hammers, axes, a machete and even a couple of guns.

Darren had never handled a gun.

'Take your pick,' Curtis said. 'Some of the fighters are easy to control; occasionally you get one who thinks he can get past you. It's our job to make sure none of them leave before they're finished. None of them speak English; this is our language tonight.' He winked, gesturing to the weapons.

Darren wondered why Marko had chosen him for the job. It was glaringly obvious why he'd chosen Curtis, but Darren was ten stone wet through. Still, a man with a weapon in a position of command would tip any balance against an unarmed man vastly outnumbered and scared. It was another test.

He looked at the weapons. He avoided the guns. Curtis took a long ugly knife, some knuckledusters and an axe. Darren decided to do the same. It felt strange packing so much metal. He didn't believe he could do this. It was highly likely that if he tried to control a fighter maddened by rage and fear, he could easily have the weapons turned on him. He wished he'd brought some vodka.

As if he could read his thoughts, Curtis opened a kitchen cupboard, where a bottle of whisky sat on a shelf.

'Virgins usually need a little help,' he said.

Darren reached for the bottle gratefully and glugged several mouthfuls. His nerves began to subside, but his guts continued to churn and he hoped he didn't shit himself whilst trying to appear dominant.

'Come on,' said Curtis, and Darren followed him into a dimly lit room that had been set up like a ring. A few men sat at tables, while others stood around talking loudly. Smoke hovered in the air and bottles of whisky were laid out. A man Darren didn't recognise coughed and said, 'Two minutes, gents, please.' The men who were standing took their seats and joked excitedly with one another.

Curtis's brothers now entered, each holding a naked man. Darren stared at them. They weren't athletic in any way; both were middle-aged and flabby around their middles. Both looked terrified. Their dicks and balls flopped around hilariously and Darren watched, fascinated by the spectacle. An excited hum elevated the noise level as men placed last-minute bets based on what they saw.

Silence settled in the room and the man who seemed to be organising proceedings slammed a gavel down on a table. The spectators began shouting and the men were shoved together. Straight away, one of them tried to run. Curtis slammed a fist into his belly and he collapsed on the floor, howling in an unrecognisable tongue. Curtis showed the other man a knife and he understood; he went to the guy on the floor and began to hit him.

Instinct kicked in and the guy on the floor started to defend himself. Flesh wobbled as the two men dived towards each other, punching and kicking. The room heated up and Darren felt his pulse racing with anticipation.

One of the fighters fell out of the ring and Curtis took out a hammer and raised it above his head. The man scrambled back into the arena to resume the fight.

Time ticked by and one of the men seemed to be tiring. It was time to help them out. Curtis threw the stronger man a long stick with bits sticking out of it. The man whacked his opponent with it, and blood spewed out of his mouth. Sensing victory, the stronger man took his chance and rained down blows on the other fighter, who was now motionless on the floor. The spectators shouted and spit came out of their mouths. It was better than *Thrill Kill* any day.

Curtis moved towards the victor, who was panting on the floor; he helped him up and took him from the room. The body of the other man was carried out, then the ring was tidied up for the next fight.

More bets were placed, and Darren wondered how many fights were scheduled for tonight. He also wondered about these men who were here enjoying the show. They had money, that was clear, and they looked ordinary enough. He couldn't imagine where Marko found them. You didn't go advertising such events in the paper.

'How many more?' he asked Curtis when he returned to the room.

'Two,' he replied.

Darren held onto his weapons and hoped none of the fighters came in his direction.

The second fight was worse because the men were pretty fit, but the third one was brutal. The fighters were evenly matched and the bout lasted twenty minutes until Curtis threw the stronger one a knife and he plunged it into his adversary time and time again. Darren was astounded at how quickly the men were willing to slaughter each other when faced with defeat and certain death. It turned them into animals. In his mind, this willingness to diminish themselves so rapidly justified their abuse. He never stopped to consider what he would do given the same options, and clearly neither did the spectators; the show was too good to ruin with philosophy. Instead they demanded more blood, shouting, swapping money and slapping each other on the back.

Again the body of the loser was carried away, and Darren wondered where they went. More importantly, though, he wanted to know what happened to the victors.

At midnight, he got his answer. All three men were tied up and gagged in the back of Curtis's van, ready to be taken to Darren's apartment, where he would guard them until the next round of fights. If they caused any problems, Curtis said, Darren had Marko's direct blessing to impose restraint.

Darren kept his weapons.

Chapter 31

Kelly parked in the central parking area near the Co-op in Ambleside. She walked down Rothay Road, past the Thwaite Hotel, which looked abandoned and neglected, and on to the Troutbeck Guest House. Ambleside was busy, and tourists meandered maddeningly on and off the pavements in front of her.

The guest house was in full breakfast swing. A man was sitting at reception and looked up when Kelly approached.

'How may I help you?' he asked politely; his name badge read: *George, Reception*. It was the same design and colour as Anushka's.

Kelly introduced herself, and George was more than happy to help. The general manager, Mrs Joliffe, wasn't available again, as was becoming her habit. Kelly already had her number, which she had been calling without success, and George suggested that she try Christine Day for an address, given that she now owned the place.

Kelly showed George the photo of Anushka.

'Ah, everybody knows her, they call her Nush. She was a live wire, that's for sure. Couldn't stick at the job; you know the type, think they're above that kind of work.'

'Yes, I was informed she'd been sacked.'

'I don't know anything about that. In trouble, is she?'

'We just need to speak to her with some urgency, and she seems to have disappeared. What about him?' She brought out the photo of Darren.

'He looks familiar, but I can't be sure,' George said.

'Can you have another look? His name's Darren Beckett, and this photo's about four years old, so he may have changed a fair bit.'

George took the photo and studied it closely.

'There was a man here the other day, loitering about the staff rooms on the second floor. He was much older than in this photograph, though, perhaps forty. He was very dirty and looked like a down-and-out, whereas this fella looks so... healthy. Although he did say he was looking for Nush, and claimed she was his girlfriend. I can't see it myself. Nush thought of herself as a bit classy, if you like.'

'Thank you, George. Are there any other staff about? I know the breakfast staff are busy, but perhaps some cleaners or porters who I could speak to? I'd also like to see where Anushka was staying.'

He showed her to Anushka's room before leaving to see if there were any staff members free to speak to her. The room was bare except for three single beds and two wardrobes. It was a sparse existence indeed. Kelly opened a few drawers, but the place had been cleaned out. Wherever Anushka had gone, it had been planned.

After interviewing three more staff members – all of whom knew Nush but not where she'd gone – she left the photograph of Darren, along with photos of the ring and the Rolex watch, with reception, and left the hotel to visit Mrs Cork, Anna's mother, who lived a mile away from the hotel.

'It's been three days and she's never not come home before. She has friends, of course, and sometimes stays over, but she always tells me.' Mrs Cork wrung her hands and her brow was deeply furrowed. Kelly doubted she'd slept in the last two days.

'So when was the last time you saw her, Mrs Cork?'

'She came home very upset, saying the police had closed the hotel. She was worried about her job, you see. She's always found it difficult to find work. She... can't read very well. It's hard you know; everyone expects it now that everything is computerised.'

'So you found her the job cleaning at the hotel?'

'Yes.'

'And how did you come across that?'

'Mr Day, of course. He was a family friend. Very sad what happened.' Mrs Cork looked away.

Funny, thought Kelly, how so many people held Colin Day in high esteem, given what she knew about him. But that could all change very soon.

'Do you think finding Mr Day's body like that has perhaps affected your daughter more than you realised and she needs some space?' she asked.

'Well, she was very shaken,' Mrs Cork said.

'So, when she came home from work for the last time, what did she do? Did she go out?'

'She went to her room and then, about five, she said she needed to go and buy cigarettes. I never approved, but what can you do?'

Kelly herself was an erratic smoker, but she fully understood the need when the craving took hold. She tried to limit her intake, but sometimes it crept up. She nodded.

'And did she return?'

'No.' Mrs Cork looked away and her anguish took hold of her once again.

'What was her relationship with Kevin Cottrell, the hotel manager?'

'Who?'

'The manager who was on duty the morning Anna found Mr Day; his name is Kevin Cottrell.'

'Oh. Anna never mentioned him. I asked her about work colleagues but she was always very unwilling to give details, so I didn't push.'

'Did Anna ever talk about Mr Day?'

'No, not that I can remember. We saw him in town one day and I reminded her to thank him for getting her a job.'

'And how did Mr Day seem?'

'What do you mean?'

'Did they seem to know one another? Was it awkward? How was Anna's behaviour?'

Mrs Cork thought about the question.

'I suppose he was pleased to see her. Now that I think back, they were quite friendly. He said she was doing a fabulous job. I didn't think about it at the time. Do you think it's important?'

'I don't know, Mrs Cork. I just need to ask as many questions as possible to get an idea of why Anna has gone off like this. Did she have a boyfriend?'

'No.'

'Has she ever expressed any desire to move away?'

'No.'

Kelly wondered how well Mrs Cork knew her daughter. It reminded her of her relationship with her own mother. She had never told her the truth about her whereabouts. If she had, she would've been banned from all the best parties and naked midnight swims across Ullswater. She doubted if many mothers really knew what their daughters got up to.

She wished she could give Mrs Cork some sort of assurance when she left: a promise that Anna would come walking through the door at any moment, well and happy. But of course she couldn't. She never could.

She cast her mind back to her interviews at the Thwaite Hotel and decided to visit Kevin Cottrell next, also in Ambleside. But when she rapped on the door of his flat, there was no answer. She tried his mobile but it was switched off, so she popped a note through his door.

As she walked back to her car, she called Mrs Joliffe's number again, to no avail. It seemed that she was getting nowhere today, until a call came through from Eden House. It was DS Umshaw. Apparently there was a wrangle going on between the British and Bosnian embassies. Nedzad Galic, an ethnic Bosniak from Sara- jevo, was wanted in connection with war crimes dating back to 1993, and Jovana was to be used as bait. The age gap between them raised eyebrows: Jovana's husband was fifty two years old, but it might mean nothing. The Home Office was sending someone to interview her. The case might be off her hands before too long, thought Kelly.

'What about Marko Popovic? Anything from Phillips?' she asked.

'No hit, I'm afraid, but I did speak to someone at the embassy who said that a lot of guys who fled the old Yugoslavia with something to hide changed their names years ago.'

'Thanks, Kate. I'm done here. I'm meeting the Crawley son when I get back, so I'll see you after that.' She hung up.

Each time Kelly had driven over Kirkstone Pass recently, she'd looked up to Caudale Moor and felt it beckoning her. Now she stopped at the Kirkstone Inn and got out of the car. The air was fresh up here, and it was a perfect day for hiking. She looked at her watch. What was it her father always said? If you have one foot in the past and one foot in the future, you piss on today. Fuck it. Her walking gear was always in her car, just in case, and now she took it into the inn and went to the toilet to change.

From Caudale Moor, she had seven routes to choose from, and she could make the hike as long or as short as she wanted. She remembered being dragged up here, aged seven, by her father. Every bloody weekend they'd have to climb something, but it was only now that she was learning to appreciate it. If she ever had kids, she'd drag them up here too.

The ascent wouldn't be overly taxing – the inn stood at fifteen hundred feet, so it was an easy walk to any of the surrounding summits – but she hadn't come up here for a challenge. She'd come to focus and clear her mind. During any investigation, one of the most common problems was sheer overload. They'd reached a point in this one where they had so much information that Kelly could feel herself going round and round in circles, and it wasn't just a matter of taking a day off: that wouldn't help. She needed peace, and she could think of nowhere better than up here.

She was on the summit of Caudale Moor in under twenty minutes and decided to carry on to Hartsop Dodd.

She felt her fogginess clearing and it strengthened her attention to detail. She stopped on top of Hartsop Dodd, and as she sat looking down on Brothers Water, flanked on all sides by crag and fell, her thoughts turned to the girl with the red hair. She saw her bouncing up and down on Colin Day and wondered where she was now. She was the key to all of this. She wondered how quickly the lab was working to match the hair samples, and made a note to befriend someone at the lab, a small outfit in Carlisle. Maybe a conversation with the chief coroner would hurry things along.

It was time to go and meet Dave Crawley, and after her diversion, she believed herself ready to face him. Her feet pounded the steep rocky path, and she felt her blood pump satisfyingly and her breathing quicken. She hadn't been out on a proper fell walk for perhaps five years, and it felt good. Sometimes, abandoning work for a couple of hours was just what was needed to zero in on what was important.

The peaks gave panoramic views of the whole of the Lakes, and she stood with her hands on her hips regaining her breath before beginning to circle back. As she reached her car, she realised that she was smiling. Everything was clearer than before, and she jumped into the driver's seat and headed back to Penrith.

Chapter 32

George stayed way beyond the end of his shift to speak to Gabriela. He was fond of her, and couldn't help feeling protective. When he told her that the detective had come to the hotel looking for someone called Darren, she went pale.

'What is it? Do you need to speak to the policewoman? I have her card here, look,' he said.

'No, George, it's all right.' But she took the card anyway.

'Is there something you want to tell me?' he asked softly. She wrung her hands, and he knew she wanted to share something. 'A problem shared is a problem halved,' he added.

'I beg your pardon?' Her English was good, but there were certain phrases she didn't understand.

'It's an English saying. It means that if you get a problem off your chest, it feels better.'

'Off your chest?'

He laughed. 'It's another saying.'

'You have lots of sayings, George.'

'Don't you have them in Poland?'

'Yes, but they aren't strange like yours.'

'Do you plan to go home someday, Gabriela?'

'Yes, George. Always.'

'You must miss your family.'

'Yes, I do.' She looked away before turning her gaze back to him. 'You saw the man, George. Is it him?' She gestured to the photo of Darren Beckett that DI Porter had left with him.

'I really can't tell. The policewoman said it was an old photo. It could be the same man.'

'But the name. Darren. I've heard it before. Nush used it the last night I saw her; she said that if Roza came back, I should tell her Darren.'

'Tell her Darren what?'

'Nothing, just say Darren, she said. One word.'

'Here,' George said. 'The detective left these as well.' He showed Gabriela photos of a watch and a ring, and Gabriela's neck turned pink. She was sure now what Darren was after. But how did he know?

'We need to tell Mrs Joliffe,' said George.

'No.' Gabriela was firm.

'Why?' George was surprised.

'It would only cause trouble. She might blame me.'

'I don't know, Gabriela. I'm not sure I can keep any of it from her. It's her hotel.'

'No it's not. It belongs to a man called Colin Day. I've seen the paperwork. What do you think I do all night? I need something to read. It's the man who died in the hotel down the street, I read a newspaper about it. It was the same day Nush disappeared.'

'Now you're being dramatic. You really have been tucked away haven't you?'

'George, will you promise not to talk about this? Please,' she pleaded, and he softened.

'I'm not sure. Mrs Joliffe will want to know what I said to the police. I can't change that.'

'Yes, but about Darren?'

'But it might not be the same man... All right, I'll keep it to myself, but if he comes here again, I'm calling the detective.'

'Agreed.'

George went home. He was unhappy about leaving Gabriela alone at night with an open door. But he was dog tired, and he was working seven days back to back this week. Besides, there were other guests and staff at the hotel, so she wasn't really on her own.

—

After George left, Gabriela photocopied the photos and hid them under a file until her shift was over, when she could add them to the contents in the envelope under her bed. She was jumpy all night. She took more notice of who came through the door, and she kept the mobile phone given to her by Mrs Joliffe in her pocket at all times, along with the policewoman's card. She knew which one she would try first.

She recognised most of the faces now, and she studied the girls more closely, just in case. Her memory was excellent and she could draw minute details that anyone else would forget. She remembered the meal she had cooked when Nikita had been born, and the names of all of her elementary-school teachers. When she played the game with her mother where she had to memorise items then look away, she always won. She'd been four years old. At three a.m. a man walked into reception whom she didn't recognise, and she froze. Her heart pounded but she collected herself. He wasn't as old as the usual residents and he didn't look affluent. She didn't know what the girls were paid, but all the men wore suits and boasted pot bellies, indicating their plentiful lifestyles. They wore gold watches and carried expensive briefcases, and when Gabriela looked out into the car park, she saw BMWs, Mercedes and Land Rovers parked like a row of cash machines.

'Morning,' the man said.

'Good morning, sir, can I help you?' She studied his face to be sure, taking in as much as possible and committing it to memory. He was skinny and he smelled bad. His hair was mousy and unwashed, his eyes were bright blue, and he was roughly five foot ten tall. He kept his hands in the pockets of a black padded coat. He wore boots, but she couldn't say if they were the same ones she'd seen under her door. But she was sure he was the man in the photograph, the man called Darren.

'I'm not sure if you can. I'm looking for Nush,' he said.

'Nush?' Gabriela's heart beat against her chest.

'Anushka. Red hair. Big lips.' He grinned, and she could see his yellow teeth.

'She's gone,' she said.

'Really? Where to?'

'I have no idea. She doesn't work here anymore. I didn't know her very well, I just remember the red hair.' She'd added too much detail and piqued his interest.

'I need to get into her room. She has something of mine.' He grinned again.

'I'm sorry, sir, I really can't do that. I don't know who you are.' She wondered if he could see the pounding pulse in her neck. She toyed with the idea of showing him the empty room, but she didn't want to be alone with him upstairs.

'Well, let me introduce myself. I'm Kieran, Nush's boyfriend. She had something that's mine and I'm not leaving until I get it.' His demeanour turned sour and Gabriela sensed danger. She noted his use of the past tense and her gut turned over.

One of the regular guests entered the hotel and smiled at her.

'Good evening, Mr Peacock!' she said enthusiastically.

'Gabriela, good evening.' He looked at Darren. 'Is there a problem here?' he asked.

'Not at all. This gentleman was just leaving, weren't you, sir?' Gabriela said.

Darren looked at the older man for a moment, then muttered something under his breath and turned towards the door.

Once she was sure both men had left, Gabriela took the photo of Darren Beckett that she'd copied and quickly drew on more hair, a large jacket and gaunt cheeks. There, it was perfect.

–

Outside, Darren walked down the road, frustrated. But something about the receptionist's name had jogged his memory. Nush had spoken of a girl called Gabriela. Miss Perfect, she'd called her.

'She's got it coming one day, Miss Perfect,' she had said viciously.

Well, maybe she had.

Chapter 33

Dave looked nervous. He wore a baseball cap and sunglasses, but this simply made him more conspicuous inside the café at the services. Kelly had to stop herself from laughing out loud when she spotted him, but decided to respect his tension rather than play off it. Besides, she was here on serious business.

Katy Crawley, Dave's wife, was a combination of unsophisticated brawn and powerboat jaw. Kelly had no idea why Dave had fallen for her and she wasn't sure she wanted to know. If Katy found out they were meeting in secret, Dave would be in serious trouble. Kelly wasn't concerned for herself, but the man before her was different: he'd got used to being told what to do, and it pained her.

She walked to his table and sat down with her coffee. His eyes darted around but eventually settled on her. He smiled and seemed to relax a little.

'I'm sorry to put you through this, Dave. I wouldn't do it unless it was important. I need to speak to you about an investigation I'm working on.'

Dave sighed. He seemed relieved and disappointed at the same time.

'I've reason to suspect that Crawley Haulage is hiring out lorries, which are then being used to transport illegal immigrants from Europe.'

Kelly let the information sink in, she wanted to tread carefully. She couldn't go accusing Dave and his father of smuggling or trafficking; besides, it was obvious that Dave wasn't earning the lucrative sums associated with the trade. He was too depressed and downcast for that to be the case.

Dave sat up defensively, but his tone remained nonchalant: a curious combination.

'Really? That's highly unlikely but our lorries do get contracted out all the time. It's nothing new. My dad could be working with a whole host of companies all over the world. But I'm sure I'd know about it if this was really happening.'

'We have a witness.'

Dave's eyes turned dark and Kelly felt his discomfort.

'I need your discretion, Dave. Have you ever heard of a company called Tomb Day?'

'No. Who's the witness?'

'An illegal immigrant has said that she was brought here in a lorry carrying the name Crawley on its side.'

Dave's eyes widened.

'We also have large sums of money being transferred to Crawley Haulage from this company Tomb Day. I wanted to give you a chance to explain.'

'Christ, Kelly, what are you suggesting?' His voice sounded panicked, and Kelly kicked herself for not making her enquiry formal and sending someone direct to the Crawley offices. Sympathy was hardly helpful during an inquiry.

'How do you vet your drivers?' she asked.

'Er... the usual ways... references...'

'And are the vehicles tracked?'

'No, we can check mileage and speed, but we don't track them as such. We do keep a log of which driver is supposed to do which route, though.'

'OK, so could you get me a list of the drivers coming from Europe, via any route, back to Penrith on the day or night of the sixteenth of September? This one came from Budapest.'

'That should be easy, yes.'

'Good. And could you also let me know what each of those drivers was supposed to be delivering or picking up, and where?'

'Er... yes, no problem.'

'Thanks. That's all I need for now. You do understand that I have to ask these questions?'

'Yes. Of course. You're so serious when you... what do you call it... interview?' He changed the subject, catching her off guard.

She laughed. 'It wasn't exactly an interview, but I know what I need so I just come out and ask for it.' She instantly regretted the wording.

'I know,' he said, grinning.

'It's good to see you smiling,' she said. 'You were looking... well, down.' He glanced away. 'How are the kids?'

The mention of his children lifted him, and he smiled again.

'They're great. Josh is fantastic at football and Courtney is a drama queen.' They both laughed.

'I'd offer you another coffee, but I guess you'd prefer to be here for as short a time as possible,' she said.

He looked at his watch, and Kelly followed his gaze momentarily.

'I can stay a while. What brought you back, Kelly? I thought the big smoke was calling.'

'It did for a while, and then a job came up here and I realised I missed the Lakes. London is suffocating. Don't get me wrong, it was exciting for a while, but it was full on, case after case of lunatics stabbing and shooting one another, or worse.'

'Isn't that why you left here in the first place? Not enough murders in these here hills?' He gestured behind him in the direction of the mountains and affected a sinister accent.

'I'm beginning to think that there are plenty of criminals roaming round those hills. They're the perfect place to hide.'

'You're not getting paranoid, are you? We're all harmless folk up here.'

She half smiled and wondered if she was indeed being paranoid. The last thing she needed as she settled back in up here was to make up dark deeds where there were none, but she'd stumbled upon something and she knew it. It was just a case of fitting together the pieces.

Dave looked at his watch again.

'So, do you think one of my drivers has a sideline in the white slave trade?' He was teasing her and enjoying it, but Kelly spoke seriously.

'Well, what if they were? What would you do about it? It's a lucrative trade. Some studies reckon girls can be sold for as much as ten thousand quid each, if they're taken to order.'

'Oh, come on! Now you're being ridiculous. With respect, Kel, don't you think I'd know if a steady flow of sex slaves was being churned through my business?'

'I thought you worked for your dad?' she said. Kelly hadn't mentioned sex or slavery.

'Wait a minute, are you suggesting that if this is going on – which is ludicrous – my dad knows about it?'

She'd gone too far. 'No, I'm sorry, that's not what I'm suggesting at all, but what I do know is that Penrith is full of haulage companies, the Lakes is full of illegal workers and plenty of places to hide them, and they don't come in by aeroplane. I may have just uncovered the tip of the iceberg.'

'I didn't think of it like that,' he said, and looked at his hands. 'Kelly, Dad's ill. This would kill him. Can you be discreet too? Come through me. Please don't involve him.'

'I'll do my best, but I can't promise anything. I've got a job to do. I'm sorry about your dad, though. What's wrong?'

'Cancer. Inoperable. He's got about four months left. I shouldn't have mentioned it, not what after happened with your dad…'

'Hey, it's fine. Cancer's shit; it seems to get everyone eventually. I'm just sorry I wasn't here in time for my dad.'

'He always talked about you, couldn't shut him up.'

'Since when did you socialise with my dad?' She already knew the answer. Dave was the son her father had never had, and he'd always held it against her that he'd lost him.

'We still went for our Thursday pint, right up until… He loved you, Kel.' She started to argue but he cut her off. 'I know you find it hard to believe, but he was so proud of you.'

'Funny way of showing it.'

'What did you expect? You left him all alone with that sister of yours; no wonder he was mad.' He smiled, and suddenly Kelly saw the younger Dave in his eyes. She desperately wanted to ask if he was happy, but she was afraid to cross a line that was already crumbling.

'Look, Kel, I need to get back. Josh has got football.' He looked at his watch again. Kelly was sure now that it was a Patek Philippe model; Matt the twat had been obsessed with them.

'Of course you do. Where are you living now, Dave?'

'Oh, Mosedale.'

'Really? Nice.' Mosedale was a quiet hamlet of stone cottages and expensive barn conversions.

He got up to leave, and she followed him discreetly to the door and watched him walk across the car park. He disappeared behind a van, and she moved to another section of the café to see him, then watched as he climbed into a Range Rover Sport.

Chapter 34

'Ted Wallis speaking.' The chief coroner sounded distracted as he answered his phone.

'Hello, Mr Wallis. My name is Kelly Porter and I'm a detective inspector with Cumbria Constabulary. I'm chasing a few cases and I wondered if you had a moment to chat?'

'Well, well, well, I haven't heard that name in a while. John Porter's girl?'

'The same. You knew my dad?'

'I did. So you followed him into the force? He'd be proud. Are you based here in Carlisle? You should have dropped in. How is your mother?'

'She's good, thank you.' Kelly was taken by surprise; she hadn't realised she was calling an old family friend. 'Actually, I'm calling from Penrith, but I noticed that your name is on the autopsy reports of two of my cases and I have reason to believe they're linked by a person of interest.'

Ted sounded intrigued. 'I'm listening,' he said.

'In 2012, you autopsied Lottie Davis. She was—'

'Ten years old, went missing from Haweswater on a family outing to spot rare eagles, found in a red party dress dumped in a ditch above Dobbin Wood. Her father was innocent but committed suicide a year later.'

Kelly was impressed. She'd spoken to many coroners and they usually came across as aloof and condescending, but not this one.

'That's the type of case one can't forget. It was truly awful. Am I right in thinking that you're reviewing it? Please say it's being looked at again.'

'Yes. Yes it is, and I suspect it may be connected in some way to a new case.'

'Which one?'

'You were the reporting coroner again, a Mr Colin Day?'

'Yes, I was, but I'm confused. How could they be connected?'

'Er...' Kelly faltered. She didn't know Ted Wallis at all, and here she was hypothesising with just shreds of evidence and a good old-fashioned hunch. She decided to tell him her theory.

'Did you hear about the Bosnian woman who abandoned her baby near the Greenside lead mine?' she asked.

'Of course. The story was covered on TV.'

'She said she and her husband were brought from Europe by lorry, but they were tricked and her husband was allegedly forced into another vehicle. We can't find him, but she remembers that the lorry that brought her up the M6 belonged to a local haulage firm. Then Colin Day dies of a heart attack, induced by the enthusiasm of a young woman named Anushka Ivanov – an illegal. We can't find her either. She was an employee at the Troutbeck Guest House, less than a mile from the Thwaite Hotel, where Colin Day died. He was the owner of both hotels, plus five others. Colin Day was an astute man, and taped the encounter, possibly for insurance purposes.'

Kelly took a deep breath. 'I believe Mr Day was running an illegal brothel. There is video evidence and a paper trail to indicate that this is the case. But I think it's bigger than just a one-man operation. He was turning over hundreds of thousands of pounds a year via an umbrella company in the Isle of Man.' She was getting used to the financial jargon; before, she'd known nothing of such companies where people could legally dodge tax and other laws.

'I knew Colin Day personally,' Wallis said. 'I don't know what to say. How does all this link to Lottie?'

'A man named Darren Beckett knew that Lottie would be eagle-watching that day. Haweswater is isolated and difficult to get to. She needed to be taken away at speed – probably by car. It's my belief that it wasn't an opportunistic abduction, and I suspect that Beckett is acting as a go-between for a more serious outfit. He's disappeared too, though I have evidence that he was sniffing around the Troutbeck Guest House looking for Anushka Ivanov. I believe that if I find Darren Beckett, I find the illegals. He's my link.'

'Where do I come in?'

'I wanted to ask you your personal opinion on Lottie's cause of death – the things I can't get from a report. I don't want science, or medical terminology. Just your thoughts when you examined her.'

'Well to start with, she had a full face of make-up. I mean, adult stuff, not something a little girl would wear.'

'As if applied by someone else?'

'Yes. I remember thinking that she looked like a doll. I'm sorry, it really was the worst case I've ever had. When I heard that she could have been taken for some kind of paedophile ring, it sickened me to my stomach. I've got two daughters myself. They wasted a lot of time on the father, didn't they? I always told myself that strangulation would have been quick at her age. I hope I was right.'

'Mr Wallis, there's something else you could help me with, if you would.'

'Of course.'

'The bright red hairs you pulled from around Mr Day's wedding band.'

'Yes, go on.'

'I managed to gain access to Darren Beckett's last known address via his landlord in Barrow-in-Furness, and we found long bright red hairs there. They're at the lab in Carlisle now, but they don't know me there and it's taking an age. I'm a newbie round here, I've only been back a few weeks. I was wondering if you could speed things up.'

'You're looking for a match?'

'Yes. And a possible DNA profile.'

'I know the lab well. Consider it done.'

–

Ted Wallis sat looking at his phone for a long time after he'd spoken to DI Porter. Eventually he made a call to the lab, who promised him they'd have an answer for him by close of play today.

He couldn't carry on with his work now. He'd have to go to the flat and look for something.

It had been after a party, some five years ago now. Colin had invited Ted to these affairs because he looked good: professional and authoritative; he liked the kudos that came with influential friends. The party had been a stiff event, and afterwards Ted and Mary were invited back to Colin and Christine's, along with a few others.

Ted had admired the house and noted that Colin had done rather well for himself, though he never knew how at the time. Perhaps now he was beginning to understand.

The men went off to play snooker in what Colin referred to as the billiards room. It smelled of stale smoke, cigars and whisky, and Ted remembered feeling envious of the other man's wealth and success. The women stayed in the drawing room. Colin was very drunk and the talk turned to sex. Colin asked Ted if he had ever tried Viagra, because he had some rather powerful ones from Germany.

Married to Mary, Ted had about as much use for Viagra as he did for football boots, and he'd laughed and said that sex with Mary wasn't an option. Instead, Colin had passed him a card. A card that he knew he still had. It was black, and simply embossed in gold with a mobile number and a single word: *flower.*

Chapter 35

There'd been several sightings of Darren Beckett in Barrow-in-Furness in the past few days, and Kelly considered them. Darren and Nush's photos had been printed in the *Westmorland Gazette* and the *Evening Mail*; they had also been on the evening news. The police had received perhaps a dozen calls. Two stood out.

One was an old school friend who said he'd seen Darren filling his car with petrol in Ulverston; he'd waved but Darren hadn't responded and the man had got into his car, dismissing the rudeness as pretty normal for Darren Beckett. He described the car as black, small and probably a Ford. He couldn't remember the night. It might have been 21 September. He wasn't sure. He had seen Beckett leave the petrol station and turn towards the A590.

The other was an ex-girlfriend who was a timid creature and scared out of her wits. She said she'd seen Darren walking close to Barrow Dock, also on the 21st, but earlier, around eleven p.m. She said his head had been down and his hands firmly in his pockets, but there was no mistake. She'd been with him for two years and she'd never forget him, not after he'd punched her in the stomach when she accused him of stealing from her mother. The woman had been asked how good a likeness to Beckett's current appearance the photo released by police was. The answer was not a lot. She said he'd grown shaggy hair that covered his eyes, and he looked gaunt, and older. She thought he had been returning to his car, and it stuck in her memory because there was no reason why anyone would be walking down there at night. She'd been stuck at a red light near the museum, and had been staring right at him. Luckily he hadn't appeared to see her. She was sure about the date because she was covering a late shift for a friend.

She was a credible witness. Kelly knew Barrow Dock; though it was frequented by dog walkers during the day, it was deserted by night. Darren Beckett didn't strike her as the kind of person who might take a stroll along the promenade to clear his head, nor did he own a dog, as far as they knew, and he certainly wasn't a fitness enthusiast taking advantage of the long stretch of smooth pathways.

She called Lockwood to see if he could find out if either the garage or the museum had CCTV. The museum didn't, but the garage did, and it was on a ten-day loop, so film from the 21st should still be there. Lockwood sent a DC to examine it, and got back to Kelly within three hours, having found footage of Darren Beckett filling up a black Ford Fiesta. He also added that he'd taken the liberty of enhancing a still from the footage, and emailed it to her. Kelly faxed it over to the Troutbeck Guest House for the attention of George, and it was also released to the press.

In it, Beckett seemed to be a different person entirely. He appeared frail and hunched over, and looked like a tramp. Kelly guessed that years of drugs and alcohol had taken their toll; he easily looked forty, like the man George had seen at the hotel.

She called Lockwood to thank him. 'I need another favour,' she said.

'No problem. Go ahead.'

'I think we should lean a bit harder on Dennis Hill while his sister isn't around.'

'She won't like that.'

'I know, that's why I'm asking you to do it. I want to push him to see if he can remember anything about Darren. He was friends with Wade, so he might have known Darren too.'

'OK, I'll see what I can do. How's the other case going? Do you still think they're linked?'

'Yes, I do. I've got evidence that a lorry firm is being paid a lot of money from one of Colin Day's companies, but I don't know why, and I've got video footage of women being paid for sex, though none of them are traceable. Darren and Anushka are my missing link. Her because she is evidence of organised prostitution, and him because he knew Lottie through Wade. If Beckett is working for whoever organised Colin Day's extracurricular activities – including Day himself – then he would know people who'd snatch a girl to order.'

'Is this connected to the woman in hospital as well?'

'I can't say for sure, but she said she was dropped off by a lorry driver who worked for the same haulage company.'

Lockwood whistled. 'I didn't think Darren Beckett had it in him to get involved with the big boys.'

'When you were in Manchester, did you know anyone who worked trafficking? We certainly don't have a department like that here, and I could do with throwing my ideas around with an expert. Someone who knows about money trails and how this kind of operation works.'

'I'll have a dig around and get back to you.'

'Thanks, Lockwood. I'll be in touch.'

'Call me Craig, Kelly, for God's sake.'

Kelly rang off and turned back to her computer. A new email pinged into her inbox. It was from the lab in Carlisle. The hairs matched and they'd extracted a DNA profile. It wasn't in the database, but the contents of Anushka's bag had been sent off too, and soon she'd know.

Chapter 36

The three men moaned continually through the night, and Darren slept fitfully, knowing that if they could break out of their room, they'd kill him. Curtis had done a good job securing them, but they stank. They weren't allowed to wash, and every time they wanted to piss or shit, Darren had to escort them to the bathroom with a knife.

Two of them were pretty docile, not wanting to court the danger of further injury to add to those sustained during the fights; but one was a belligerent shit. He stared into Darren's eyes and never looked away; even when spitting into the sink, he glared at him through the mirror. Darren felt constantly sick, and only vodka took the edge off. He'd eaten some fried chicken when he'd had a chance to leave the flat and try and get into Nush's room but he'd brought it straight back up. His eyes were sunken and he sweated profusely, despite the evening being bitingly cold.

'I speak English and hear every word,' the belligerent man said.

'Shut your mouth,' said Darren in reply, bringing the knife up to the man's back.

'Why you do this? I see how they treat you, you get all the shit jobs. You're a *pas*, no?'

'Shut up, you fucking Paki or whatever you are,' Darren spat. He didn't know what to do.

'What is Paki?' asked the man.

'Scum, migrant, whatever. Fucking hurry up, if you understand English,' Darren ordered. He felt dizzy.

'You English think everyone is Paki, you *pas glup*. Stupid dog.'

The man laughed and Darren punched him in his right kidney. He coughed but he didn't falter. Darren walked him back to the living room roughly and replaced his gag.

The man looked at the other two, and they nodded back imperceptibly.

The next night, during another bathroom trip, the captive spoke to Darren again.

'What they pay you?' he asked.

'Shut the fuck up, or I'll let you shit your pants next time!' Darren had had stomach cramps all day long and hadn't seen a soul. He was desperate to get out of the flat. Surely a short walk to the corner shop wouldn't hurt, he thought.

'I pay more,' said the captive.

'How you gonna do that with no fucking money?' Darren asked.

'My name is Nedzad. I have money. You like money and you are bored. You are also very ill, my friend.'

'Shut up!' Darren was consumed by a coughing fit and the knife fell out of his hand.

'I have a lot of money in English bank. You see. You know I tell the truth. If they make me fight and I lose, it will sit there forever.'

Darren stopped coughing.

'Where?' he asked. His mind whirred. He knew he was ill. His body was failing him from years of abuse. He'd seen a new picture of himself in the *Westmorland Gazette* and had taken to wearing a hat and sunglasses together with big jumpers even inside the flat, despite them making him sweat even more. The thought of going somewhere like Thailand and living the rest of his days lying on a beach and paying hookers was an attractive one. Marko would dump him at the bottom of a lake when he'd finished with him, of that he had no doubt.

–

Nedzad knew he'd struck a chord and didn't say another word. It was only a matter of time. He went back to his place obediently and didn't bite the fucker's hand like he wanted to. He knew how to play the game. He needed to avoid the evil bastard with the big head and bigger hands.

Darren went to his bedroom and slammed the door. Nedzad raised his eyes to the other two, indicating that the time might come soon. A few minutes after that, they heard another bang; they'd worked out enough about the flat to know that it was the sound of the front door closing. They heard no voices, and Nedzad suspected that it was the stupid dog leaving rather than anyone else arriving.

He retrieved the plastic razor he'd taken from the sink when Darren was having his coughing fit and broke it into pieces, leaving only the blade. He worked quickly, and within five minutes, he was free. Their tethers displayed sloppy work. In his country, hostages would be tied up properly, if they weren't already dead. He began working on the other two, and the second man was almost free when they heard the door again.

Nedzad took a gamble that it was only the dog returning and not anyone else, and he was right. Darren peered around the door to check that they hadn't moved, and found all three men where he'd left them, their hands behind their backs, gags in.

Nedzad knew the dog's routine well and smelled the alcohol on his grimy breath. He would soon be in a stupor, and if they could wait, they'd have more chance of putting distance between them and the flat. He had no idea where they were; all he knew was that it was a fucking cold and miserable place. They were supposed to be heading to London.

This was not London.

Of course, the risk with waiting was that the big bastard would turn up, and even Nedzad wasn't convinced they could overpower him, though perhaps with the element of surprise… After all, they'd all fought to the death in the ring.

They waited for half an hour.

Nedzad had no idea where the other men were from; they didn't speak English and he didn't recognise their languages. One could have been Chinese; the other was white European. They worked together purely from instinct, and within half an hour they'd padded around the flat and found coats, two kitchen knives and a spanner, though only two pairs of shoes. The small man who looked Chinese indicated that he could go shoeless.

They all nodded their readiness and Nedzad tried to communicate with his hands that every man was on his own when they left the flat. The other two seemed to understand; they both gestured to the outside and then 'away' with a flick of an arm. Nedzad held out his hand and they all shook.

They entered the hallway. The sound of a TV was coming from one of the other rooms. It drowned out any noise the three men made opening and closing the front door. The escapees padded gently down the stairwell and went off in different directions. Nedzad looked both ways. It was freezing. He hadn't a clue where he was, but he'd soon find out. He'd been on the run before, and this was just England, where no one except criminals carried guns; England, where anyone could live comfortably as an illegal; England, the laughing stock of the world with her outdated allegiance to liberalism, tolerance and justice.

In Bosnia, he'd seen men stoned to death for stealing a pig; starving wretches put out of their misery by a more dominant species. He was a survivor, and for now, all he needed was shelter and water. He heard the distant rumble of traffic and walked towards it, sticking to the shadows. He looked nondescript, and in the overcoat and trainers he'd taken from the flat, he blended in. One of the first rules of survival was looking as though you belonged; it could be in your walk or the way you crossed the road, but you had to do it with nonchalance.

He was hungry, but that could be controlled. The mind made the body strong. He thought of revenge only momentarily; it was desirable but ultimately counterproductive. Only the weak sought revenge to their own detriment.

He turned a corner and the land opened up before him, lights twinkling in the distance. He decided that it was a decent-sized town: good, more places to disappear. Further away, there were mountains, and he was shocked. He'd always envisaged England as a drab place full of cities made of metal and concrete, teeming with people living grey lives. This scenery was a revelation. In Bosnia, he'd received the most generosity of spirit and heart in the countryside, where people lived simply, immune to what the press and the government told them.

Perhaps he'd head towards the mountains.

Chapter 37

'This has all happened since Kelly got back, Mum,' said Nikki. She was sitting with her mother in the outpatient waiting room at the Penrith and Lakes Hospital, waiting for an appointment: another check-up.

'That's not true, Nikki. Kelly has helped me get the house back into shape and she's busy at work. This has nothing to do with her; she can't make me ill. Now go and find me some tea. I might be in there for hours, knowing their tests and retests. And pass me a magazine.'

Wendy Porter looked at her elder daughter and wondered where she and John had gone so wrong. Children could be born into the same family and raised in exactly the same way, but turn out so differently. She didn't favour one daughter over the other, although it was true that her relationship with Kelly was volatile, because she was just like her father.

Wendy had had a lot of time to think during her stint in the hospital. She'd done her best for both her daughters, and for John. How could she have known what lay ahead? How could anybody? You left school with a head full of dreams, met a boy, got married and became consumed by babies, then they grew up and suddenly you realised that you'd just been a vessel for human life.

John had thought he was the thinker, but Wendy was the one who watched the news and saw it getting worse and worse. She'd cried when troops went to Iraq and again when they went to Afghanistan because of all the mothers who'd be burying their sons, and of course it had come to pass. It always did.

And gradually she'd witnessed the war between her own daughters escalate to the point where they barely spoke. Kelly left, Nikki stayed. Kelly followed her heart, Nikki her duty. Kelly freed herself and Nikki became imprisoned. Now Kelly lived and Nikki brooded.

Secretly Wendy wished she herself had been more like Kelly, but she hadn't had the courage. She'd watched as John and his younger daughter shouted at one another. Wendy wanted her punished for not being just plain ordinary. Now she understood that ordinary never broke records, ordinary never got a pay rise, ordinary never travelled to the moon, ordinary walked the same path for fifty, sixty, seventy years, and she was glad that that wasn't Kelly's destiny.

When Kelly had left for London, Wendy knew that she would survive. It was Nikki she feared for now, with her reliance on the ship being forever solid. She looked at her elder daughter, with her thick make-up and her pinched-in mouth, telling her mother who she was going to blame for the ward being too cold, or the toilet not being clean, or the consultant being late. She wondered who'd looked after Nikki's three children in her absence, and if Ria would ever stop wetting the bed.

Wendy had told neither daughter of her illness and what it meant, and she'd instructed the hospital staff to respect her wishes and do the same. She'd known for three months. When Kelly had suggested she might move back to Cumbria, Wendy had jumped at the opportunity to enjoy her younger daughter for a while. The palpitations, and other nagging conditions, would continue to get worse until she had to stay in hospital for the last time. She wouldn't tell them until she had to.

'I thought Kelly might have come,' Nikki said. She was still standing there, with her hands on her hips. Wendy knew that what she really meant was that Kelly was selfish for not being here. Her elder daughter was making her melancholy, and Wendy wished she'd talk of something positive for once, instead of complaining all the time. It was tiresome staying at her house and she wanted to go home.

'Well I'm going to speak to the consultant today, Mum. I'm going to give him a piece of my mind. We need to get to the bottom of this. If you don't get results today, I'll explode.'

'You're not coming in with me, Nikki.'

'What?'

'I want to go in alone. The last thing these doctors want to hear is complaints from someone who has no idea what real suffering is.' It was out before Wendy could help herself.

Nikki's mouth opened and closed.

'But Mum! It's unacceptable! This hospital has always been useless. When I had Ria, I was left for twelve hours screaming in agony, and given nothing for it.'

'I'll call you when I'm done.' Nikki began to say something, but Wendy stopped her. 'I mean it, Nikki. I want to be alone. Please.'

'But what about your tea?'

'I'll survive, thank you, love.'

Wendy watched as her daughter left the waiting room.

After she was sure Nikki had gone, she got up and went towards the toilet. The outpatients' toilet was busy, so she went along to the main ward, where she was known to the nurses. They told her that of course she could use the loo. Rules were bent for patients who'd had bad news, and they all liked Mrs Porter.

She walked to the end of the corridor and turned the corner. A policeman was standing outside a door.

'I'm sorry if I shocked you, ma'am,' he said. Wendy laughed and shook her head.

'You startled me, that's all. Just ignore me!' She carried on to the toilet.

When she opened the door, she was faced with the sight of a woman standing on a chair, trying to get out of the window. Wendy rushed to her.

'My goodness, are you all right?' she asked.

The woman babbled in some foreign language.

'I'll get help,' said Wendy.

'No!' the woman whispered.

'You speak a little English?'

The woman gave up struggling to climb out. She stepped off the chair and fell to the floor, where she began to weep. Wendy sat down next to her and put her arm around her.

'Where are you from?' She spoke slowly, as if this would break down the language barrier. The woman simply stared at her.

'Scared. Baby. Out.' She spoke with sad eyes, and pointed to the window.

'You have a baby? Where?' Wendy gesticulated, pretending to nurse a swaddled baby.

'Yes,' the young woman said. She began to cry. Wendy thought her baby might have died and she was suffering some terrible postnatal grief.

'I'll go and get help.'

'No!' It was emphatic, and Wendy stopped. 'Out.'

Wendy climbed up onto the chair and looked out of the window. It wasn't a big drop, but she wasn't sure she had the strength to help the young woman to get out.

'What is your name?' she asked. She gesticulated again, pointing to herself. 'I am Wendy.' She repeated it a couple of time until the young woman understood.

'Jovana.'

Wendy was unsure what to do. She remembered the policeman. 'Police, outside.' She pointed to the door and the woman's eyes grew wider.

'No! Bad!'

'Bad?' As the wife of a police officer, Wendy found it difficult to understand how anyone in uniform could be anything but helpful and reassuring, but she knew that was just fanciful. Even John had made mistakes. So had she.

This was her chance. Her chance to do something not ordinary.

'You, out?' she asked, and pointed to the window.

Jovana's eyes changed and Wendy saw something that she only saw in her grandchildren: a pure and unshakeable trust. She made up her mind. They both got to their feet, and she gestured that the woman needed to take off some of her clothes. She understood.

There was a knock at the door.

They ignored it and sped up. Wendy screwed Jovana's spare clothes into a ball and secured them with a jumper, then pointed to the chair. Jovana stepped up onto it and Wendy stood behind her. The young woman grabbed the window and Wendy pushed her from behind. Her fingers, wrists and shoulders screamed, but she hadn't been so sure of anything for a very long time. She stood strong and tall, and heaved upwards.

Jovana climbed out of the window and Wendy threw the clothes out after her. She stood on the chair and watched her gather her things and run into the trees, stopping to look back once and wave. Then she saw a figure come forward and take the woman into his arms. They were lovers! She was going to her lover!

'Go and find your less ordinary,' she whispered, smiling to herself.

Wendy went to the toilet and washed her hands. When she left, the policeman was outside, still waiting and looking extremely anxious.

'Is there a woman in there?' he asked breathlessly.

'No, no one but me. Good morning, Officer,' she said, and turned to walk back to the waiting area.

Chapter 38

Darren woke from his fug. His phone was ringing and his head was banging. Christ, he could hardly see. The phone stopped, but in the time it'd taken to ring out, he'd found some sense of who he was, where he was, and whether he was dead or alive. He established that he was well and truly alive, although he wasn't convinced that was necessarily a good thing. He coughed and looked at his phone; he didn't recognise the caller. It rang again and he answered. He didn't make a habit of picking up to unknown callers, but he wasn't thinking straight.

'Yep.'

'Who is this?'

The man was well-spoken and sounded senior and kind of authoritative.

'Who the fuck is *this*?' Darren fell to his default setting of basic primate behaviour.

'I want a flower,' said the caller.

Darren swallowed. It was always tricky negotiating with a new customer about whom he knew absolutely nothing; it could always be a trap.

'Who's your contact?'

'Colin Day.'

'Nice try, he's dead.'

'I know, but he gave me this card before he died.'

'Flower's closed.'

'Shame.'

'You couldn't afford it anyway.'

The man laughed. 'Oh, I think I could.'

'Well, like I said, it's closed, but I'll take your details in case that changes.'

'Sure. I'm interested. I like... young ones.'

Darren laughed. 'OK, nothing wrong with that. I'll pass you to someone who deals in that shit. Name?'

'Mickey Mouse. You have my number.' The caller hung up.

Darren was used to old perverts giving Disney names; they thought they were being ironic, but Darren thought they were just sick. He'd never been interested in that sort of thing, but he had to admit it made money. The person to ask was Marko.

He padded to the bathroom to take a piss. While he was there, he swallowed four paracetamol. He remembered his mother warning him not to overdo the painkillers, and this made him laugh because of the forty per cent brandy she threw down her throat every day. He washed his face and glanced in the mirror; he looked fifty.

The flat was quiet as always, and noise travelled up from the street: revving cars, barking dogs, and domestics. Everything was normal.

Until he opened the door to the lounge.

He began to shake and rubbed his eyes, as if it would make the men reappear where they should have been. Their restraints had been left in bundles on the floor, and he searched through them desperately, hoping to find the men underneath. His stomach tightened. He knew he was in trouble.

Again.

But this time he wouldn't be allowed to make it up. Marko didn't give third chances. Darren shivered. Images of death at the hands of Curtis or Sasha swirled through his brain and assaulted him. It would be painful and slow.

He made up his mind and rushed out into the hallway, where there was usually a mass of bags, shoes and coats. They'd been gone through and there were no shoes and only a couple of coats left. He swore and grabbed a bag and took it to the bedroom, where he shoved whatever was to hand inside it and zipped it shut. He dressed quickly, catching his finger on his trouser zip.

'Fuck!'

He checked his wallet and phones, leaving his keys on the side. He took a baseball cap and pushed it onto his head. He'd been growing a beard but it was still straggly. It would have to do. He threw on his new coat and left the room.

The front door was unlocked, and he remembered vividly now that he hadn't locked it last night. He was in big trouble and there was no chance he could talk his way out of it this time. Those guys made Marko a ton of money and he'd let them walk.

He closed the door behind him and prayed Curtis wouldn't turn up for a good few hours – ideally a day or two. He rushed down the stairs and walked past his car. He wanted no trace left at all. It would take him twenty minutes to reach the main road, and from there he'd hitch to Ambleside. He had nothing to lose now, and he needed Nush's money. She'd had ten quid on her the night he suffocated her, and he knew she'd earned a hundred times that. She was a stupid bitch for leaving it behind for Roza

233

to keep safe. That was her insurance and it'd done her no good at all. For all he knew, the room had been cleaned out already, but it was his only chance.

He checked his wallet and counted forty pounds in notes and seven pounds in change. He picked up a newspaper at a petrol station; there was a new story on Colin Day. The police were asking for information on two items of jewellery, though the piece was cagey and didn't directly suggest that they were linked to the guy's death. In the time that Darren had been checking the papers daily, nothing had been mentioned about the old man being fucked to death. If he'd been a scumbag from Barrow Island and not an ex-mayor and public do-gooder, his shit would be all over the press; it would probably even have made the *Daily Mail*. He'd call the papers later to try and squeeze some cash out of the story.

For now, he had some items to retrieve from the Trout-beck Guest House. This time, he was armed with the formidable weapon called 'don't give a flying fuck'. He'd be in and out in under half an hour. He knew the routine. He'd wait until about three a.m., when all the Colin Days would be asleep after their strenuous activities, and most of the whores would've left. And if that stuck-up bitch gave him any trouble, he'd punch her in the face before she could even open her mouth.

Chapter 39

Dave Crawley came back to Kelly with lists of drivers and their schedules. He also told her he'd looked into his father's accounts and seen a few payments to Tomb Day but didn't know what they were for. He hadn't wanted to push his father due to his illness. Kelly couldn't really argue with that, but it left her with no option: she had to begin an investigation into the payments. Dave took the news badly and she felt guilty.

She drove with DC Hide to a housing estate on the outskirts of Penrith and parked outside the address of a lorry driver called Jack Croft. He'd worked for Crawley Haulage for ten years. In the past four weeks, he had been on the road for twenty-three days, most of it in Europe, including the week of 10 September, when he'd travelled from Zagreb through Budapest and then Munich, on to Belgium and home.

'Any news on Jovana Galic?' Kelly asked DC Hide.

'No, guv.'

'She must have had help. I don't understand how she could simply vanish, and without her baby. She must have been terrified. It's bad news for us, because she could have ID'd the lorry driver. Damn. Anyway, come on. Let's see what we've got.'

They got out of the car and approached the house.

The small terrace stood out because there had been no attempt to make the front yard attractive. Other people along the road had pots and flower beds, or even a tiny patch of grass; this one had nothing, and it was an indication that Jack Croft not only travelled a lot, but that he also lived alone.

Kelly knocked and rang the bell at the same time for good measure. It took a few goes, but eventually a figure came towards the door. The man who filled the doorway wore scruffy jeans and a white T-shirt. His hair was dishevelled and he had about a week's growth of stubble on his face. He looked to be in his mid-fifties. Typical lorry driver, Kelly thought. He was the right age, build and height for the description they'd managed to get from Jovana, but then so were thousands of other lorry drivers in England. He scratched his chin and she got a whiff of unwashed body.

'Good morning, sir. We'd like to speak to Mr Jack Croft, please.'

The man looked wary. 'Who wants to know?'

'I'm Detective Inspector Porter and this is Detective Constable Hide. We'd like to ask him some questions. Is he in?'

'I'm in. I'm Jack Croft,' he said. His demeanour was shifty.

'May we come in?'

'Sure,' said Croft and moved backwards. It was clear to Kelly that he was trying to appear helpful. She'd learnt long ago that were two types of interviewees: those who simply told the police their story, and those who tried to convince them of their story. The latter were always liars.

The hall was tiny, but they shuffled along and into the front room and Hide closed the door.

'Can I get you a drink?' Croft asked.

'No thank you, we're fine. May we sit down?' said Kelly. She really didn't want to sit down on the grubby sofa, though she'd seen much worse. She certainly didn't want to drink from one of his cups.

'So you work for Crawley Haulage, yes?' she asked.

'Yes.' Croft coughed.

'And I see from your schedule that on the sixteenth of September, you returned from a long trip to Zagreb, via Belgium. Can you remember the journey in question?'

Croft scratched his chin again, stalling for time. The detectives waited.

'What day of the week was it?' he asked.

'It was a Sunday,' Kelly replied.

'I've done a lot of trips recently. I don't remember that particular night.'

'Well, I've got your log from Crawley Haulage, Mr Croft. So either you did it or someone did it for you in your lorry. Which is it to be?'

'It must have been me,' he said, shifting butt cheeks on the sofa. The stench of body odour was becoming unbearable.

'Have you ever brought people into the country illegally, Mr Croft?'

'No!' He was indignant but too hasty.

'And you've never accepted cash to do so?'

'No! Wait a minute, what's going on here?'

'It's simply an investigation. I'll be asking all your colleagues exactly the same questions,' Kelly said calmly. 'You must have seen the news, Mr Croft. Someone helped that woman into the country. She didn't speak English and she was heavily pregnant. But it's her husband we're most concerned for. Do you recognise either of these people?' She handed him the photographs of Jovana and Nedzad Galic.

'No.'

'Are you sure?'

'Sure.'

'Thank you, we'll call back if we need anything else. Oh, one more thing, Mr Croft. Are you aware of any of your colleagues bringing illegal immigrants into Britain via their regular routes for cash?'

'No.'

'None at all?'

'No.'

'Thank you.' They got up and left. Jack Croft looked pale and clammy as he closed the door.

'What do you think, guv?' Hide asked her boss.

'He's lying. Do we know when his next trip is?'

'Tomorrow.'

'I know someone in the Home Office who does border control. I'll send her an email with his details. It'll speed things up. They can't physically check every lorry coming into Britain; he might have slipped through dozens of times. He's playing with fire. Something has to lead to the person calling the shots. Let's hope it's this.'

Their next port of call was the Troutbeck Guest House, and they weren't leaving until Mrs Joliffe showed up. They'd had enough excuses. As Hide drove them towards Ambleside, Kelly's phone rang.

'DC Phillips, good morning.' She put him on speaker.

'Guv, I spoke to a DS at Merseyside yesterday about what Marko Popovic might have been up to during his time there. He was a suspect in plenty of cases involving stolen goods, drugs, possession of firearms, and GBH/ABH, but whenever they got close, either witnesses would retract their statements or the police lacked hard evidence to convince the CPS. For whatever reason, he was never charged with anything, although he was arrested a few times and his DNA is on the system. It was flagged up to us that he was headed our way, and it turns out we even had him followed, but funding cuts stopped all that and he doesn't appear again. He has legitimate cover; he was given asylum in 1997. And get this, he draws disability pension for anxiety.'

'Christ, you are joking?' Kelly couldn't believe it. 'Wait a minute, is it paid electronically?'

'Yes, guv.'

'Bingo! Find me the details. Did you get anything from Elite Escapes?'

'Yes. Apparently Colin Day or his wife book the same property up to four times per year. They're good clients: the place is always left clean. They drink a lot of booze. When I asked about other clients, she was unwilling but I leant on her. Turns out Harry Chase and Barry Crawley have booked through them – and get this, guv, they've booked together.'

The small hairs on Kelly's arms stood up. Harry Chase.

'Thanks, Will, good job. I want you and DS Umshaw to drop everything else and work on this link. We need to see if the three of them were linked in other ways: companies, financial deals.'

As she was speaking, Kelly was glancing through her notes.

'Fuck.'

'Sorry, guv?'

'HCCD Art Handling. Harry Chase/Colin Day. Bingo. Look into it.'

'Yes, guv.'

'Me and Emma are in Ambleside all day. If I don't get to see Mrs Joliffe today, I'm putting a warrant out for her arrest for wasting police time and evading an investigation. Just to confirm, the phone number found amongst Anushka's belongings is Joliffe's?'

'Yes, guv.'

Hide put her foot down, sensing her boss's urgency. Soon they were passing the Kirkstone Inn and cutting across to Ambleside.

To Kelly's surprise, Teresa Joliffe was waiting for them at the guest house. She took stock of the woman, and decided she was the kind of smooth operator who would never miss calls by accident. She also struck her as someone who didn't quite fit in here. She didn't look like a hotel manager; more of a nightclub owner, all black garb and dripping in diamonds. Her make-up was overdone for daytime, and she reeked of perfume.

'We've been trying to get hold of you for several days, Mrs Joliffe. We've got a few questions that we'd like to ask, and it could take some time. Do you have any other engagements, or may we proceed?'

'Please. I'm free for a good hour. I oversee other hotels, which is why I haven't been here when you've called before. I do apologise.' Her voice was well trained and controlled, as if she were used to public speaking. They all remained standing.

'Let's begin, shall we?' Kelly said. 'Which other hotels? All owned by Colin Day?' Hide took notes.

'Oh, I wouldn't know about that.'

'Who pays you?'

'I get paid by a company called Forward Holdings Ltd.'

Hide wrote it down. They hadn't come across that one.

'What was your relationship to Colin Day?'

'I never met him.'

'He paid your wages: Forward Holdings was his company.' It was a stab in the dark. Hide held back a smirk.

Teresa Joliffe shrugged. 'The Queen pays yours, but I don't suppose you've met her, have you?'

The two women locked gazes and Hide bristled.

'What is your relationship to Anushka Ivanov – your ex-employee?'

'Just that. I sacked her because she was never on time.'

'Were you aware that she was in the country illegally?'

'No.'

'Do you know where she went after you dismissed her?'

'No.'

'Why would she have your personal mobile number?'

'I probably gave it to her on one occasion I wanted her to actually give me notice when she never bothered to turn up. She obviously kept it.'

'Do you know this man?' Kelly showed her a picture of Darren Beckett.

'No.'

'This one?' A photo of Harry Chase taken hastily off the internet.

'No.'

'These women?' Photos of stills taken from Colin Day's USB sticks.

'No.'

'Is money ever handed over for sex on these premises, Teresa?'

'No, don't be absurd.'

'Wouldn't you like to know why I asked? Surely you would want to know that your employer is legitimate.'

'I don't need confirmation. I'd never make that mistake.'

'But you said you'd never met him, so actually you know nothing about your employer? Which is it?'

Joliffe remained stony.

'This man.' Kelly held a photo of Barry Crawley, received from Phillips on their way over here.

'No.'

'Who's Marko?'

Teresa Joliffe's right eye quivered and Kelly saw it.

'I don't know anyone called Marko.'

'Would you swear that on oath?'

'Yes.'

'You are aware that this interview will be recorded and any change in statement could go against you in the future?'

'Are you threatening me? You've come into my hotel, made accusations, and now you imply that I'm lying. This interview is over. I've got nothing more to say unless it's in front of a lawyer.'

'*Your* hotel?'

'It's… a figure of speech.'

'It sure is. What accountancy firm does the hotel use, Mrs Joliffe?'

'Off the top of my head I can't remember. I don't get involved in the finances.'

'But you're the manager.'

'Well, I collate the figures but then some accountant turns up – a different one every year – and I hand them over. It's always been like that.'

'I don't suppose it's Chase and Chase in Workington, is it?'

'Could be.'

'Have you ever heard of a company called Tomb Day?'

'No.' The answer was too quick. 'Oh, wait a moment. How is it spelled?'

Kelly thought the woman might be stalling for time. She asked for Hide's pad and wrote the name down on a piece of paper.

'That's funny,' Teresa said.

'What?'

'Colin Day has a son called Tom. I was checking out my new employer years ago – yes I did do some background – and I read an article on Mr Day. I think the son is in prison. I don't know what the B is for, though.'

Kelly was floored. Tom B. Day. Could it be? She was angry with herself that they hadn't known, but also puzzled why Teresa Joliffe would tell her, unless she had no role in this whatsoever and genuinely didn't know any of Colin Day's business.

'We'd like to look through the hotel accounts, please.'

'I'm afraid there aren't any held here. They all go to the accountant.'

'It's not year-end and you're telling me that you have no records on the premises?'

'Are we done?'

'I think you should be more careful with the type of people you employ. We're looking into all of Mr Day's affairs very carefully indeed. We'll see ourselves out.'

–

Teresa followed them to the door and waited until they'd left. Then she swore under her breath and went to her office to call Marko. She hadn't wanted to come back here. He'd forced her. He wanted to know how much the police knew. She was about to tell him that they knew virtually everything. She was encouraged by one thing at least. She had made up Forward Holdings, plucked it out of thin air, and the detective had pretended that she had heard of it; that it was owned by Colin Day. So they didn't know everything. Yet.

It was time for her to move on; she'd done it before. And she wanted Tom Day out of her life for good. She really should be spending the afternoon closing the Trout-beck operation down, but that was no longer her priority. By the time the detective had worked everything out, Teresa Joliffe would be long gone.

Chapter 40

George waited for Gabriela in the foyer. He'd slipped a note under her door at four p.m., hoping she might be awake. He'd tried to speak to Mrs Joliffe several times about his concerns, but she'd either been too busy or too irate to discuss anything. She'd wafted him away angrily and George concluded that he should never have bothered making an effort to do her a favour; he was only trying to keep her business safe. She'd left in worsening mood and he was glad to see the back of her.

When Gabriela finally appeared at reception, he handed her the fax from the detective.

'That's him,' he said.

'I know.' They turned their backs to the reception area, and pretended to be busy when a guest or member of staff walked past. Car horns tooted outside on the busy street, and the phone rang constantly. They spoke in hushed voices.

'How do you know? You never saw him.' George was puzzled. He rearranged papers on the reception desk.

'He came here last night, but a guest interrupted him and he left.' Gabriela fiddled with a vase of flowers.

'Why didn't you say? Gabriela, this is serious. I think you need to speak to the policewoman. I already have. I told her it's definitely him.'

She looked scared.

'What are you frightened of, Gabriela? He's wanted by the police and he's harassing you.'

'Because Mrs Joliffe has my passport and I don't have a work permit. Can I make myself any clearer?' she whispered.

George folded his arms and stroked his chin. He felt for the girl, she was a good kid. It wasn't true what people said about immigrants; he'd never met anyone so hard-working. But he could tell she was scared.

'Do you think Mrs Joliffe is involved?' he asked.

'In what way?'

'Well, they seemed keen to talk to her, and she was in a foul mood this afternoon – has been all week.'

'You know the man who died in the Thwaite Hotel?'

'The one you said owns this place?'

'Yes. Mrs Joliffe must have known him. I overheard some of the girls whispering about him. They said Nush bragged about gifts she'd been given by him, really expensive ones.'

'Gifts?'

'In return for things.' Gabriela's cheeks flushed and George slowly caught on. He felt embarrassed for her, and he coughed.

'Oh. Do you believe it?' he asked.

'That was the morning she left. She threw up all over that Japanese couple, then said she was going. That's when she said to tell Roza one word: Darren.'

George smiled. 'You are quite the detective, Gabriela; that policewoman would like you. You have no choice but to tell her all of this. I'm serious. Look, we're a civilised

246

country, you won't get into any trouble. It's the right thing to do.'

Gabriela seemed to think about his words. Eventually she came to a decision.

'I'll do it, George. I'll talk to her.'

'Good, you make sure you do. Her number is on the card I gave you.'

'I know, I have it.'

—

Back in her room, Gabriela spent the rest of the afternoon fretting about how to start a conversation with a policewoman in a country that wasn't hers. She went back and forth over possible starters, and each time came up blank. Her stomach churned as she imagined the likely outcomes.

Her shift started without incident, and every now and again, she'd stare at the card. Each time, she would talk herself out of it. The evening was quiet and she found herself without anything to do: she'd tidied the office, shuffled papers, even sketched Anushka and Roza from memory. Bored, she left the reception desk and went to Mrs Joliffe's office, round the back of the foyer. She tried the handle but it was locked, just as she'd expected it to be. She peered through the window in the door, but saw nothing of consequence. Maybe she could take her drawings to the police, she thought. A wire crossing the floor caught on her shoe and she tripped, ending up sprawled on the floor. She stayed there for a second and shook her head at how jittery she'd become since Darren Beckett had tried to get in to her old room. He looked like trouble, and Gabriela shivered at the thought of what might have happened to Anushka and Roza.

She got up and straightened her clothes, and went back towards the reception office to get a pencil sharpener. She fiddled with the pencils in her pocket and decided that she wanted to draw a portrait that was hung on a wall in the entrance. It was a scene of a lake with mountains behind it and it would probably take a while to complete, thus taking her mind off Darren Beckett. She walked to the front door, and peered through the glass and into the dark night; no-one was around. As she approached the reception office, she heard a thump and it made her jump. The noise came from upstairs, and it sounded as though somebody had dropped something and she stared at the ceiling. There was only quiet. She took a deep breath and stepped through the door.

The light had been switched off and Gabriela couldn't remember doing it. Before she could back track in her mind, a hand was clamped over her mouth and a man's voice whispered roughly in her ear. 'Don't make a sound and I won't hurt you, bitch.'

He let her go and she swung round. It was him. Darren. He held up a knife.

'I'm not gonna hurt you,' he said. 'I know you shared Nush's room; she told me.'

Gabriela had her hands slightly in front of her, as if to ward him off, and her eyes darted about, scanning the room. She noticed a hefty paperweight sitting on a table to her right. Her heart threatened to jump out of her chest. Of course he'd come back! Why had she been so stupid?

'What do you want? You're Darren Beckett. The police are looking for you. Your picture is everywhere. They're going to catch you.' She kept her voice low.

'OK, Gabriela — it is Gabriela, isn't it? I know that Nush and Roza never came back. And they won't. I also know that they left stuff behind; my stuff, stuff that I want. If you let me into their room to get it, I swear I'll leave you alone.' He was sweating heavily.

'I moved rooms. I never touched their stuff. I have no idea what it is that you want.' Gabriela raised her voice, hoping that a client might walk into reception and hear her panic.

'Keep your voice down!' he said. 'Who's in that room now?'

'I don't know,' she lied.

'Take me there now,' he demanded.

She didn't move.

'Do you know what it feels like to have a knife in your belly, Gabriela?'

She swallowed. Darren was small, but he was still a man, and the knife was large. She didn't know what to do. Her phone was in her pocket, but she couldn't move without him seeing.

They heard the front door bang, and a minute later, the bell rang in reception. She looked at Darren. He put a finger to his lips.

'Hello?' a man shouted.

Darren nodded backwards and raised his knife. 'Go, and not a word,' he said. Gabriela walked past him slowly with her hands raised, and he pointed at her, showing gritted yellow teeth.

Two policemen were standing at the desk. Gabriela froze. She didn't know what to do. Why weren't British police armed? She couldn't understand it.

'Hello, miss,' said the older of the pair. 'Your manager called one of my colleagues earlier to say that there was an intruder on the premises yesterday, so this is just a routine visit to make sure that you're OK.'

Gabriela felt a wave of gratitude towards George. He must have suspected that she wouldn't have the nerve to call the police herself.

'I'm fine, thank you.' Aware of Darren only metres from her, she picked up a pen and pulled a sheet of paper towards her. It was the only way she could protect herself. She knew Darren was lying when he said he wouldn't hurt her. She couldn't worry any more about what Mrs Joliffe would say about her talking to the police.

She wrote: *There is a man in the office, he is dangerous, and he has a knife.*

The officer took the pen from her and wrote: *Stay calm and slowly walk away from the desk.*

They took out their truncheons and cuffs and approached the office.

'Sir, this is PC Crick of Ambleside Police. I'd like you to come out and surrender your weapon,' the officer said loudly. Gabriela prayed that no one would walk in at this moment.

The order was met with silence.

'Sir, I am calling for other officers to join me right now.'

As the policeman began to speak into his radio, Darren emerged from the office with his hands held out in front of him. He glared at Gabriela, who looked at him triumphantly.

'Turn around, please, with your hands behind your back,' the PC shouted.

'I haven't done anything wrong,' whined Darren. 'This is my girlfriend. We had a fight.'

'I am not his girlfriend!' Gabriela said indignantly.

'Sir, I'll ask you again, put your hands behind your back and turn around.'

Darren tutted loudly and began to turn, but before anyone could approach him, he made a run for it, darting towards the stairs. The two policemen swung into action, with one sprinting after him and the other speaking urgently into his radio. He only got to the top of the first flight of stairs before PC Crick caught up with him. The officer cuffed him and read him his rights, then brought him back downstairs, holding onto him tightly.

'Sir, do you have a weapon?'

'No,' Darren muttered.

'He's lying! He had a huge knife.' Gabriela marched into the office. 'It's in here somewhere.'

Despite the policeman's remonstrations, she quickly searched the small space. 'Here, he put it in a drawer,' she said proudly, slamming the knife onto the reception desk. She took the photos from under the counter and put them on the desk as well. 'Look, he's Darren Beckett, wanted by the police. I knew it was him; that's why he's here, to shut me up.'

Sirens could be heard in the distance, and within moments they had stopped outside the hotel. Two officers came in and PC Crick gave them an update.

'Looks like this guy is wanted for questioning. Take him in, we'll stay with the girl.'

As Darren was led away, Gabriela realised that she was shaking. PC Crick pulled up a chair and guided her to it. The other officer stood by the door.

'Can I take a statement from you, miss?' he asked.

She couldn't speak. She had to get rid of them. She had no idea what would happen next and what they'd do when they found out that she was here illegally.

'I want to talk to Detective Inspector Kelly Porter,' she said. 'She's the officer who was looking for that man.'

'I'll get a message to DI Porter as soon as I can.' PC Crick glanced at the photo of Darren Beckett. 'How do you know him?'

'I don't. He came after me when he found out that I was his girlfriend's roommate. I think he did something to her, because I haven't seen her for almost two weeks. She's the other one wanted by police, here, look.' She pointed out the photo of Anushka.

'And the other photos?' PC Crick was looking at the pictures of the watch and the ring. 'Are these connected?'

'Detective Inspector Porter gave them to us together, so I guess they are.'

'You've never seen these things?'

'No.'

'OK, miss. Can you call your boss and get someone else to work tonight? I can stay with you until somebody comes.'

'No, I'm all right now that I know he's with you. Will he be released?'

'No, don't worry about that: he'll be staying with us tonight.'

Crick put on some gloves, then went to the desk and placed the knife in a plastic bag.

'Where are you from, miss?'

'Poland.'

'Summer job?'

'Yes.' She smiled, willing him to leave.

'I'll need to take a statement from you. Can you tell me your full name, please?'

'Gabriela Kaminski.'

'Gabriela, OK.' He gave the knife to his colleague, took out a pad and pen, and sat down in front of her. 'So, Gabriela, let's go back to the beginning. When did DI Porter bring you the photos?'

'Er... about a week ago.'

'And when did this Darren Beckett turn up?'

'He was in the office when I went in to get something and he grabbed me from behind and threatened me.'

'With the knife?'

'Yes. He said if I took him to Anushka's old room he could get what was his and he wouldn't hurt me. Then you came in.'

'Did he say what he was looking for?'

'No.'

'How did he know you were her roommate?'

'He recognised my name. Anushka must have told him.'

'And where is Anushka now?'

'I don't know, but he said she was never coming back. I think he might have hurt her.'

'What makes you say that?'

'He spoke as if she was already gone, perhaps even dead.' It sounded dramatic. She looked down at her hands and picked at her skirt.

'Don't you lock the hotel door at night?' he asked.

'No.'

'I think you should. You have an intercom, right?'

'Yes.'

'So use it,' he ordered, and smiled. 'Are you sure you're OK?'

'Yes, I think so.'

'Could you read through this and sign it if you're happy.' He handed her the pad on which he'd written her statement. She read it and signed her name.

'Do you live here, Gabriela?' asked the PC.

'Yes.'

'Have you any reason to expect anyone else tonight?'

'No.'

'OK. We'll call you tomorrow. If it isn't the detective herself, it will be another officer. Now,' he stood up, 'make sure you lock this door behind us. When does your shift end?'

'Five a.m.'

'Right. We'll swing by again before that to make sure you're OK.'

She walked the two officers to the door and closed it behind them, locking it.

–

Further down the street, Sasha watched from his car. It hadn't taken him long to track down Darren Beckett, but he hadn't expected the turn of events that had just occurred. His father would be enraged.

Sasha spoke into his phone, then, satisfied that the police were long gone, got out and walked to the hotel. He peered through the door and saw a girl sitting at the desk. Her head was down but he could make out certain features. Nobody else was about, and he surmised that if any other member of staff was on duty, they'd be busily discussing the unfolding drama at the front desk, overriding any other duties in the quiet night. But there was no one.

Chapter 41

Kelly flicked on the kettle, and dropped two tea bags into cups. Her mother was back home. Kelly had tried to keep a straight face when Mum had told her about her stay at Nikki's. They'd laughed conspiratorially, then felt guilty afterwards. It was diverting having someone to make tea for again. Her neck ached and she stretched. She'd been up until gone midnight updating her notes. When she'd got the call this morning about Darren Beckett being in custody, she'd fist-pumped the air and it had given her a boost.

She took the tea to her mother.

'How'd you sleep, Mum?'

'Much better in my own bed, love. Have you got a busy day?'

'I'm afraid so, but I can pop back at lunchtime to check on you.'

'You don't need to mollycoddle me, I'll be fine,' her mother said. 'Have you heard anything about that woman who left hospital?'

Kelly sat down on the edge of the bed, sipping her tea.

'I still can't believe she left her baby. She's a potential witness in an important case; I think they're illegal immigrants. We'll catch them soon enough.'

Wendy shifted position uncomfortably. 'Them?'

'She came with her husband, who's wanted in Bosnia.'

'She must have been terrified. I didn't know she'd left her baby, I thought he died.'

'Died? What are you talking about, Mum?'

'Ah, nothing. I'm just confusing her with something I read.'

'It's another headache I don't need; she could have identified someone for me, that's all. Right, I'd better get going. There's no washing to do, the house is clean and I've put some nice stuff in the fridge for you, so you don't have to cook,' said Kelly. She took the towel off her head and shook her hair out. 'I'm sure Nikki will be over, but don't let her tire you out,' she added.

'I can look after myself. Go on, you'll be late.'

Kelly felt anticipation building inside her. She had so many questions for Darren Beckett, but no guarantee that he'd talk, or tell her any truths she could work with. She also needed to speak to the night manager at the guest house – the young woman from Poland – who'd need handling carefully. It sounded as though she knew plenty but was petrified of that hag of a boss Teresa Joliffe. She'd also had a terrible shock last night. Joliffe was firmly a person of interest in the investigation, and would remain so until Kelly found out how involved she was with Colin Day.

Agencja Wywiadu, the Polish foreign intelligence agency, had confirmed that Anushka Ivanov was a Polish citizen, and they were looking into her last-known whereabouts. There was no evidence that she had entered the UK, nor indeed had a work permit. What Kelly wanted to know was if she was dealing with a random set of unconnected events that the girls organised themselves, or one organisation that planned it all, and thus potentially international and highly organised.

She had to see Christine Day again. It was feasible that Colin Day had used his wife's name to make bookings through Elite Escapes without her knowledge, but it was also possible that she'd been duped by the hard-done-by widow.

When she arrived at work, there was an email waiting for her from Ted Wallis. It was marked as 'sensitive'. It was short, and simply asked her to call him when she had time. She looked at her watch and figured she had five minutes for the helpful coroner.

'Mr Wallis, it's Kelly Porter.'

'Kelly, I've been thinking about what you said, and it's a long shot but I think I might have something for you. Many years ago, Colin Day gave me a card. I thought nothing of it at the time and threw it in a drawer somewhere. After our conversation, I found the card and called the number, and a male voice answered and intimated that he could provide a certain service. The memory of Lottie Davis has never left me, you see.'

'Service?' asked Kelly.

'Yes, the card simply says "flower", and I'm pretty sure it's a service offering, er... prostitution.' He coughed.

Kelly was shocked. Her thoughts bounced from Wallis's compassion towards Lottie to the fact that he had been harbouring this information. Slow down, she told herself. He hasn't done anything wrong.

'And you've never given this information to the police before?' she asked.

'No.' The implication sat between them, but she understood. Ted Wallis's moral fibre wasn't her concern; after all, he was doing the right thing now.

'What gives you the impression that it's a sex service?'

'My call to them. I, er... said I wanted a young one. I felt sick to my stomach when I said it.'

'So the service is still operational?'

'The man informed me that it's not, but I managed to come across as quite legitimate, and he said he knew someone who could help and he'd be in touch.'

'I don't suppose he gave you his name and address?' she asked sarcastically.

'Sadly no.'

'And did you give him your name?'

'I think we both know that in these cases, no one gives their real name. I said I was called Mickey Mouse.'

'Colin Day used his own name,' said Kelly.

'He'd become arrogant. I think he thought that at his age he could get away with it.'

'Quite. Can I take the number? And could you scan the card and send it to me? By the way, Darren Beckett is in custody in Ambleside; he was caught harassing a young woman at another hotel who had recognised his photo.'

'That's great news. It sounds like you're almost there.'

'Was there anything else about Colin Day that struck you as odd? Was that the only time he offered his services?'

Ted paused. 'There was a woman he was close to, and I don't think Christine cared for her much. She's a local businesswoman, or she was. It's probably nothing. But she and Colin got on well, and when Christine wasn't there, they had a lot to talk about.'

'Can you remember her name?'

259

'I'm trying to think. It was Teresa, I think, but I can't recall her surname.'

'Joliffe?'

'Yes, that's it.'

'Thank you, Mr Wallis. I'll try to be discreet about my sources, but if this goes the way I imagine it will, you might be dragged in.'

He hadn't committed a crime, but details like this had a habit of being leaked. Social media now did the job of the old witch hunts, and no one, not even the law, could prevent it. Dealing with malicious communications was in its infancy, and as the internet grew bigger by the day, the law trailed behind. Everyone knew what was at stake.

DC Hide poked her head around Kelly's door, then came in and placed a coffee beside her.

'Thanks, Emma. I was just thinking about caffeine. Could you get me the list of numbers called from Colin Day's two phones, please.'

'Will do, guv. I thought you might like to see this. My mum is a Daily Mail Online addict, and this came up today.'

DC Hide handed Kelly her iPhone. Sloppy, unchecked journalism could sometimes be a handy thing, and Kelly had to admit that she used the app from time to time. It was all well and good reading a broadsheet from cover to cover, but she knew no one who had the time. The gutter press served a purpose. If one could stomach the articles about sex on *Love Island*, soap actresses' buttocks, and celebrity infidelity, then a sweeping ten-minute grasp of the news could be gleaned with not much effort.

'Scroll down about three articles,' Hide said. Kelly did so and her eyes widened.

SCANDAL IN THE LAKE DISTRICT: LOCAL PHILANTHROPIST'S FINAL BINGE WITH 'PROSTITUTE' the headline read. Inverted commas forestalled libel; the newspaper wasn't that stupid. A photo of Colin Day was emblazoned above the article, and there was one of his wife and kids too.

Bastards, she thought. This kind of thing could never be undone. The paper had a readership of over two million, and then there was the gossip fallout on top of that. It would only take one person from Ambleside to read it and the whole town would know. Christine Day's worst fears had just been realised.

'Do me a favour,' said Kelly. 'Get on to the *Daily Mail* news desk and find out the source. They should give it to you; they know the score. I doubt any real names were used, but it might be helpful.'

'I'll do it after I've got you those numbers.'

Kelly had been right. The number for 'flower' appeared on Colin Day's statements.

'Let's go and pay Christine a visit on our way to see Mr Beckett, shall we?'

DC Hide drove as always, so Kelly could make calls and update her computer. Thank God for HOLMES. It did the work of a hundred detectives, but most importantly it used dynamic reasoning, and nothing was left out. Just one word could flag up a whole bunch of leads. Kelly typed in Harry Chase's name. She knew him from the investigation into Lottie, and hearing his name in relation to Colin Day had thrown her, he was cropping up more and more. They hadn't unravelled all of his business affairs yet, but they already knew about HCCD Art and Chase and Chase Accountants. She was looking for any links to

Colin Day or any of his business affairs, such as Tomb Day. Chase hadn't killed Lottie, they knew that much – he'd been in prison at the time – but that didn't mean he hadn't arranged it. If these guys were partying together, it might not only be Day running the show. It also satisfied a niggle in Kelly's mind: her hunch that Lottie had been abducted to order.

She opened the email that had arrived from Ted Wallis and looked at the scan of the calling card: *flower*. It suggested innocence, but that was all. If Colin Day was handing them out to friends, how much did he know about it? Was Anushka Ivanov a flower? Was Lottie?

The next name she entered into the computer was typed with trepidation. Barry Crawley was an affable giant, always quick with banter and terrible jokes, but he had been associated with Elite Escapes and she dreaded what else she might unearth about the man she'd once wanted as her father-in-law. She typed his name and three offences popped up. She'd missed a lot in the time she'd been in London and she wondered why her mother had never told her. How had the gossip not reached her?

Barry Crawley was on the sex offenders' register. He'd been accused of sexual harassment at Crawley Haulage, attempted rape and possession of indecent pictures. In the two former cases, the women had dropped charges. In the latter, he'd received a caution, which probably meant that he'd been able to prove it was someone else's computer. All three offences had occurred over ten years ago, but this kind of information stayed on the PNC forever.

'Jesus,' she said.

'What, guv?'

'Barry Crawley is on the sex offenders' list.'

Hide made no comment. 'We're here, guv.'

Kelly was shell-shocked.

'Guv?'

'Sorry, Emma. Right, let's go.'

They walked up the well-kept drive to Christine Day's house and rang the bell. Christine took her time coming to the door; Kelly wondered if she read the *Daily Mail*.

'Detective,' she said briskly when she eventually appeared. 'I thought I might be seeing you again. My daughter read the vile stuff this morning and rang to tell me. I'm appalled. I'll take legal action.'

'Actually, Christine, that's not why we're here. I'm calling about something else. May we come in?'

'Of course.' Christine wheeled backwards so the two detectives could enter. She led them into a reception room and invited them to sit down.

'Christine, this is DC Hide. Our enquiries have taken us in some quite unexpected directions. Have you ever had dealings with a company called Elite Escapes?'

'Not that I know of. It sounds very grand, though.'

'Did you ever attend any parties at this property, organised by your husband?' Kelly showed Christine a photo of the Borrowdale mansion.

'No.'

'Do you know a man called Harry Chase?'

'I don't think so.'

Kelly noticed that Christine had a smile on her face that hadn't changed since they'd started talking, odd for a woman who'd just had her dirty laundry washed in public.

'What about Teresa Joliffe?'

'No. Look, Detective, I've got a very busy day ahead.
I—'

'Barry Crawley?' Kelly interrupted her. She knew in
her gut that the woman sitting innocently before her was
anything but, and she was disappointed at her suspected
involvement; she'd felt genuinely sorry for her. 'What
about "flower"?'

Now Christine's expression changed slightly.

'Let me help you out. It's a service offering underage
girls for sex.' Kelly had no idea if this was true, but it didn't
hurt to ruffle Christine's feathers.

'I think you should leave now, Detective. Unless you
have a warrant.' Christine wheeled towards the door.
'You've put us all through enough. I'll be contacting my
husband's lawyer.'

'Is that the same lawyer that got Barry Crawley off a
rape charge?' Again, it was a guess, but possible.

Christine Day wheeled angrily out of the room and
waited by the door for the officers to leave.

'Do you know where all your husband's money came
from, Christine?'

'If you've got no warrant, get out of my house.'

Kelly knew she could have handled it better, and
perhaps got some information out of Christine by being
tactful, but she was shaking with anger. She hoped one day
to return to Christine Day's house armed with a warrant,
and wipe the fixed grin off her plastic face.

'I don't envy Darren Beckett, guv,' was all DC Hide
said.

Chapter 42

Marko knocked over a chair violently.

'That's Teresa's territory. Get her here now.'

'Yes, Papa.'

Sasha left, and Marko strutted up and down. His body-guards didn't dare make a sound. Too many loose ends had unravelled and he was nervous. His biggest problem was his own lack of judgement. He should never have trusted Colin Day. Respected philanthropist, charity organiser and all-round decent good guy, Day had been the perfect front, but he'd got complacent and had cut corners.

'I've got friends in high places, Marko. You don't need to worry about me,' he had said. Marko had watched Day carefully, and as time went on, he'd observed that he fancied himself much more important than he was. He also had a loose mouth. Marko had given him freebies to try and keep him quiet.

Day had brought in business, but it was slowing down and Marko had moved on to other clients with more promise and more finesse. Alarm bells went off when Day suggested a party at his own home. It was a step too far, and it showed that the old man misunderstood what was at stake. The big fish in his little pond had got ahead of himself.

And that led to Marko's other problem: Darren Beckett. Marko suspected Day of dealing with Beckett directly. And now Darren's ugly drug-ridden face was all over the news, and worse, the coppers had him. Marko should have put a knife in him when he had the chance. The three fighters were worth thousands in bets.

Marko was running out of chances to regain control. He'd never worried about the police before, but now they were too close. He needed the girl. There was nothing he could do but wait.

He went over in his head what Beckett knew. There were three types of people, and they could be distinguished by how they reacted to the law. The first type saw it as a mere obstacle, the second saw it as an opportunity and the third was simply honest. Beckett was far from honest, but Marko was unsure if he'd crack under pressure; he was English, after all. In England, you were either law-abiding or you were not, and the two rarely met. It made things easier in some ways, but in others not. Not one case of trafficking had been tried successfully in an English court; there was too much red tape, too much paperwork and too many do-gooders defending the human rights of the people trying to unravel the fabric of British society.

It was what had attracted Marko here in the first place, and he wasn't the only one. Only in Britain could a man stand on a street corner and preach hate while the coppers looked on. It was laughable. But now he was perilously close to risking everything.

He considered calling off tonight, but there was a lot of money at stake and he had to be there in person. Sasha could handle Teresa.

He grabbed his coat and left the grubby apartment. It was time to move. Beckett had been here, and if he was shrewd, he would give the police the address to try and save himself, but he'd regret it. The tin shed at the slate mine had been cleaned up, but the bodies were still there, and it hadn't been difficult to make sure he was linked to them. Sasha had seen to that by keeping hold of Beckett's bloody clothes after the murders of the young manager and cleaner, and leaving them with the corpses. He had also returned the dead men's IDs, to speed things up.

Marko used a pay-as-you-go mobile to call in the tip-off, then dismantled the phone and threw it into a waste bin in the car park. He got into his car. He was alone; his bodyguards were still upstairs taking care of the flat. They'd sterilise the whole place.

The roads were clear and the only ambient light came from the moon. He drove to the usual spot and Curtis appeared in the doorway.

'Curtis,' said Marko.

'Marko,' said Curtis.

'Why's the lorry still here?'

'Driver is cleaning sick off the floor.'

'Did he have to do it here?'

'It's dark, I didn't think it was a problem.'

Inside the warehouse, eight people sat huddled on the floor. Marko cared not that the journey across Europe had left them exhausted, terrified and maddened by thirst. Nor did he care that they'd been tricked.

Two children were among them. They were protected by women who could have been their mothers, but this fact didn't concern Marko. He nodded, and the children were taken away. He had buyers for both. The two women fought and struggled but were no match for Curtis's brothers, or their baseball bats. They knew they were beaten, and a bat handle shoved under a chin, accompanied by a menacing glare, was all it took to subdue them. Marko was continually surprised by these feeble-minded people who thought that entering another country illegally in the middle of the night was somehow a good start to their future.

He watched as Curtis's brothers gagged the women one by one and secured their hands behind their backs with cable ties. Even if they kicked and screamed, he'd still be able to sell them on one way or another. If they didn't shut up of their own accord, then a shot in the arm would do it, and at least they'd be good for one of his many houses where girls were drugged and tied to a bed.

After they were secured, Marko surveyed his goods. They were all suitable, and he nodded to Curtis and his brothers to ready them for the next leg of their journey. The women were wrapped in blankets one at a time and loaded into a van. Marko smoked a cigarette while he waited. He wandered outside and looked at his watch. The lorry had gone. With loading complete, the men climbed into the van and drove away, leaving Marko to pay a visit to Teresa Joliffe.

–

The van's onward journey to Workington took forty minutes. It pulled into a private garage connected to a four-storey town house close to the port. Curtis got out and flicked the garage light on, then went to check upstairs. The room was ready. The men took off their coats: carrying bodies up flights of stairs was hard labour.

The women were left on the floor of a room that was empty apart from a few beds. They'd have to share.

In the kitchen, a man worked diligently at the table. He took small white pills and crushed them with a gas lighter, tipping the powder into a plastic cup then mixing it with enough water to dissolve it. Once satisfied with the emulsion, he took a syringe, placed a filter over the tip of the needle and drew the liquid up into the barrel, leaving a semi-solid substance at the bottom of the cup. When he'd filled six syringes, he placed them to one side and began preparing more.

After he'd prepared another six, he gathered the cups and began adding water to the residue that had adhered to the bottom of them. He took another syringe and drew up the liquid from the first cup, then emptied it out into the next, swirling with the thumb of the syringe to liquefy the residue from that cup. After he'd done this five times, he felt satisfied that he had a strong enough solution, and he casually injected himself in the arm. This was his wage. Then he went to lie down on a single bed in the corner of the room, under a shelf laden with pots and pans. He didn't notice Curtis come in to collect the syringes, and Curtis didn't disturb him.

The women were injected before they were unwrapped; it might get too tricky if they tried to do it while they were struggling. As soon as an arm or leg was exposed, it would be stuck with the needle. They had to be careful at first, as these women were highly likely never to have been near a narcotic in their lives before, so it was strictly minuscule doses to begin with. Gradually they would become dependent upon the substance and easier to control.

Once they'd all been injected, they were taken to the beds and attached to the headboards so they couldn't leave. They'd get used to it.

'Welcome to England,' Curtis said.

Chapter 43

A car was dispatched to Kirkstone slate quarry. They'd been up here several times before. Pissed-up kids loved to prank the police, and incidents were on the up. They didn't use blues for this one: if it was a hoax, they'd just wake people up; if it wasn't, they'd find corpses. The tip-off was untraceable.

After 450 million years in the making, the stone of Kirkstone had ceased to turn a profit, and the mine had closed in 2012. The two PCs kept a lookout for obstacles as they drove carefully up the hill. The place was like a deserted town and no one had bothered tidying up, but adventurers and thieves occasionally came and dragged lumps of stuff they found valuable off in vans and car boots. They drove past an old sign leaning at a ninety-degree angle; it read: DANGER: WORKING QUARRY.

The call had simply mentioned an abandoned tin shed. It frustrated the PCs working the night shift, but at least it gave them something to do. They parked next to some buildings that looked like working sheds and got out. They put coats on and fetched torches from the boot, then separated and took a look around. The place was eerie and felt like the remains of a village after a nuclear war.

Three large vessels, the shape of torpedoes, gleamed under the torchlight in the first shed; another dilapidated sign read: DANGER: FLAMMABLE LIQUID. The officer moved forward to where blocks of dark slate were piled up next to a rusty truck. A table and chair sat next to an old map, as if the guy sitting there had just popped out to take a pee. Electric controls hung from the ceiling, and he read another sign on the wall next to a lever: IN CASE OF FIRE TURN OFF VALVE.

Somewhere a tap dripped, and the PC shivered. He had to admit, it would be a good place to dump a body. No one would ever know it was there unless someone wanted them to. Deciding he'd found nothing of worth, he headed back into the bitter night, where he heard his colleague shouting his name. He followed the sound to another shed, and his colleague shone his torch into a corner where a huge contraption of thick pipes and old scaffolding stood, still erect despite the neglect. Underneath it they saw two mounds about the size of bodies. It could still be a hoax; they could easily just be rolled-up carpet. The mounds were covered in what looked like blankets and plastic sheeting.

It was no hoax.

As they went forward to investigate, the PCs smelled something familiar. It was the same smell as a sheep rotting on the fells being picked at by crows. They looked at one another and walked closer. The smell became stronger. One man held both torches as the other bent down and moved an old blanket and some plastic sheeting.

He leapt backwards.

'Jesus!'

'What is it?'

272

'It's a face. Oh God, I want to be sick.' The PC rushed to another corner of the shed, where he doubled over and retched. Meanwhile, the other man bent down to see what his colleague had found. Being the owner of a stronger stomach, he was able to reveal more of what was underneath the covers, confirming what his colleague had said, and moved on to the next one. Both victims were male. The second one was on his back and his open eyes stared up through the plastic. Both looked as though they'd suffered huge trauma to the head and face. Given that the bodies had been wrapped up, the assumption was homicide, but they'd have to get detectives and medics here as soon as they possibly could.

They radioed in and requested a medical team. They'd have to wait here to secure the area, and it could take a while. Their shift had just become busy.

–

It was DC Phillips' turn to be on call that night, and he wore gloves as he examined the bodies, or what he could see of them. A forensics officer was already working in the small shed, and lights had been erected. The two PCs guarded the door. They were freezing.

'Looks like executions,' one observed.

'They obviously pissed someone off.'

'Poor bastards.'

Phillips searched the victims' pockets and found ID. Unless it had been planted, he could be looking at the bodies of Kevin Cottrell and Tony Proctor. He shook his head. Porter would be pleased. He also found a business card for the Thwaite Hotel, a broken mobile phone and a pile of bloody clothes.

He stepped outside.

'All right, lads. Not a nice discovery. Make sure you look after yourselves.' He knew what sights like the one inside the shed could do to coppers. In the past they'd been expected to take it stoically on the chin. Nowadays there were certain services that could help after such cases.

After five hours, the bodies were removed in black bags. They'd been wrapped in forensic sheets that would make sure any evidence wasn't lost in transit. The heads, hands and feet were wrapped individually. The forensics officer had been to the scenes of RTAs, stabbings and domestics, but he'd never seen anything like this. He'd tentatively suggested blunt-force trauma – knowing he was stating the obvious – but nothing would be certain until the coroner had done his work.

Phillips left a message for Kelly to tell her that he'd be in late, and gave her a precis of his nocturnal activities. He made sure that a separate investigation was opened, until the bodies could be formally identified. Then he went home to bed.

Chapter 44

When Dennis Hill got off his bike and wheeled it to the back of his little house, Craig Lockwood was waiting for him.

'Good afternoon, Dennis.'

Dennis stopped and stared at him in silence.

'Dennis, my name is Craig and I know your sister.'

'Jenny.'

'Yes, Jenny.'

Dennis's expression didn't change. He looked odd with his cycling helmet perched on his massive head.

'Dennis, I'm a policeman.' Kelly had told him to go slow and not overload the man.

Dennis looked away.

'I'd like to talk about your brother-in-law, Ian.'

Now Dennis looked at him and his brow knitted.

'Ian,' he said blandly.

'Yes, Dennis. Ian. He was accused of killing your niece, Lottie, wasn't he?'

Dennis sucked in air. 'Yes, he was. It wasn't true, though.'

'I know, and that's why I need your help.'

Dennis sat down on the concrete and took a Mars bar from his pocket. He unwrapped it and chewed. Craig

275

turned over a crate and sat on that. His mobile buzzed but he ignored it.

'I saw Wade Maddox, and he told me that his friend Darren liked Lottie's pretty red dress too,' he said.

Dennis stopped chewing. 'Darren?'

'Yes.'

'Wade's friend Darren?'

'Yes.'

'He played Xbox with me. He always beat me, though, he never liked me to win.' Dennis smiled cheekily.

'That's a shame. That you never won. What was Darren like?'

'Bad.'

'Bad?'

Dennis nodded.

'You know, Dennis, we're trying to find out who took Lottie so your sister can be at peace. It's all we care about.'

Dennis started to chew again, but his face crumpled and he began to weep. Melted chocolate dribbled from his mouth.

'Bad. Bad,' he said, rocking gently back and forth now.

'Who's bad, Dennis?'

'I'm bad.'

'Why? Have you done something wrong?'

'He just wanted to play with her, and she beat him at Xbox to teach him a lesson so he'd stop being mean to me.'

'Who wanted to play with Lottie?'

'Darren.'

'Where was this, Dennis?'

'At Wade's house.'

'You took Lottie to Wade's house?'

'Only once! Jenny let me take her to the park and it wasn't far to Wade's house. She came with me and we played, but I got into trouble because Lottie told Jenny she played Xbox.'

'Did she tell Jenny where?'

'No. Lottie was my friend, she stuck up for me. She never told.'

'Smart kid.'

'Smart, not like me.'

Craig felt terribly sad as a series of events formed in his head.

'Did Darren know Lottie was going eagle-spotting, Dennis?'

'I think so.'

'You think so?'

'I wanted to go really badly. I had to work. I told them I didn't want to work because I wanted to go with Lottie. Darren said I was a pansy.'

'Why don't you see Wade any more, Dennis?'

'He was rude. He called me names and told me never to call round again.'

'And when was this?'

'When Lottie didn't come home.'

'Thank you, Dennis. I think you should go inside and take your hat off now,' Craig said quietly.

Dennis got up and went towards the back door. The interview was over. Craig drove to Barrow Island, his fists clenched around the steering wheel. This time, he didn't knock. The lads were sitting in the same seats they'd been in last time.

'Fellas,' he said, 'you should keep your door locked, or the big bad wolf might come and get you.'

They all froze.

Craig strode over to Wade, who braced himself.

'Don't worry, lad, you're not worth it. The rest of you, fuck off. Now!'

They were gone in under ten seconds.

'So, Wade. Darren Beckett met Lottie Davis, and she kicked his arse at Xbox.'

Wade's eyes widened in terror.

'You little piece of shit! You've known this all along and that family have been going through a hell that you'll never understand. The dad killed himself, for God's sake!'

Wade had backed away, and now he crushed himself up against a wall, desperate for an escape route.

'I didn't know!' he squealed.

'You're a liar!' Craig's eyes were glittering and he used his huge frame to intimidate the young man. It was out of character for him, and he had to strain with every fibre to hold himself back. He should beat the living daylights out of this piece of shit. But sanity won through. There was no point throwing his career away for scum. He hadn't felt anger like it since he'd found out about his wife and his best friend.

He turned away.

'This is your last chance, Wade. Tell me what you know or, by God, I'll frame you so you make Compton look like a saint.' Goggs Compton, a Barrow boy, had gone down for twenty years for fucking up a burglary and killing an old woman three years ago.

Wade began to tremble.

'He said he knew how to get the kid back for humiliating him, making him look like an idiot. Dennis went on and on about them going eagle-watching and Darren asked him loads of questions, but I didn't think about it at the time. I didn't think he'd do anything to her. It's disgusting, I never knew he was into that shit.'

'I don't think he was,' said Craig.

Wade looked confused. 'What?'

'She was stolen to order, you fuckwit, and whoever it was, Darren led them straight to her.'

'He was with us that day!'

'I didn't say he was there, but he passed the information to whoever did it.'

Wade's mouth opened and closed.

'You need to tell me everyone who Darren ever bragged about knowing. These are mean bastards, probably with a lot of money. Was he in debt to anyone? Did he struggle for cash and then suddenly not?' Craig had calmed down, but he was left with the dull sadness of realising that a ten-year-old beating a twenty-eight-year-old on Xbox had led to her torture and death.

'Yes! That's when he started going to the Lakes. He said he worked in posh hotels and there were girls hanging off him,' Wade said, breathless.

'Did you believe him?'

'No, but I didn't see him much after that.'

'Liar! Tell me the fucking truth, or help me God...'

'He got me a job driving.'

'Driving what? Miss Daisy?'

'Girls.'

'Where?'

'Hotels.'

'You drove girls in between hotels?'

Wade nodded.

'For what?'

'I don't think they were cleaners.' Wade clearly thought his joke was funny, but Craig disagreed. 'Darren took a bit of money off them. He said it was his sideline, before the big boys got their share.'

'The big boys?'

'Who he worked for.'

'And who might that be?'

'Some guy called Marko.'

Craig turned away. He needed to tell Kelly.

'Listen to me. I'm going to write a statement, and you're going to sign it, understand?'

Wade nodded again. He hung his head. His mum would kill him. Darren would kill him.

'One more thing. Has Darren ever asked you to get rid of anything for him?'

'What?'

'You heard. He worked for Marko, delivering girls; what else did he do?'

Craig could almost hear the cogs turning as Wade scrabbled around in his head trying to remember. Suddenly his eyes lit up.

'He loved to play Manhunt.'

'The video game?' Craig knew it well; he'd taken a copy off his son and slapped him over the head with it.

'Yeah.'

'Go on,' Craig said.

'He always said it'd be easy to get rid of the dead bodies here in the Lakes. You know, the people he killed on the game.'

'And? Did he have a favourite place?'

'Not exactly, but he said the dock would be good.'

'Barrow Dock?'

'Yeah.'

'Have you ever thought about maybe getting some new friends?'

Wade shrugged.

'Keep your door shut and stay out of trouble, and if I ever hear your name again, I swear I'll kick your head in, do you understand?'

Craig left, slamming the door behind him. The cool air was refreshing. He hoped his son never met anyone like Wade Maddox or Darren Beckett. It was a pipe dream, he knew; soon enough he'd be on his own, making life-changing decisions for himself. He hoped he stayed away from lowlifes, but could only pray that if one did walk into his life, he'd have the good sense to know it.

Chapter 45

'Hello, Darren.'

Kelly sat down. She looked at Beckett for a moment. He was in a shit state: he stank, and he coughed frequently. The interview room was small and sparse, and his odour pervaded every inch of it.

'Can you confirm your full name and date of birth for the record, please?'

'Darren Paul Beckett. Third of the fourth, eighty-nine.'

'Thank you. Darren, what is your relationship to Anushka Ivanov?'

'She was my girlfriend. I haven't seen her in ages.'

'When was the last time you did see her?'

'I can't remember.' He fidgeted continually as he spoke.

'Is she a prostitute?'

No answer.

'Does she work for you?'

No answer.

'Does this ring any bells?' Kelly placed the 'flower' business card in front of him.

He shook his head.

'Do you work for Marko?'

The faintest flicker, but still no answer.

'Why were you visiting the Troutbeck Guest House last night?' Kelly realised that the man wasn't going to

282

respond to anything she asked, but she ploughed on for the record. 'Who did you deliver Lottie Davis to five years ago?'

This time his mouth fell open, but he closed it tightly again. Kelly could tell that he was shocked that she knew so much. After Craig had called, she had walked out of her office, sat on the wall opposite Eden House and cried.

'Was this all about Lottie beating you at Xbox?'

She noticed that small beads of sweat had formed on Darren's forehead, and he shifted in his seat.

'Do you recognise these?' She held up a clear plastic bag through which bloody and soiled clothes could be seen.

'No.'

'That's funny, because we have CCTV footage of you filling your car up at the Arrow station in Ulverston on the night of the twenty-first of September, and you're wearing an identical jacket. That's a lot of blood, isn't it? You know, we have something these days called DNA testing. I'll know in under an hour whose blood it is. Is it Anushka's?'

Darren swallowed. There was a cup of water in front of him and he sipped at it. His hands shook.

'Or Kevin Cottrell's?'

Darren looked down.

'Did you rape and strangle Lottie Davis?'

'No!' Finally, a response, and Kelly reckoned it was the truth. He slammed the cup down.

'You just delivered her?' she continued. 'Could you open your mouth, please?' Darren looked confused but did as he was told. He didn't think to question it when she scraped DNA from the inside of his mouth and placed it in a tube. He hadn't been arrested, but his acquiescence would count as permission in court.

His breathing became laboured and he coughed some more, hacking and spluttering, to Kelly's disgust. She gave him a few minutes to compose himself.

'Why were the following items in your Barrow Island flat: Anushka Ivanov's phone, wallet, driving licence and various items of clothes?' Kelly read from her pad for effect.

'I told you, she was my girlfriend.'

Kelly paused. 'Darren, look, Wade has told us everything already. It would be easier for all of us, including you, if you stopped wasting my time and simply told us what you know.'

He stood up, and the uniform behind him shoved him back down into his seat.

'Who do you think might have tipped us off about two murdered males left in the Kirkstone slate mine? Are they Tony Proctor and Kevin Cottrell? Did they know too much? You were set up, Darren; is there somebody who'd like to see you behind bars?' Kelly knew that Darren was a mere cog in the wheel. She needed something else.

DS Umshaw came into the room and handed her a piece of paper. The dentistry department at the lab in Carlisle had gone all out and identified one of the bodies as Kevin Cottrell from his dental records. Plus there was a printout from Anushka's phone. Kelly quickly scanned it; she knew what she was looking for.

'Well, well, well. It would seem that Anushka called your number on the evening of the twentieth September at exactly eight fifty-seven p.m., two minutes before she left Colin Day for dead in his hotel room after robbing him and being paid for sex. Was she asking you what she should do? Did she panic? She called you a lot, didn't she? Daily at least. Until the twenty-first, when the calls stop. Where did she go without her phone?'

Darren wiped his top lip with his sleeve and loosened his collar.

'What happened to the cash, the Rolex and the ruby ring?'

'What? I never took any of those things!'

Interesting. Anushka was a clever girl; she'd hidden them from him. Possibly in her room, and that was what he'd been after at the guest house. But her room was empty.

'It has now been confirmed that one of the men found at the mine was the manager of the Thwaite Hotel, Kevin Cottrell. What did he know?'

Silence.

'Didn't you mind your girlfriend having sex with other men?'

'She wasn't my...'

'Ah, I thought you said she was,' said Kelly. She was rattling him. She was almost there.

'This ring any bells?' She put the photo of Lottie's dead body in front of him and he stared at it for a long time. He closed his eyes.

'What about this?' It was a photo of Anna Cork.

'This?' A photo of the mutilated corpse of Kevin Cottrell.

'Oh God.' Darren bent over and threw up all over the floor. Kelly got out of the way just in time, but within seconds, the sour aroma of vomit filled the room. She fought back her desperate desire for fresh air. She had to keep going.

'Can I wash my mouth out?' Darren looked at her with pleading eyes. Sweat dropped off his chin and ran into his straggly beard.

'No.'

Kelly dragged the table away from the sick and instructed Darren to move his chair.

'Do you know any of these girls, Darren?' She spread ten photos in front of him taken from the USBs found in Colin Day's office. She picked them up one at a time and held them up. Darren stared at them all blankly, turning away only once.

'So, you know this one, do you?' Kelly wrote on the back of it that Darren seemed to recognise it.

Silence.

'How many hotels are you aware of that double as brothels, Darren?'

Silence.

'You are aware that a jury would put you away for life for the torture and murder of a minor?' She stopped the recording. 'You do know what happens to sex cases in prison, don't you?' The uniform behind him smirked. 'It gets difficult to walk after a while,' she whispered. 'On the other hand, drugs – which we also found at your flat – could make you quite popular inside. I know which I'd choose.'

She resumed the recording.

'How much did you get paid for delivery of Lottie Davis?'

'I didn't deliver her!'

She ploughed on.

'Were you the one who leaked the Colin Day story to the *Daily Mail*? Come on, Darren, if you don't give me something, you'll be hung out to dry. Are you really prepared to take the rap for everything? It all started to unravel with Colin Day's death, didn't it?'

'He should've kept his dick in his pants!' Darren blurted.

'Quite an outburst, Darren. His death must have been an inconvenience to you.'

'Not to me.'

'To your boss?'

Kelly stared at him. His eyes were dead, but she could tell that he was thinking. He was scared. He looked as though he was suffering withdrawal tremors too.

'What were you doing at Barrow Dock on the evening of September the twenty-first? Bit late for a walk.'

She continued to hold his gaze, and he looked away.

'Wade said you told him it would be a great place to hide bodies.'

Darren leant over and rubbed his eyes.

'I've got divers going into Barrow Dock,' Kelly lied. 'I wonder what they might find.'

'He's called Marko.' Darren's voice was almost inaudible.

Kelly sat up straight. 'Marko who?'

'I don't know.' She was getting straight answers to straight questions now.

'Address?'

'He's got places all over.'

'I have plenty of time.'

Darren recited details of a number of addresses. He sounded exhausted, and Kelly made one final push.

'What exactly is Marko's role, Darren?'

'He's in charge.'

'Of what?'

'He gets girls.'

'From where?'

'All over. None of them are British.'

'Except Lottie Davis.'

'Look, I told Marko's son about her when I was angry, but I swear I had no part in it.'

'Name?'

'He's called Sasha.'

'Did you tell him about the eagle-watching trip?'

'Yes.'

'Associates.'

'A guy called Curtis and his three brothers.'

'How big an operation is it?'

'I don't know. He's into dog fighting, street fighting and high-class sex parties. He uses a big house in Ullswater.'

'This one?' Kelly showed him the photo of the mansion booked through Elite Escapes.

'It could be.' Darren studied it. 'The driveway looks familiar. I only ever saw it in the dark.'

'What really happened to Nush?' Kelly asked.

Darren's expression was sly. 'Sasha killed her and gave me her stuff.'

'Where's her body?'

'Could I please have a fag at least?'

Kelly nodded and he reached in to his pocket, pulled out a packet, and lit up. Kelly fancied one herself. She waited.

'He told me that he wanted a package taken care of, but when he turned up with it, it was big and heavy and I had to help him carry it from his car to mine.'

'Why didn't he simply discard it himself?'

'So he could pin shit on me, I guess.'

Kelly acknowledged this as plausible. 'Did you know what was in it?'

'He said it was *that* red-haired bitch.'

'What happened next?'

'We took some weights and chains and threw it in the dock.'

'Barrow Dock?'

'Be more specific.'

Darren exhaled deeply. 'The old dry docks.'

Chapter 46

Altcourse Prison held just over a thousand men, on what the prison service classed as Category B offences. Tom Brian Day should've been Category A, but Daddy had pulled some very long strings.

He sat on his bed and read a magazine. He was anxious. They'd taken his laptop again. Without it, he became paranoid and aggressive. It wasn't because of what was on the computer – far from it, that was safe as houses; it was more the fact that Tom Day was addicted to screens and had been since he was fifteen years old. Every time a new gadget came on the market, it would be bought for him; so that now, he knew his way around any machine blindfolded.

His mother had confiscated DSs, iPads, phones and TVs for weeks on end, but he always found a way to get in front of a screen, any screen.

Now, without one, he didn't know what to do with his hands, and the magazine was dull, as they all were. Not being able to interact, connect headphones or surf was killing him, and the guards knew it. They liked to play with him every now and again, just to keep him in no doubt of who was in charge.

They all came to him for advice on online banking, compensation, PPI, investment schemes and anything else to do with financial management. After years of finding ways to hide money for his father, he was an expert.

He smiled. And now it was all his.

He had possibly two months to wait out in this shit-hole, and then he'd be able to get out and spend it. Every penny was safe. Every little bit went through Tomb Day, with its non-existent board of directors and its mailing addresses in Canary Wharf. The ultimate shell that he'd created. When he got out, he'd sell the idea and the protection pathways. It was way more sophisticated than foreign subsidiaries, and with international law becoming a pain in the arse, he had people queuing up for it from Mexico to Azerbaijan. He'd pissed his pants when the Azerbaijan laundromat had crumbled. It never would have done on his watch.

He'd already made several contacts who were inter-ested. It was easy to spot shell companies and even easier to track them, but not his. He could tell when someone was trying to hack into Tomb Day, but they hit the firewall every time. They'd never get in.

He compared himself to a builder of foundations – the more solid the work, the longer it would last – and he used his time wisely. Except when they thought it was funny to take his laptop for a day.

He'd completed his sixty daily press-ups, twenty pull-ups and three hundred sit-ups, and he was mind-numbingly bored. They'd be let outside soon, but for now, he had no choice other than to sleep, wank or read this useless magazine. At least it had some decent tits in it.

He missed sex like crazy. That was the other reason he needed his laptop back: it kept his mind on an even keel by stimulating his senses, and occasionally he could satisfy the cravings with porn.

He sprang off the bed and paced up and down. He could taste his own frustration.

—

In the prison director's office, two uniforms were asking questions about Tom Day. The director told them that Day had been an ideal inmate who hadn't shown any signs of violence, which was why he'd qualify for early release when the time came. He kept his nose clean, had good relationships with the guards, and didn't ask for anything apart from to be left alone.

'We'll need to question him and search his cell.'

'Of course. What's it related to, Officer?'

'We're not at liberty to say at the moment, but we have reason to look into his financial affairs.'

'Financial affairs? That doesn't surprise me.'

'Why?' asked the uniform.

'Because there's not a guard here who doesn't go to Day for advice about money.'

The director made a phone call, and within five minutes a prison guard knocked on the door.

'Come in,' shouted the director. 'Spinks. Tom Day, you know him well, don't you?'

'Fairly well, sir,' the guard replied.

'What does he do all day? What's his business?'

'Sits on his laptop playing computer games mostly, sir. He helps pretty much everyone out with their serious stuff as well; you know, banking, bills, deals and shares. He knows everything about everything.'

'We'll need to seize any computer equipment as part of our inquiry,' said one of the officers.

'I'll take you down if you like,' offered the guard.

The two uniforms followed him and the director clasped his hands together.

These youngsters never learned. Two months from release and Day was up to something. Stupid, stupid man. The director shook his head. He would tell his wife about it this evening. Nature versus nurture: they discussed it most mealtimes. Tom Day had been born into a well-respected family and had had money and privilege thrown at him from birth. The director's wife argued for nurture, but he said nature. In the case of Tom Day, he suspected he might win this one.

Chapter 47

Jack Croft waited in line to enter the Channel Tunnel. His windows were closed so the wind couldn't bring in the stench from the migrant camp two miles away. This was the riskiest part of the journey. It wasn't the French he was worried about; they'd love to get rid of as many of them as possible, and although checks were regular, they weren't as sustained this side of the Channel. It was the other side that he had to worry about.

He'd told himself that this would be his last job, but given how easy the journey had been, now he wasn't so sure. The money was good and he planned to retire when he'd saved enough. He'd got away with it so many times, but the visit from the police had made him nervous.

He tapped on his steering wheel and moved along slowly. He'd be home by early morning. The back of his lorry was quiet; they were well briefed.

The journey through the tunnel was the same as always: airless and noisy, and he longed for a beer. On the other side, he saw land out of the window and jumped back into his cabin. He'd taken all the necessary precautions.

As he exited the tunnel and approached the customs checkpoint, Border Force officers waved for him to pull over. Croft wasn't overly alarmed as it'd happened a few times before. They usually checked his paperwork for contents and expected weight, and asked him to drive onto a special road scale to see if the figures matched.

He jumped out of the cabin and remained calm.

He was asked to open the back doors, which he did placidly. He attempted polite conversation with the officers. They looked like police personnel – and occasionally acted like it – but they were nothing more than jumped-up bus drivers strutting around in body armour. A bit like St John's Ambulance volunteers pretending to be doctors.

It was only when two officers leading large dogs appeared from behind him that his pulse quickened.

'Could we see your itinerary and load documents please, sir.'

He got the documents from the cabin and they checked the details carefully.

Large boxes blocked the lorry's compartment from the back, as they were supposed to, but instead of closing the doors, three officers began unloading the crates.

'Hey, mate, this is gonna put me right back. You've seen the—' Croft began.

'Step aside, please, sir.' A female officer led him gently by the arm to one side. He felt like shoving her off and making a run for it.

A gap formed between the boxes and the dogs jumped in and started barking straight away. Then another officer climbed up holding some sort of contraption in his hand. As he waved it about, it lit up like Christmas. The officers moved more boxes and Croft knew the game was up. They weren't stopping.

Once they reached the middle of the container, they came across a couple of wardrobes and the dogs went crazy. It took three men to move one of the large pieces of furniture to the side; behind it huddled a gaggle of frightened people, thirty of them crammed into the tiny space.

'Come with me, sir, please.'

Jack Croft was led away.

–

The passengers were brought out one by one as officers took photographs and checked for any injuries or illnesses. They were asked if they understood English and if they knew where they were. One man broke down and held up his dirty, worn hands. 'Please new life, please new life,' he said, over and over again.

Every day the officers found more and more vehicles like this one. They felt like bastards ending the dreams of these people who'd fallen prey to the increasing number of drivers – UK citizens – willing to risk it all to make some extra money so they could buy a sixty-inch TV rather than their fifty-inch one; have two holidays instead of one; buy more clothes, a new car, toys for their kids.

By comparison, these poor fuckers had probably fled war, seen loved ones killed, travelled thousands of miles with little food or water, only to be turned round at the last minute. It drove the officers mad when celebrities just couldn't keep their mouths shut and demanded that everyone should be taken in for the love of humanity but didn't offer to put them up in their own mansions. It just didn't work like that.

It hurt like hell when they looked these poor people in the eyes and saw only torture and anguish; it hurt knowing they'd probably end up in filthy camps hastily set up across Europe and woefully under-resourced. Immigration and

Border Force officers weren't paid well enough for what they did, but they kept on doing it because they were professionals. But like many public-sector workers, they were detested just for doing their job.

Chapter 48

Finally Kelly had enough to start chasing warrants. Beckett had been charged with conspiracy to abduct a minor, allowing the death of a minor, concealing criminal property, preventing legal and decent burial, aiding prostitution, soliciting to murder, and murder. Kelly juggled her time between the Home Office, the Foreign Office and now the UK Border Force. She and her team were worn out, but they could smell the finish line.

Gabriela Kaminski was waiting for Kelly in the foyer of the Troutbeck Guest House. She was tiny and strikingly pretty, and she spoke in a whisper. She was visibly scared. Kelly stretched out her hand and Gabriela took it tentatively. George led them into the empty dining room so they wouldn't be disturbed.

'So I believe an officer following up my investigation averted a potentially horrible situation for you?' Kelly spoke softly, matching the girl's attitude.

Gabriela nodded.

'Gabriela, are you here legally?'

'Yes, Mrs Joliffe has my paperwork and my passport.'

'Why did you give her your passport?'

'She gave me no choice.'

'So you are kind of beholden to her, then? That's a little worrying.'

Gabriela nodded. Kelly had a healthy suspicion that this petite little mouse knew a lot more than she was letting on; George had also told her that she had been Anushka Ivanov's roommate.

'I've got some photographs here, Gabriela. Could you look at them one by one and tell me if you recognise any of them.'

The girl took the pile of photographs and studied them carefully.

'That's Anushka. This one is Roza; she hasn't been back either.' The photograph of Roza was the one that Darren had seemed to recognise in his interview, Kelly noted.

'Since when?'

'A few nights before Anushka left.'

'Do you know why Darren Beckett came looking for you?'

'I think he wanted Nush's things. These.' Gabriela held up the photos of the Rolex and the ruby ring.

'And you know where they are?'

'I have them.'

Clever girl, thought Kelly. They'd been her insurance all along. She knew who she was dealing with. No wonder she was so scared.

'What exactly do you do for Mrs Joliffe, Gabriela?'

'I'm the night manager. I didn't know what was expected of me, but Mrs Joliffe showed me. Men come here, and girls meet them.'

'Could you describe any of them? Are there regulars?'

'I made sketches.'

'Sorry?' Kelly thought she'd misheard.

'I made sketches of them all. There was nothing else to do and Mrs Joliffe scared me. I thought if she ever tried to force me to do something I didn't want to do, I could use them. I'll show you. I want to study art when I get back home.'

Gabriela stood up, and Kelly followed her up three flights of stairs to an attic room, squeezing in behind her. Gabriela went to her wardrobe and took out a large bag, laying it open on the bed. Kelly looked from the contents to the girl and back again. She'd been busy. She took out the envelope stuffed full of sketches and looked at them one by one. The drawings were stunning; the girl could be a forensic artist any day of the week.

Gabriela handed her a small drawstring bag and Kelly felt inside. She pulled out a roll of cash and some items wrapped in tissue: the watch and the ring. She looked back to the bag on the bed and noticed the laptop at the bottom; she could have hugged Gabriela. She didn't need to open it to know that it was the one from Colin Day's room. And now they had his son's laptop too.

'Were you aware that Anushka worked for Darren as a prostitute, Gabriela?'

'No,' said Gabriela quietly. Her cheeks burned and Kelly acknowledged her innocence. Teresa Joliffe must have thought she was on to a winner when she chose the quiet foreigner to keep watch, threatening her with withholding her passport. She'd badly miscalculated. Gabriela was far from stupid.

'Thank you, Gabriela. You're a brave girl. I'll send an officer to take a statement from you, and this evidence, I am sure, will tell me what happened to your friend Nush.'

'She wasn't my friend.'

'Oh?'

'They were horrible girls. I want to go home.'

'I'm sure that can be arranged.'

Kelly went back downstairs. She left the hotel and walked to her car. She had enough time to visit Jenny Davis to officially inform her of the circumstances surrounding her daughter's death.

–

Across the street, three people sat in a car.

'Look. That must be her,' said Teresa.

The woman's demeanour and dress screamed police. She was of average height and slim build and walked with a confident swagger that suggested 'get out of my fucking way, mere mortals'. She wore a trouser suit topped with an overcoat that looked like cashmere; Marko hadn't thought abiding by the law paid so well.

Sasha took photos and Marko watched. The detective was just his type and he was pleasantly surprised. She was strong and had presence, and he could tell that Teresa was instantly jealous. He also smelled her fear; it happened rarely but he knew for sure that she was calculating how to get away from him, and he was damned if he was going to let that happen. He watched as the detective walked away and disappeared out of sight. This was the only window they'd have.

Marko had decided that it was time to turn up the heat and he and Sasha carried pistols. They didn't come cheap, but were relatively easy to come by, but it meant that there was no going back now. If they had to use them; he could say goodbye to his freedom for life. He had to avoid that at all costs; there was a speed boat arranged and it was on standby at Workington port. But first they needed to take care of the girl.

The three of them left the car and walked casually into the hotel, like tourists. They rang the reception bell and George came out of the office.

'Afternoon, George,' Teresa said confidently. George looked behind her at the two men, and something in his expression told Marko he was suspicious.

The foyer was quiet and Sasha took his chance. He walked behind the desk and grabbed George by the throat, thrusting a gun to his belly. George's bulk could've been a handful had Sasha not come armed. Marko reached over the desk and brought the butt of his own gun down hard on the man's head. He slumped over and the two men dragged him quickly into the office, then Teresa locked the door, leaving George inside, collapsed on the floor.

Teresa led the way upstairs and used the master key to unlock Gabriela's door. It was unbolted. The girl sat up straight on the bed and opened her mouth to scream, but Sasha was on her before a sound could escape.

'You're coming with us, and this time, no one will save you.' Marko winked at the girl. She was a little pixie and he could probably carry her with one hand. He showed her the gun and she froze, the fear evident in her eyes.

Sasha made her stand up and Marko shoved his gun into her back. She had no choice but to do as she was told. They left through the back entrance, with Marko concealing the gun. They saw no one.

Once in the car, the doors were locked and Marko never took his eyes off the girl in the back seat. Her lip trembled and she fought back tears.

'Please, I don't know what you want with me,' she whispered.

'Oh I think you do, Gabriela,' he said. 'We can't have that lovely detective talking to you again. You may have already said too much; we'll soon find out.'

'I didn't tell them anything except that Darren came with a knife, I promise!' It was a heartfelt and emotional plea, but not one that cut any ice with the three people with whom she was hitching a ride.

They sped out of Ambleside and headed into the country.

Chapter 49

Two divers from the Underwater and Confined Space Search Team readied themselves to submerge into one of Barrow's many docks. Lockwood watched Kelly climb out of her car and walk towards him. They shook hands. The wind was bitter and they both wore long coats. The dock to be searched was a long-disused Victorian one, close to Channel Side and where the ex-girlfriend of Darren Beckett had seen him climbing into his car at an unsociable hour. The witness had never mentioned a second man, but Kelly already suspected Darren was lying.

Lockwood wrapped his scarf around his neck and they walked to the railings.

'You didn't have to come,' Kelly said.

'I can't miss this; it's on my patch.'

Kelly nodded. They watched as the two divers checked their equipment. Two more police personnel sat in a van parked close by, and the area had been sealed by uniforms. A small crowd had gathered. This was big news for the local community and several camera crews filmed from a distance. Lockwood had sent them as far back as he could, but it didn't matter with modern lenses.

'When I found out who Roza was, I had Beckett leaned on back at the station, and he cracked. She's in here too.'

'They know they're looking for two,' said Lockwood. 'Thanks Craig. Part of me hopes they're not in there.' 'I know.'

The divers performed their final checks and were satisfied they had enough oxygen for the shallow dive at only 9.9 metres. They tested their helmet radios and spoke to one another clearly. It wasn't the worst dive either man had faced; they could be called to search canals, sunken engine rooms, ponds, water-filled mines or septic tanks. Their most dangerous enemy was debris, and they both wore strong gloves. The water was murky and freezing and they wore Aqua Lung drysuits that would keep a layer of warm body-heated air between them and the inclement temperature of the dark water. They signalled they were ready and the men in the van charted their agreed grid pattern, bar air pressure and communications.

The divers got into the water clumsily, but as soon as they were in, the weightlessness enabled them to move freely and they began their descent. Looking for bodies was the most satisfying part of their job; should they find what they were looking for, it gave ultimate closure to the families and great fulfilment to the team. One of the men carried an underwater camera.

They descended to the bottom slowly and began searching in a grid formation, back and forth, turning over debris but making sure they didn't disturb too much silt and sludge. Visibility was almost zero, so they had to use their hands and headlights, and progress was slow. Only the area two feet in front of each man was illuminated by torchlight.

Hundreds of years of debris covered the dock floor, and the divers worked their way over old glass jars, tyres, pottery, anchors and rope. One of the men spotted what looked like an old penny farthing bicycle and took a picture for his son with his underwater camera. After fifteen minutes, they had covered an area of only five square metres. The dock was tidal, so if there were bodies in there, they could have moved.

They carried on.

Amongst the mass of piping and jumbled shapes, they had to be vigilant. Bodies could be wrapped, dissected, disguised or decomposed. Their job was mostly a silent one, with the odd crackle of communication and the occasional joke when they found a condom or a clown mask.

The two men turned a corner on the grid and began a new ten-metre column. The silt was thick and they tugged items free of the clinging dirt to take a closer look or a photograph. Pieces of rolled-up carpet and other household items told the pair that the dock had been used as a dump site for many years until the development of the Channel Side for leisure purposes meant that tipping now carried a heavy penalty.

They peered into every vessel or piece of piping that looked as though it might be big enough to conceal a body or body part, then moved on to the next item. Their gloves hindered them, but it was better than immobile freezing fingers; it just took more time.

One of the divers stopped above a bulky article and rubbed off some gathered silt; it shone black and looked to him like bin bags had been secured with duct tape. He ripped a little hole; beneath was what appeared to be a coloured blanket. He continued ripping and ran his hand along it to see how long it was. It was tough, and resisted his prodding. It took four minutes for the silt to clear, and he called to his buddy to help him. A chain wrapped securely around the middle of the object disappeared into the silt. The divers cleared the area slowly and discovered an item poking up from the bed; it was perfectly round and looked like a gym weight. There was another one close by. The detective had said that the suspect had used weights to sink the bodies.

–

They had something. The radio barked into life and Kelly heard the exchange from where she was standing, close to the open door. She and Lockwood climbed into the van and looked at the screen, staring at the images streamed directly from the camera.

The divers connected an inflatable buoy to the item and awaited instruction; the buoy inflated and hit the surface, and a flurry of activity rippled through Channel Side. People pointed and filmed on mobile phones; some took selfies with the buoy in the background.

Lockwood nodded to the head of the unit, who asked for an update from the divers of their air pressure remaining: anything less than forty bar was a risk. They both had over that and so the dive carried on. Besides, the bodies might be close together. He then instructed for a tent to be erected close to the drop-off, where a member of forensics could perform an initial assessment without the press being able to see what was going on.

–

The two divers felt a renewed sense of purpose and willed away the cold that had begun to seep through the thick rubber. They couldn't rush. But fifteen minutes later they agreed that it was time to ascend and give up for now. They'd only covered twenty square metres or so, but they'd found something worth investigating, and that was worth the painstaking process. They'd be back in the water in three hours, the length of break necessary for this depth and duration of dive.

As one of the divers went to rearrange his buoyancy, which would enable him to ascend, one of his fins struck an object. He hoped it hadn't been sharp enough to pierce his suit. His foot throbbed, but he couldn't feel a rush of cold water, so he was pretty sure he hadn't done much damage. He looked down.

His colleague followed his gaze. Beneath them, a perfectly round object protruded from the silt. They checked their bar again and it was dangerously low; the exertion required to investigate the second find would take too much air. The diver made a split-second decision.

'Requesting an old job, sir,' he said into his radio.

'Did he say old job?' Kelly asked.

'He did. It's a good old fashioned mask and snorkel, he's nearly out of air, so we need to get it down to him,' said the head of unit. Kelly looked alarmed.

'It's risky in deep water, but he knows what he's doing.'

He took charge and grabbed a mask and snorkel as requested. One man on the surface always had to wear a rig just in case, and it was his turn today. He checked his secondary demand valve; his colleague would need it.

'I fancy a swim,' he said.

He descended quickly and reached the divers in seven seconds. As one diver ascended safely, the other waited for his superior and he removed his own demand valve and sucked on the spare. He'd checked his equipment one last time and was down to about a minute of air remaining. They set to work quickly, clearing the silt away from the second find to reveal a package roughly the same size as the first, and also wrapped in black plastic. The chain was attached to the weight and there was no doubt that whatever was inside had been disposed of by the same person. A second inflatable buoy was attached and their job was done. The head of unit passed the diver the snorkel and mask, who removed the secondary demand valve, allowing his boss to ascend. The remaining diver blew out of his nose before he too ascended.

When they broke the surface, they were grinning.

'Good fucking day.'

'Good fucking day,' he agreed.

Chapter 50

Four teams were dispatched to four separate addresses supplied by Darren Beckett, who now lay coughing and sweating on a cot bed in a bare cell. With no drugs or alcohol, his demons punished him and his head was a maddening place to exist.

The first address was a warehouse in Penrith. Each team was followed by a forensics officer, but the uniforms went in first to secure the building. It was a damp and isolated place and there wasn't much to see, except for long tubes of industrial plastic wrapping, the odd chair, and tea- and coffee-making facilities.

After the lights were dimmed, however, the luminol that the forensics officer had sprayed over the surfaces lit up like swarms of fireflies, indicating that a person or persons had lost a lot of blood in there. It looked like a phantom slaughterhouse that would delight children on the ghost train at the fair.

The second address was a flat on the outskirts of the town. This one was harder to secure; there were lots more places to hide in a residence and the officers approached the door cautiously. On the wall there was a peace sign sprayed in blue, and various scrawled phrases; one said *Fly me to the moon*, another *No way back*. A ladder was leant against a cement wall. The door had to be broken down, but it soon became clear that the place was deserted. It had been cleaned, but the protein in blood can't be washed away, and the luminol showed blood spatter in the bathroom and two of the bedrooms.

The third address was a crumbling pile just outside Ambleside. It too was deserted. The kitchen was set up for the occasional visitor and the fridges were full of beer. It reminded officers of various dog-fighting set-ups that they'd seen, though the ring in the main room – chairs and tables placed around a roped-off area – would have been more secure if it was used for dog fights. The forensics officer picked over the place, removing microscopic fragments as well as clothes, rags, playing cards, beer bottles, ashtrays and a human tooth. The place would make a perfect training ground for apprentice forensic detectives, and the officer left with a full vehicle of items that would be laboriously processed in the coming weeks.

The final raid was on an address in Workington, where Darren said he'd driven on occasion with Curtis. Unmarked vans pulled up at three o'clock in the morning and officers jumped out armed with battering rams and body armour. The sound of splintering wood and shouts in the night startled the neighbours, and within minutes, the incident was caught on mobile phones and posted on YouTube. Officers found twenty-nine women in squalid conditions, attached to beds and delirious. Five arrests were made, including the junkie who slept in the corner of the kitchen.

Back in Penrith, an incident room had been set up, and forces from all over Cumbria sent personnel to join in the mammoth task. The number-one priority was finding

Marko Popovic. Merseyside police had provided an old photo of him.

In Barrow, the atmosphere inside the tent was tense as Kelly and Lockwood watched the two forensic examiners cut open the soaking items set before them on makeshift slabs. If they contained human remains, they'd be removed for full examination to the coroner's office in Carlisle, fully intact. Each layer of rug, blanket and plastic wrapping contained its own micro-world that needed to be examined in sterile conditions to prevent contamination, but first they had to see what was in there.

The smell assaulted their senses first, and the two detectives covered their noses, but they still had to be sure. Confirmation came when one examiner located a hand, and then a scalp. Lockwood lowered his head. Darren Beckett, you fucking scumbag, he thought.

In Penrith, officers visited the home of Barry Crawley. This was one visit that Kelly had had to delegate. She wouldn't have been able to look Barry in the eye as she asked him if he was a paedophile with a penchant for little girls.

Patricia Crawley made the officers a cup of tea, and they were shown into a makeshift bedroom in what was normally the lounge. A hospital bed was rigged up in the centre. Barry wanted to die at home. Two Macmillan nurses checked the syringe driver that delivered morphine to him on demand. He was desperately pale and looked small and fragile in the bed.

The officers took their time and tried not to overwhelm him. He stared at them and then glanced at his wife, suspecting what was coming. He closed his eyes, wondering just how much they knew.

'Sir, one of your lorries was stopped at Crewe yesterday, and another one at Folkestone. Both were full of people trying to enter the country illegally. Two of your drivers have been arrested. We also have evidence that a trafficking organisation is being run through your company and those associated with Colin Day and Harry Chase.'

Barry struggled to breathe. Patricia was livid.

'What on earth are you talking about? My husband can't be subjected to this kind of interrogation. You can't do this!'

The nurses kept their eyes down and left the room quietly.

'I'm sorry, ma'am. We have to ask your husband some questions as owner of Crawley Haulage. It might be best if you wait outside.'

'Barry?'

'It's all right, Pat. I know what they want. Go next door.' His voice was raspy and weak.

In London, a search of the Home Office database showed that Gabriela Kaminski did not have a work permit, there was also no record of her having entered the country using her passport.

Chapter 51

'Could I have a drink of water, please?' Gabriela asked her captor. He was a strikingly large man who they called Curtis. She'd committed him to memory, noting every detail of his face, his hair, his clothing and jewellery, and his mannerisms. She did the same with the other one, who they called Marko. She had worked out that Marko was in charge. If she could get hold of a pen or a pencil, she could draw their faces perfectly. She might never get the chance.

Curtis wasn't very bright, but he was exceptionally intimidating. He was English; she recognised the accent. She reckoned he was in his early twenties. The other man was called Sasha and he called Marko 'Papa'. Gabriela could tell that Marko and Sasha were not English; they were from somewhere Slavic. Their voices rose and fell in a similar fashion and they had eyes that might have seen something terrible. Both reminded her of men who belonged to gangs back home, with their black clothes, dark eyes and chunky jewellery. She committed Marko's rings to memory; anything that might help if she ever got out of here alive. She took in her surroundings. She'd noticed two young girls who'd each brought food and drinks for her captors, after which they'd disappeared into other rooms, neither making eye contact with Gabriela.

Curtis watched her. He shook his head.

'Please, I am so thirsty. Please.'

He looked towards the kitchen, and to his gun. Gabriela could see him debating with himself. Eventually he made his mind up and disappeared for a minute or so, coming back with a cup. She took it gratefully and gulped the whole lot in one. She had no idea where she was or why, only that they suspected she'd talked to the policewoman. Every time they tried to catch her out, she denied it. She stuck to her story: that she'd identified Darren Beckett and that was it.

Now and again, Mrs Joliffe came into the room for a chair or a blanket. She never looked at Gabriela. Gabriela tried asking her why she was here, and what the men would do, but she never answered. Gabriela noted that she looked different: instead of her signature black wardrobe, she wore casual jeans; she tied back her hair and wore little make-up. It made her look like a different woman altogether. Perhaps that was the intention. Gabriela wondered if Mrs Joliffe was in trouble, because if she was, then her own chances looked slim. To Gabriela, Mrs Joliffe looked as scared of the men as she felt, and that worried her.

Her heart raced and she couldn't still her anxiety. Terror. That was what it was. Not being in control. Not being in charge. Not knowing what might happen next. Curtis looked at her with hungry eyes and she knew what it meant. Gabriela wasn't hurt, but she was very afraid. She was miles away from her home, and no one knew where she was.

Marko came into the room, and the whole atmosphere changed. Curtis became more alert and stood taller. Gabriela prepared for attack. He knelt before her, smelling

315

strongly of cologne, and held her chin with his hand. He was strong. Scarily strong. His eyes bored into hers and he grinned.

'When should I let him have you, little Gabriela?'

Her breath quickened and tears came to her eyes. Marko had deep lines etched into his face and his grip was vicelike. She studied his rings, which were inches from her face; anything to not look into his eyes. The gold and diamond one looked expensive, but the other one didn't, although it was the more distinctive of the two. It was made of a dull pewter metal and had black, purple and green squares of something, possibly enamel, set into it. He never took them off; they must mean something to him.

—

Marko noticed how much the girl was taking in, and he knew they shouldn't keep her long. He yanked her chin upwards so she had to look at him. His options were fading fast. The lorries, Crawley, Beckett, the newspapers and that fucking infuriating detective. There was no way back. He couldn't afford to take anyone with him. They had to split up. But if he was going to go down, he'd go down with a fight, and Gabriela was the perfect bait. She was innocent and pure and would fetch a great price if he could arrange it, but he doubted after the dust settled she'd still be saleable. He'd seen the way Curtis looked at her. It was always the same: the innocent ones, the young ones, the ones that were quiet and polite. Curtis was one sick motherfucker. Any moment, he could pounce, but Marko wouldn't let him, not just yet. He let go of the girl's chin and stood up, pacing the room.

'Your friend the detective should be here soon, little one, and then I think I'll let my charge here have his fun.' Marko thought about the detective.

He didn't care about her fancy badge. It was just a title. People in this country went crazy over the death of a police officer, but to Marko, it didn't make any sense. Anything that happened to them, they brought on themselves. For him, harming a law enforcement officer was a treat. A rare treat. He left to go and find Teresa. Gabriela's head slumped to her knees.

Upstairs, Teresa paced up and down.

'I disagree, Marko,' she said. 'If they catch us, it'll be life, no question. I won't have anything to do with it.'

'You'll do as you're told, Teresa. This is your fault, remember, hiring that cool drink of water downstairs in the first place.' Marko was angry and needed to vent.

'Bullshit! This is about that worthless piece of shit you hired to tidy things up. Beckett forgot about a body! I won't have anything to do with it. I'm out of here.' She went to make her way to the door, but Marko blocked her.

'Sit down, Teresa.' He stood over her and her eye twitched.

'I never signed up for kidnap,' she said. 'What's going to be next?'

'What did you think we'd do with her? Give her cake? Besides, you led us right to her, so you're involved whether you like it or not. Sit down,' he repeated.

'Let me go,' she said firmly, and tried to go around him again. The back of his hand struck her on the cheek and the force of it knocked her sideways. She fell with a thud and Marko stood over her with his hands on his hips. He opened the door and shouted for Curtis to come up.

'Take her to the other room,' he ordered. 'Watch her like a hawk and don't let her leave.'

Curtis didn't hesitate. He picked the woman up by the arm and dragged her out. She tried to fight back, but he was far too strong for her to have any effect whatsoever. He bent her arm around her back so forcefully that she squealed. She shot Marko a look of hate and they stared at one another until she was out of sight. Marko went back downstairs, checked on the girl and beckoned Sasha into another room.

'Folkestone?' asked Marko.

'Done,' replied his son.

'Penrith?'

'Done.'

'Ullswater?'

'Done.'

'Rydal Water?'

'Done.'

'Good. What about Crawley?'

'He was taken into custody this afternoon. They've charged the old bastard but apparently he'll be dead in a week anyway, so he shouldn't talk. The cops got Workington and a few others.'

Marko nodded. 'There are too many loose ends,' he said. 'We have to leave.'

He stared out of the window while his son waited for his next instruction.

'We can't stay together, Sasha. And you shouldn't take anyone else. Understand?'

'Yes, Papa. Where will you go?' The port in Work-ington was too risky now, but there were other options.

'I don't know yet. You know what to do, and where the money is, right?' Marko said. He looked suddenly older.

Sasha nodded. 'Let's just leave now,' he pleaded. 'We could be out of here in twelve hours.'

'No. I can't. I won't walk away until I'm satisfied. But you must go, Sasha.'

'Yes, Papa.'

The two men embraced.

—

Sasha walked outside and got into his car. He didn't look back. In the boot was a bag full of personal items and the keys to safety deposit boxes in and around the Manchester area. By the time he'd emptied them, he'd be a very rich man. He knew his father wouldn't make it. He was too stubborn. They couldn't both get away, and Marko had chosen to save his son.

He pulled away from the cottage and drove to the end of the gravel driveway. The local radio news was appealing for information on a Mrs Teresa Juliffe, who was thought to be associated with the haulage company trafficking people from Europe.

Sasha smiled. He knew that every trail led to Teresa; they'd made sure of it. Even Tomb Day. At four p.m. he'd call the police like his father had told him and give them the address. That gave Marko six hours to decide what to do with her. He also had the number for the detective.

Chapter 52

At the end of another long day, Kelly drove back to Penrith. She'd had to let Johnny down again, but he'd understood when she told him that she was at a crucial point in the case. Johnny had hinted in their short time together that being away for months on end serving his country and disappearing with only twelve hours' notice was what had ended his marriage. He didn't want her feeling stifled. Kelly smiled; there was nothing she'd like more than to hide under his duvet for the next twenty four hours. She hung up and took a call from her mother.

'Kelly, what's going on with the Crawleys? What have you done?'

'What, Mum?' She didn't know how much her mother had heard.

'Nikki told me. Katy is inconsolable. Did you know that Barry is gravely ill?'

'Mum, hang on. What are you talking about?'

'Nikki told me that you've got Dave and his dad in trouble. I hope it's not true. Pat Crawley is a lovely woman.'

'What else did Nikki tell you?'

'That the police dragged poor Barry off his deathbed and Dave has been arrested. Why would you do something like that, Kelly? Is Nikki right? You've done it because Dave didn't marry you?'

'Oh Christ, Mum! How could you believe such bullshit? You were married to the force for Christ's sake!'

'Don't swear at me!'

'I'm not swearing at you! Nikki is full of shit. The Crawleys are in trouble for good reason. Reasons I can't go into. I'm a policewoman, you know that. Didn't Dad ever piss anyone off?'

'You must have got it all wrong. I can't imagine what Pat is going through.'

'Her husband should have thought of that,' Kelly muttered.

'What?'

'Sorry, Mum, I need to go.'

She hung up and took the waiting call. This one was from Ambleside police. A distraught guest at the Troutbeck Guest House had discovered the male receptionist locked inside the office, dazed and bloodied. Initial enquiries had elicited that Mrs Teresa Joliffe and two unknown males were responsible.

So now the woman was wanted for assault. What are you up to, Teresa Joliffe? Kelly asked herself.

'Do you have descriptions of the two males?'

'Yes, guv.' One matched the details they had for Marko Popovic.

Kelly was almost at Penny Bridge, so instead of carrying on to the M6, she turned onto the A5092, north to Ambleside. She had nothing to go home for and she certainly didn't want to see her mother. Her last conversation made her want to stay the night at Johnny's even more. On the way, she called Eden House for an update.

She'd checked her iPad several times and kept up to date with inputs, but nothing beat real-time. They had a steady stream of charged suspects coming in all over the Lakes, and she was pushing everyone to dig deep until they found the pin holding everything together.

'What's the progress on the paperwork, Will?' she asked.

'Guv. We've traced the money to an umbrella company in Jersey.'

'Jersey?'

'Yes, guv. There's several offshore accounts paying three owners of Tomb Day via the Isle of Man. We're still fitting everything together, but this accountant we're using is a machine. I don't understand the links, but he's working on the exact routes. Incidentally, the numbers in Colin Day's office were bank accounts. Christine Day is a signatory on all of them.'

Kelly had the best people she could get in cyber-crime working on the two laptops – Colin Day's and his son's – but so far they had failed to get into the closed files on either.

'I'm stopping off in Ambleside, Will. Mrs Joliffe had her receptionist beaten up and she's gone AWOL, but I'll be back around six.'

The information surged around Kelly's head and she felt overwhelmed. One step at a time, she told herself. She had more questions than answers, and one of them was why Christine Day had so willingly handed over all the information in her husband's office if she was herself involved. The only explanation she could come up with was that the woman was genuinely livid that he'd been caught with a prostitute, as well as pilfering her mother's ring. Hatred could affect judgement and even override self-preservation. Maybe she hadn't expected Kelly to get the bottom of it all and was regretting her impulsiveness now.

Kelly parked outside the guest house and found two uniforms inside reception. George had already been taken to hospital. The hotel seemed to be operating normally, but the guests Kelly saw looked worried and uncomfortable. As well they might. A few local journalists had got hold of the story and had to be prevented by the uniforms from harassing guests. A few customers were demanding their money back at reception, and the girl behind the counter looked as though she had absolutely no idea what she was doing.

Kelly flashed her badge and climbed the stairs to the third floor. Gabriela's door was open, but there was no one inside. She looked around. Next to the door there was a small chest of drawers, and beside it, on the floor, was an overturned glass, liquid staining the floor around it. Gabriela's room was otherwise spotlessly clean and tidy. She wouldn't leave a glass on the floor like that. Kelly ran down the three flights of stairs and pushed breathlessly to the front of the reception desk queue.

'Gabriela, where is she?'

The girl looked overwrought; her day was going from bad to worse. 'She left with Mrs Joliffe.'

'What?' Kelly slammed her hand down on the desk and the reception area fell quiet. 'Did you see her leave?'

'Yes.'

'Was anyone else with them?'

'Two men.'

'Oh Jesus.' Kelly ran out and leapt into her car, calling ahead to get Phillips to put out a description of Gabriela to all units. 'Her name is Gabriela Kaminski, she's a Polish national and she's nineteen years old. It's time to release details of Mrs Teresa Joliffe too. Put it in the PNC.'

'Yes, guv.'

'I want the Troutbeck Guest House closed. There are two uniforms there on their own; they'll need help. There are a few journos hanging around too.'

'Yes, guv.'

A previous background check on Teresa Joliffe had revealed that she was the owner of three cars and four hotels, but no address and no record had showed up. They did however have a photo: it was from an article published in the *Westmorland Gazette* two weeks before Colin Day's death, a promo piece for the local secondary school, where Teresa Joliffe had spoken to the students about women in business. It was a good photo, and Kelly would make sure it made the evening news.

Chapter 53

Kelly took a deep breath.

On the other side of the interview room door, Dave Crawley was sitting waiting.

She could have run it past her DCI. She knew that he would have allowed her to step aside; to get someone else to interview him, but she wanted to look him in the eye and ask him why.

She took a deep breath.

'You all right, guv?' DS Umshaw asked.

'I went to school with him.' It was only slightly bending the truth.

'Do you want me to do it? I've plenty of experience.'

'I know you do, Kate. I absolutely know you could nail this, but the fact that I know him makes me want to do it more.'

Umshaw nodded.

They went in. Dave shuffled in his seat.

'David Crawley, for the record, my name is Detective Inspector Kelly Porter, and—'

'I know who you are.'

He caught Kelly off guard. His voice was different, as were his eyes.

'As I said, for the record, I am Detective Inspector Kelly Porter, and I am with Detective Sergeant Kate

Umshaw. We will be conducting the interview of David Barry Crawley today, the twenty-ninth of September 2017. David Barry Crawley, of number five, Mosedale Mews, Penrith, can you confirm your date of birth?'

Kelly had started laboriously on purpose. She wanted to disarm him, she wanted to settle her own nerves, and she wanted to make him think that she was amateurish. Now she knew why he'd never liked her being a copper. She wondered what he really thought of her father.

'Do you know why you are here, David?' She had to keep this formal.

'I guess it's about those two lorries that were stopped. I had no idea, and no one I know of at the firm did either.'

'If that's the case, why is there an intricate paper trail of accounts, all signed off by you or your father, travelling through Jersey and the Isle of Man, making you very rich indeed? For the benefit of the tape, I am showing the suspect accounts from Crawley Haulage showing the discrepancies mentioned. I don't believe your father acted alone.' She placed photocopies of accounts containing the signatures of both Crawleys, father and son, in front of him on the table. She looked him in the eye. He looked away.

'I don't know anything about foreign money. I didn't know our lorries were being used like that.' He was making it hard.

'Is that your signature?'
He didn't answer.
'Both drivers said they took instructions from you.'
Again no response.
'Did your mother know about any of this?'
He looked down at his hands.

'Let's try something else, shall we? How well did you know Colin Day?'

'Not at all.' Dave held her gaze.

Kelly took a deep breath, she looked into his eyes looking for a hint that he was telling the truth, but she knew he wasn't.

'Were you aware that your father is on the sex offenders register?'

Without warning, he was over the desk and on her, his hands around her throat. Umshaw shouted for help. Two uniforms rushed into the room and restrained him. Kelly held her throat and gulped for air.

'You fucking idiot,' she said. 'Was it worth it?'

She got up and left the room. Umshaw followed her.

'Christ, guv, you OK? He's a lunatic!'

'Fucking arrest him.'

'On what charge?'

'Assaulting a police officer. As well as all the other shit. I'm going to see Teresa Joliffe's ex-husband as planned.' Kelly calmed herself and straightened her blouse.

'Don't you think you need to—?'

'No. I don't. I'm fine. I'll be back in an hour.'

She walked out of Eden House and towards her car, rubbing her neck. Once she was in the driver's seat, she put her head into her hands and cried.

Chapter 54

The man who opened the door was handsome and well dressed. He also had impeccable manners. Kelly had hastily wrapped a scarf around her neck, which had turned red and blotchy. It stung.

'Do come in. The boys are at college. So you're trying to find my ex-wife? Why on earth would you want to do that?' Jacob Joliffe's eyes twinkled playfully. 'I'm sorry, is that crass? Personally, I wish she would disappear. The boys wouldn't notice and it'd give my bank balance a rest. Can I make you a cup of tea or a coffee? I never used to like coffee, but I went on a trip to Italy and came back in love with the stuff. Look, this is what I treated myself to.' He showed off his De'Longhi proudly.

'Do you know where your ex-wife lives now? I can't seem to find a home address, just businesses.'

'Well, I can only tell you what the boys tell me, but I believe she still lives in the house I bought for her near Dockray, on the Grizedale Road. Very smart.'

'Grizedale Road? What number?'

'There are no numbers on the Grizedale Road, just names. It's very pretentious. The house is called Grey-stone.'

'Can you tell me about the hotels, Mr Joliffe? We have evidence that she was employing illegal workers, and at least one hotel was used as a brothel.'

'Ha! Well bugger me – not literally, obviously, please excuse my language. Is that so? No wonder she could afford to keep the house. Just heating the damn thing costs a fortune. Bloody hell, you've stumped me on that one. I'd like to help, but I had no idea. Crikey.'

'It sounds like you were very generous in your settlement. Why did she keep your name?'

'Her maiden name is Smith. She liked the sound of Joliffe. When we were married, she called herself Joliffe-Smythe. It was most embarrassing.'

'I'm getting the impression that your ex-wife likes money,' Kelly said.

'That's an understatement. She'd do anything and climb over anyone for the damn stuff. It all stems from the fact that when she was growing up, her family had nothing. She was blessed with only one thing: her willingness to climb from one bed to another, taking what she could and moving on when she got bored.'

It was a scathing portrayal, but went some way to understanding the motives of a woman who would trade men, women and children for profit.

'Do the boys have a recent photograph?' she asked.

'I'll go and see. Their rooms are a mess, I don't usually go in, but you might be in luck. I know there's a box of photos on the shelf in the study. In my haste, I might have forgotten to burn them all.' His eyes glinted as he left the room, and Kelly couldn't help smiling.

He came back with a photo. Kelly looked at it and shivered. Teresa's smile was broad, but her eyes were dead. It must be exhausting keeping up the pretence, she thought.

'Has Teresa been in trouble with the law before, Mr Joliffe?'

'Not that I know of, though there was a man she lived with for a while a couple of years ago who went to prison. Tom someone?'

'Tom Day?'

'Yes! That's it. I don't think the boys liked him.'

'We're already looking into Tom Day. We think he's been laundering money from prison for his father. Were you aware of why he was in prison?'

'No.'

'He blinded a man in a fight.'

'Gosh.' Jacob grimaced. 'She was even less responsible than I thought.'

'Have you ever heard your ex-wife or your boys mention anyone called Marko or Sasha?'

'Sasha, no, but Marko definitely. That's who she used to go to when we fought. He lives somewhere near her. I have no idea the nature of their relationship and I never met him. The boys might have done, though.'

'When do they get in? I'd like to speak to them if I could.'

'Twenty minutes. Why don't you wait and I'll make you a coffee.'

'All right, I'd like that,' she said. She touched her throat; it was damn sore. She couldn't work out which hurt more: her neck or her ego. Dave had been her lover, they'd almost got married. It turned out that all he cared about was money, and he'd do anything to make more of it. She felt betrayed.

When the boys arrived home, they both kissed their dad, and the intimacy touched Kelly. It was unusual for children to choose to stay with their father after a break-up. Having met Teresa Joliffe, though, Kelly knew who she'd rather live with. She chatted to them about their mother.

'There were plenty of people in and out, but Marko was cool,' said one of them.

Jacob Joliffe rolled his eyes and Kelly asked, 'In what way cool?'

'He drove an Aston Martin,' he said. Kelly raised her eyebrows as if impressed. It kept the boys on side.

'What else?'

'He wore all black and sunglasses, like a movie star.' The boys laughed and their father rolled his eyes again.

'He should be easy to find in Cumbria,' Jacob said.

'Could you help a police artist, do you think?' Kelly asked. The boys looked at one another.

'What's he done?'

'I'm not sure, we just need to speak to him. When's the last time you saw your mother?'

The boys glanced at their dad. 'About a year ago.'

'They decided to stop making the effort, and Teresa didn't object,' Jacob said, and the boys looked away, embarrassed.

'Thanks, lads. I'll arrange for a sketch artist to get in touch.' At the moment she'd do anything for a lead on Marko.

The boys went off to their respective rooms to do whatever teenage boys did, and Kelly thanked Jacob for the coffee and gave him her card.

She was in no mood to check her emails or look at HOLMES. Instead she decided to drive to Grizedale Road. Just to see. In all likelihood, no one would be home. Teresa's last known whereabouts was the Troutbeck Guest House, collecting Gabriela: a bold move suggesting that she and Marko were panicking. Kelly mused that perhaps Tom Day had been violent with Teresa as well, and that was why she'd given her the lead about the name of the company. Teresa Joliffe certainly wasn't stupid; and on that note, Kelly didn't expect to find her any time soon.

Chapter 55

Their priority was Gabriela, and the whole team was working frantically to nail down where their suspects might have taken the young girl. They all knew how important the first twenty-four hours were in an abduction case. They'd closed in on Crawley Haulage, and Harry Chase was being questioned in Liverpool, but they still had to find Teresa Joliffe and Marko. Chances were they'd still be together. Gabriela's drawings were attracting much attention, and Eden House was inundated with calls about sightings. The task seemed impossible, but Kelly knew that if they were methodical, it would reap rewards. It was a shame that Gabriela had never drawn her own face, but then why would she? Who could have predicted that it might be needed?

From what George had told them, it must only have been minutes after Kelly had left the guest house that Gabriela was taken. She hoped with all her heart that the girl was unharmed. There was something about her that she admired: her grit in particular. She knew now that Gabriela was here illegally, but that didn't matter. Without her, they wouldn't have the wealth of information they now had, and might still be trying to join the dots.

DC Phillips called while she was on the road to let her know that they'd been given another possible address for

Teresa Joliffe. It was in Newton and that was half an hour away from Dockray.

'Thanks, Will. I'm just coming up to Dockray now, so I'll call into the Greystone address first.'

'Right, guv, you want backup?'

'No, don't worry, I'll be fine.'

'Are you sure? I mean—'

'You mean what?' Kelly wasn't thinking straight. The incident with Dave had got under her skin, and now Phillips was questioning her.

'Nothing, guv.'

'I'll let you know if I need you. I don't want to waste resources. Get someone to the other address and I'll stay in phone contact.'

Dockray was a tiny hamlet of scattered dwellings that had probably been around for hundreds of years. It was hemmed in on all sides by fells and dales and was about as remote as you could get. Kelly had hiked here many times as a child. It was on the road connecting Ullswater with the A66 and could occasionally get busy, but that wasn't the case now as she searched for the house. The light was fading and she stopped the car repeatedly to check the wooden signposts that pointed the way to grand houses situated at the end of long private roads. Her mind was wandering and she was tempted to call it a night. But she was here now and she might as well see it through.

As she reversed the car and drove out of yet another private road, a thought struck her. It was too much of a coincidence that she had just missed Joliffe and the two men at the guest house. Christ. They must have been watching. So they knew that she'd been to see Gabriela, and now they'd be trying to figure out what the girl had told her.

And they'd probably seen her face.

Her phone rang. It was Phillips again.

'Guv, a call came in at four p.m. saying that the girl is at an address in Glenridding. It was anonymous and untraceable, but the operator said the voice was foreign.'

Kelly was in a dilemma. She had three addresses now, and she was at one of them alone. She knew she'd reached a point in the investigation where she needed solid backup. She'd had a lapse in concentration because of Dave Crawley, and she was pissed off. It had clouded her judgement.

'I need DCI Cane to agree to armed response,' she told Phillips. 'It's highly likely that these guys are armed, and certainly dangerous. You have to go to Carlton Hall on this one. Tell Cane everything we've got and get him to call me if necessary. Wait a minute, I'm turning round again. I think I just drove past a sign. See if you can get authorisation for all three addresses.'

Sure enough, a small wooden signpost, almost hidden behind bushes, pointed the way to 'Greystone Lodge'. How respectable, she thought. Kelly stopped the car, short of the private driveway. She had no choice but to wait for back up. Her phone rang again. It was an unknown number.

'I know where the girl is,' said a male voice. It was certainly not English. In fact it sounded strikingly similar to the accent of Jovana Galic. Kelly looked around her. The lane was quiet and she saw no vehicles and nothing out of the ordinary.

'Marko?'

'No, but he wants to meet you.'

Kelly's pulse quickened and she knew she'd been right: they'd watched her leave the guest house. Marko was betting that using Gabriela as bait would work, and he was right. Of course he was right. Kelly would do everything she possibly could to keep the girl safe.

'Has Gabriela been harmed?'

'Go and find out for yourself. You know the Grizedale Road, near Dockray? Look for a house called Greystone.' He hung up.

Shit, they were supplying different addresses. Was the house she was approaching the correct location to find Gabriela, or one of the other two addresses? It took less than a second for Kelly to decide. She called Phillips again and told him what had happened.

'DCI Cane has authorised armed response. Where's the priority?' He waited.

'Greystone Lodge on Grizedale Road. I'm going in,' Kelly said.

'No, guv! We can get them there in ten minutes. You mustn't go in without backup.'

'By then she might be dead. He wants to see me.'

'Guv, please. It's not my place, but I really think it's the wrong thing to do. We'll never be able to explain it.'

'Get armed response here as quickly as you can.' She hung up.

It was a deadly gamble. If this was the correct address, she had no idea how many people were in the house. She had no idea if they were armed. She had no idea if it was another hoax. She had no idea if Gabriela was already dead. She knew how a fox must feel being chased through a forest by a pack of hounds lusting for blood.

Whoever Marko was, and whether he was in Greystone Lodge or not, Kelly was responsible for bringing down his empire and that of his three accomplices – Crawley, Day and Chase – and it was unlikely he wanted to share a friendly chat.

But she'd made up her mind.

Chapter 56

Teresa watched as Marko made preparations to leave. He went in and out of rooms, gathering items, and he wore his coat. It was clear that she wasn't invited. She suspected that they'd wasted too much time. Surely it wouldn't be long before the police tracked them down. Sasha had left already, she'd watched him drive away, no doubt as a result of some pact between father and son. How touching, she thought. She wanted to tend to her face. It stung like hell. It wasn't the worst she'd ever felt, though. Tom Day had been far more violent.

She'd never pressed charges.

All her life she'd been pulled to the bad boys. Jacob was the exception. His money kept her interested for a while, but she soon became bored with him and the babies. He hired a cleaner, a cook and a housekeeper, but still she was bored by domesticity and began going out. She went out a lot. That was when she met Marko.

He'd never hit her before now. It had come out of the blue and it terrified her. That colossal pig of a man that Marko had insisted on bringing here watched her carefully, and she daren't move.

She was fretful and it made her twitchy. Marko always had an answer, but this time he didn't. Perhaps she should have persevered with him and made herself indispensable, but she knew that was never going to happen. She'd tried once and he'd spurned her, a feeling that had taken a long time to fade. No one had ever said no before. Marko had a type and she wasn't it. That was all. She could tell that he had his eye on the detective instead, and it galled her. But Teresa knew that her age was beginning to show in her face, while the detective was strong and vital, and Marko loved a good match.

'Curtis, for God's sake, I need to go to the bathroom and take a goddamn shower. I need some privacy.'

'Wait,' he said. He left the room and locked the door. All the damn doors in this place had locks, and she regretted keeping it that way, but she could never have guessed that it would come to this. She still thought it could be different. If she could just get away from this house, she might be able to escape and re-emerge somewhere else. She'd reinvented herself so many times before; she knew she could do it again. She'd already made the necessary arrangements, and she even had a passport. Terry Smith. She liked the sound of it. But she knew she'd have to get past Marko in order to leave.

Curtis came back. 'Marko said you've got fifteen minutes, but I'm locking the door behind you. Do what you need to do.' He slammed the door and locked it.

She got up and grabbed her washbag and a pile of clean clothes, and walked in to the grand ensuite, kitted out on Jacob's money. It was a relief to be away from her guard for a moment. Whenever she felt Curtis's eyes on her it made her feel uncomfortable. She knew what he was capable of. Where did Marko find these thugs he surrounded himself with? she thought. She wondered where his brothers, the other three bullies, were; they were usually inseparable.

She showered quickly, then got dressed and looked in the mirror. She no longer looked like Teresa Joliffe, proprietor of the Troutbeck Guest House; now she was Terry Smith, artist and traveller. She tied her hair back, checked her watch, and looked around. She'd destroyed everything else; the last thing to do was clear her laptop. She opened it and began erasing files. She'd take it with her and abandon it somewhere random. She'd decide where later.

The two bedrooms at the back of the house overlooked the garden, and their windows led onto the flat roof above the orangery. The drop from the roof was a good twelve feet, and Teresa toyed with the possibilities. If she broke her legs in the fall, she'd be going nowhere, and He–Man outside her door would probably teach her a lesson. So she'd just have to make sure she didn't break her legs. She knew how Curtis taught women lessons, and how Marko allowed it. She'd become his latest liability. That was why she had to get away.

She climbed onto the roof and peered over the edge. It was a long way down. There was no grass, just paving stones. Perhaps she could shin down the drainpipe, but she wasn't sure it would hold. She was doubting herself, and it was costing her time.

The doors to the orangery opened beneath her and she froze. It was Marko. She daren't breathe. He lit a cigarette and blew smoke into the darkening sky, then walked towards the garden. Teresa was now in full sight; if he turned around, she'd be seen. She tried to tiptoe back-wards, but she stepped in a pile of old mushy leaves and slipped, clattering to the floor. Marko threw his cigarette away and spun round, checking where the noise had come from. Oh God, thought Teresa. Her time had come. She kept down and clung to the roof, making herself as flat as possible. She couldn't see him over the lip, and he couldn't see her.

'Curtis?' he shouted. 'Go and check on our lovely Teresa will you.'

Marko threw away his cigarette and marched back indoors, heading upstairs.

Teresa was wet through and lying in a pile of rotting vegetation. In her current state, she'd attract attention. She had no vehicle – Marko had her keys – and no way of putting a decent distance between herself and Greystone. She punched the flat roof and her hand hit a puddle, splattering mud onto her face.

She got up quietly and crept back inside, knowing that her options were dwindling by the second. Before she was three steps inside the room, the door opened and Marko burst in.

'Going somewhere?' he asked.

Chapter 57

As Kelly walked quietly but swiftly down the track, she noticed that there were three vehicles parked outside Greystone Lodge. One of them, she knew, was registered to Teresa Joliffe. It was a brand-new BMW X6, and she had read in the file that it had been bought on credit card for over sixty grand. She slowed her own car to a gentle roll and brought it to a halt next to a wall, away from the other vehicles. She quickly snapped shots of them on her phone, and did the same for the front of the house, then put her mobile back in her pocket.

The evening was drawing in and grey clouds sat on the fells all around her. The isolation made her chilly. Little Mell Fell and Great Mell Fell sat like watchkeepers, and she wondered if there were any walkers around at this time of the day. She doubted it.

She decided to check the exterior of the house first. After all, the man who'd called her – who she assumed was Marko's son, Sasha – had had no idea she'd been so close already. She could have been driving from Penrith or even Barrow for all he knew. It was the only advantage she had over Marko, who would be waiting for her and would have planned everything out in his head already.

But she was getting ahead of herself. It was possible that the call had been a hoax, and that Marko Popovic was out of the country by now and Gabriela was lying seriously harmed, or worse, inside the house. Kelly didn't know which scenario she hoped for. Some criminals, when faced with the end game, became reckless and made mistakes. Others disappeared sleekly and silently. Something about Marko's MO suggested to Kelly that he would want to stay and fight, but she couldn't be sure.

She went around the rear of the property, treading carefully and quietly. The area was walled and secluded, making the garden private. A light was on upstairs and she heard muffled shouting. She approached a downstairs window but all the curtains were drawn, although she could see lights on behind them.

She strained her ears but heard no sirens. The time had come to make up her mind. She went back to the front, took a deep breath, and knocked. After a few minutes, a young woman answered. Beyond her, the hall was dark. Kelly showed her badge.

'Good evening. I'm Detective Inspector Porter, I was wondering if Teresa Joliffe was home?'

'Yes, ma'am.' The girl spoke with an accent that Kelly didn't recognise. As she opened the door wider, Kelly noticed some bruising on her forearms. The girl saw and covered them up.

Kelly's phone went and seeing it was Phillips she answered it straight away.

'Kelly, we're still about six minutes away, there was an accident that we had to bypass. Are you OK?'

'Yes. I'm being shown in. There's no sign of a large welcoming party. I'm absolutely fine, Will. I'll call you in five.'

She felt a flash of trepidation hoping that armed response wouldn't be too pissed off with her if she was wasting their time. Better safe than sorry. The decision had been authorised by Cane, but she hoped she wouldn't be a laughing stock. Everybody would know if she screwed up in such a small constabulary.

The girl stood back. Kelly stepped inside.

'Do you work here?' she asked.

'I no understand.' The girl looked afraid suddenly, and turned and walked away. She hadn't closed the door.

'Shall I wait here?' Kelly shouted after her, but the girl scurried off.

'Detective Inspector Porter,' said a voice behind her, and the front door slammed shut.

Kelly spun round and reached for her pepper spray. For seconds she seemed to stand with it held high towards the man in front of her. He was tall and well-built, and he wore all black. Marko. Then she walked towards him showing her badge.

'I'm arresting you on suspicion—'

He slapped it away with one hand and got her by the throat with the other. It was the second time today that she'd been assaulted, and it pissed her off. Her body left the floor and she felt as though her head would come off. She kicked him in the groin as hard as she could, and he howled in pain and let go of her. Thank God she'd worn heavy boots.

She ran in the same direction as the girl, calling Phillips at the same time. Another man stepped out in front of her. This guy was a giant, and she remembered Darren's description of someone he called Curtis. He swatted her to the ground with one huge hand.

Her mind went into overdrive. As she crawled on all fours away from Curtis's massive frame, he slipped on the shiny wooden flooring, buying her seconds. She jumped over the back of a sofa and ran into a room that turned out to be the kitchen. She grabbed the biggest knife she could find, hit the last call button on her phone at the same time gabbling as soon as Phillips answered.

'There's at least two of them. Get here, Will, yesterday!' She hung up. She had to concentrate on avoiding these men at all costs, because if they got hold of her, she was sure they'd kill her. Come on, she willed the response team.

She heard footsteps approaching the kitchen and stood with her back to another door, holding the knife. She was well aware that bringing a knife into the equation wasn't the ideal scenario when faced with men who probably knew how to use them properly, but she was flat out of options, and she might at least cause some damage. They knew she was a police officer; they'd already worked out too that she had balls, so they approached with caution, it never crossed their minds that they might need firearms to subdue a woman.

'Where's the girl?' she asked, looking from one to the other. Her voice was raspy from having her throat grabbed twice in one day.

'What are you planning to do with that, Miss Porter?' Marko looked at the knife.

'It's called self-defence, arsehole,' she spat.

Marko laughed, and Curtis joined in. They looked like mean motherfuckers. Kelly would love nothing more than for them to run out of time in their arrogance.

'Armed response vehicles are on their way,' she said.

'Tut, tut. I doubt it. They've been sent elsewhere, haven't they? You're all alone. Otherwise you wouldn't have come in.'

'It's over, Marko. We know everything. We know about Tomb Day. We know about the shell companies and the art. Clever. It was always going to end badly. Colin Day was too sloppy, wasn't he?' She had to buy time.

'Go get the girl, Curtis, let's have some fun,' Marko ordered.

Kelly watched him. He was unarmed. She could rush him, but he'd easily overpower her and turn the knife on her. She'd felt his strength when he'd grabbed her earlier. She tried to think. If 'the girl' was Gabriela, that meant she was still alive.

'Don't make your situation even worse by losing it over a police officer, Marko. It's taken very seriously in this country.'

Marko laughed.

'You English, you think you know everything! I'm leaving you here when we're done. I'll be a thousand miles away before they find you.'

Kelly realised that he had a plan and she was somehow part of it, and it bothered her. With Curtis gone, she thought she might perhaps stand a chance but she didn't yet know where Gabriela was, or if anyone else was in the property. Her gut turned over as she realised the danger she was in. She knew that she was simply collateral. These men who made a lot of money from the suffering of others would have no problem snuffing her out. Her palms became sweaty, her head pounded and her vision blurred. Still she heard no sirens.

Curtis returned with Gabriela, and Kelly felt a mixture of relief and terror. The girl was sobbing, and Curtis put his mighty hand over her face and leaned her backwards. 'Shut up, bitch!' He was English. Kelly looked her in the eye and willed her to be strong. It would be over soon.

'You are a woman of the law, are you not, Miss Porter?' Marko's question took her by surprise: now he wanted to make a fucking speech. He was standing in the same position; neither of them had taken a step forward. He folded his arms. Kelly kept the knife in front of her.

'What kind of question is that? I'm a police officer. But you know that.'

'Yes, but there are police officers who care nothing for law, and you are not one, are you? You believe in what you do. I see it in your eyes. You wouldn't have come here alone if you did not care about the girl. That's the only reason you came, isn't it? Your colleagues would have got here soon, but you couldn't wait. You had to try and save her. It's admirable. I wish you worked for me.' As he said this, his smile broadened, and Kelly knew that he meant every word.

'I'd be a damn sight better than Darren Beckett.' She tried stalling him and whatever he was planning for her.

Marko laughed. 'I'm sure you would. I should have killed him when I had the chance.'

Kelly glanced at Gabriela. She didn't look dishevelled or as though she'd been accosted in any way; just very afraid, with good reason.

'Is Teresa Joliffe here?'

'She was another mistake. She's upstairs, ready to go to prison.'

'Why are you still here?'

'Because I wanted to meet you. And I wanted you to watch something. You see, you have single-handedly fucked up my business, and I can't allow that. You must feel the loss I feel.'

'I haven't single-handedly done anything, arsehole. You would have been caught sooner or later.'

'Perhaps you are right. Perhaps not. But all I have to do is tie up a few loose ends and then I'll be gone. You English police are stupid, your government weak; they allow people like me to exist.'

'So it's our fault?' Kelly shook her head and laughed. Time was running out. She couldn't hear any sirens yet. Her mind played tricks on her and she wondered if she'd given Phillips the right address.

Marko turned to Curtis, who took something from his pocket and wrapped it around Gabriela's wrists. The kitchen was gloomy, with only a small light burning over the hob, and Kelly couldn't make out exactly what he was doing. Gabriela panicked and resisted, and Kelly's instinct was to run to her and protect her, but she knew it would be a mistake.

'Gabriela, stop struggling,' she said quietly.

'Yes, Gabriela, stop struggling.' Marko copied her.

'Leave her alone. She's done nothing. Let her go.'

'Why would I do that?'

'Look, the police will be here any minute.'

'I can't hear them. Such an isolated spot, and the lodge is quite tricky to find, isn't it?' Marko was cocky in the knowledge that the address supplied to the police by Sasha was the one in Glenridding.

Curtis took something else from his pocket and gagged Gabriela. Next, he tied a length of material around her

348

neck. She coughed and spluttered, fighting for air. Kelly watched in horror.

'Stop it! What the fuck are you doing? Why make it worse for yourselves?' She was desperate, and torn over what to do.

'Detective, you took something from me and I'll never get it back; now I'm going to take something from you that you'll never get back. Your sense of duty, your loyalty, your integrity and your peace of mind.'

Kelly had no idea what he was talking about. She was sure he was crazy – the power he'd wielded for such a long time had gone to his head – but then she heard Curtis undoing the fly on his jeans, and she understood.

Chapter 58

The two armed response units sped along the northern shore of Ullswater, heading towards an address in Glen-ridding. Adrenalin flowed as the crews readied themselves inside the vehicles. The units were governed by strict rules of engagement, and no firearms officer ever went to a job thinking he'd kill someone.

Tonight they were dispatched under the 1971 Immigration Act, and were followed by two immediate response vehicles, two convoy vans, and finally two detectives. Together they covered all bases, but it would be the ART who went in first. The vans contained rams and door-breaking kit. The atmosphere inside all the vehicles was tense, but prepared. Instances like this one were rare in Cumbria, but as drugs moved out of Manchester and Preston, the units noticed they were needed more and more.

This was a suspected people-trafficking case. It made them sick, but only one thing was on their minds: securing the properties and making arrests.

It was fully dark now, and the flashing lights came as a shock to the visitors to Glenridding who were enjoying a pint or an evening meal in one of the many pubs. People stopped what they were doing as the vehicles sped past, sirens blaring. Everybody wanted to know what was going on.

The convoy picked its way through the dark lanes behind Glenridding, then slowed as the lead vehicle checked the computer. The tiny tracks around the area were notoriously desolate, and time wasn't on their side. A colleague was missing and hadn't been in contact with her fellow detective for a good twenty minutes. She was unarmed and vulnerable, and Eden House couldn't be sure which address she was at.

The address was located at the end of a small dirt road, and the vehicles halted. The crews jumped out and began preparing to enter. Several officers went to the rear of the property to assess entrance methods and line of sight.

A designated officer approached the front door and shouted: 'Police! Open the door!'

There was no response.

Over the radio, the commander of the unit ordered them to enter and ascertain any presence of persons or arms.

The teams prepared to ram the door, and two armed officers readied themselves to be the first in. The two detectives had arrived, and waited on the driveway for the unit to enter and the address to be secured.

The door broke apart and the two armed officers entered the building. They shouted warnings into every room and it took them only a matter of minutes to establish that no one was home.

–

Phillips took the call; he knew that Kelly was now only a minute away. He'd lost contact with her over ten minutes ago, and as they approached the Greystone property, his gut tightened. He'd read all about Marko Popovic, and he'd seen first-hand what he was capable of during every step of the investigation.

Ten minutes was long enough to die, and Phillips hung his head in shame as he realised that he should have pleaded with Kelly – ordered her even – not to go in. But she was in charge. She was his boss, not the other way round. It was highly likely that after it was all over, there'd be an investigation into what had gone wrong. He willed his car to go faster but the last thing he wanted was to crash into a wayward sheep or a stray deer. The lanes were narrow and winding, and it was taking them a long time to find Greystone Lodge.

The black night didn't help, and the vehicles up front were on full beam. Finally it came across on the radio that the driveway had been located, and they began moving more quickly.

Eventually they parked up. Now all Phillips could do was wait. He watched the armed response guys get ready and the rams being taken to the door. Other officers disappeared round the back.

He closed his eyes and said a prayer.

Chapter 59

'You do that and I'll cut it off,' Kelly spat.

Curtis laughed. Gabriela was kicking and thrashing about, and the big man stood over her, rubbing himself. Kelly thought she might vomit, and bile came up into her mouth.

Marko was enjoying himself; it was better than a dog fight.

'If you go for a man over six foot tall with a knife, Detective, that leaves you exposed at the back, and that's where I come in,' said Marko.

Kelly hoped it might all be a game to scare her and Gabriela. She stared at Marko. He was right, she couldn't overpower either one of them, but she might disable him. She should be hearing sirens by now, and she racked her brains to work out why they weren't here yet. On that road from Penrith, they could have encountered any obstacle: sheep, cows, lost tourists, broken-down caravans. She strained her ears: still nothing.

Maybe Phillips had hit red tape and armed response wasn't authorised after all; maybe their evidence was too flimsy. Most of it was in her own head and not written up yet. Damn. Phillips might be arguing the toss with the armed response commander right now, and as each second ticked by, Gabriela's safety and her own spiralled rapidly downwards. She was losing faith in herself and her team.

She made up her mind.

She studied the two men for less than a second: where they were positioned, what they were focused on, and their proximity to exits. She noticed that Curtis had gone into some kind of aroused haze, meaning that in that moment Marko was one man down as his giant pal contemplated rape. He'd done it before, that much was obvious. Had he done it to Gabriela yet? She didn't know. The girl was tiring, and it looked to Kelly as though she might be resigning herself to her fate.

Kelly knew some martial arts and boxing, but these were two fully grown males with the advantage of height and strength. And when Curtis came out of his fug, he'd be a formidable opponent. She realised that she stood no chance. But she had to try.

She swung around with such speed that Marko didn't see the blade. She slashed towards him and caught his arm.

'Fuck!' He winced. 'Bitch!'

Curtis seemed transfixed by his victim and barely heard his boss cry out in pain. Marko made a dash for Kelly, but she ducked out of the way and managed to make it to Gabriela. Curtis was on his knees. She jumped on his back and plunged the knife into his body, and he squealed and rolled over, crushing her beneath him. They wriggled together, but Curtis couldn't quite manoeuvre himself properly and Kelly got free.

'Run!' she screamed to Gabriela. The girl froze. 'Run!' she repeated, but it was too late. Within the seconds it had taken to stop Curtis, Marko was now fully in charge. He grabbed Kelly and punched her in her side. It hurt like hell and forced the wind out of her. Now Gabriela got up and ran to the door, but Curtis tripped her with his hand; he was mad as hell having been denied his prize and he got up despite the wound Kelly must have caused. Marko still held Kelly, but she was able to bite him hard enough for him to let go, and she stood panting, figuring out her next move. Curtis's eyes were murderous.

'She needs to be conscious; now hurry up!' Marko said.

'Please! No!' Kelly begged them. In her moment of weakness, Marko grabbed her by the arms and she stopped resisting. She no longer had a weapon and she had no choice but to watch. She *had* to watch: closing her eyes would be abandoning Gabriela.

'This is your fault, Detective, and yours alone. You need to consider if you're in the right game,' Marko mocked her.

Curtis was in pain, but his lust was more powerful. Gabriela was cowering in a corner of the kitchen where she'd fallen, and he went to her and stood over her. The girl was terrified. Kelly could see sores and scratches around her wrists where she'd thrashed against the ties.

'Gabriela, look at me. Look at me!' she said. But the girl closed her eyes tightly and tears rolled down her cheeks. Kelly struggled, but she couldn't shift Marko, who wasn't going to let her go for a second time. Maybe it would be her turn soon.

Suddenly she stopped moving and turned her head to the door: sirens.

'Don't worry, it'll take them ten minutes to get in, and by that time we'll be gone,' Marko said, and smiled. 'Pity we don't have time for you, though,' he whispered in her ear. She threw her head back in to his face, connecting with his nose. He let go of her but brought his hand round with so much force that when it connected with her cheekbone, it rattled her head.

She heard a whimper then, and spun round to look at Gabriela. The sirens hadn't stopped Curtis, and he was forcing her legs apart. Kelly had never felt such a failure in all her life than in that moment. She kept talking as she walked around the kitchen keeping one step ahead of Marko; anything to try to distract them.

'You pathetic cowards! Is that all you've got? Come over here and I'll show you. Get off her, you fucking animal!'

Curtis was once more engrossed in his desire and Kelly looked around for a weapon. In under a tenth of a second, she made her decision.

Marko came at her again as Curtis got on top of Gabriela, but he missed her as she side stepped and took three paces towards the kitchen dresser, grabbing what looked like a heavy vase and swung it over Curtis's head. She'd timed it perfectly, connecting directly with his temple, and she heard the crack as he was knocked out cold and the bone-chilling thump as his body landed on the floor next to Gabriela, who screamed. She tried desperately to roll out from under him. Kelly spun round and realised that Marko was taking the stairs. Instinct told her that he was either fleeing or he'd gone to grab a weapon. She heard a woman scream. Christ, how many people are in here? she thought.

She ran to Gabriela and heaved against Curtis's body; he was out cold. Eventually she got her free and dragged her over to the kitchen door. She grabbed the knife that Curtis had dropped and cut the girl's wrist ties, then removed her gag. Gabriela's shoulders heaved up and down.

'Stay here,' Kelly told her. 'The police will be here shortly. Stay on the floor, and don't get up.'

She pulled herself away and looked around waiting for Marko to appear again at any moment. Her biggest fear was that he'd gone to get a gun.

The sirens grew louder. Nearly there. She ran to the front door and flung it open, she saw the lights and ran to the end of the lane. She was spotted and she waved her arms frantically. Two vehicles sped up the drive and Kelly sprinted after them. Breathlessly she explained the situation, and the condition of Gabriela, and armed officers entered the property.

On the first landing, the officers pushed doors open but found only empty rooms, until they burst into one and came face to face with Marko Popovic. He was holding a pistol against the head of a badly beaten woman who could barely stand.

'Back off!' Marko shouted.

The Specialist Firearms Officer held his semi-automatic carbine steady as his colleague gave Marko one warning.

Downstairs, Kelly heard the splintering of wood, loud bangs and voices as the response team secured the house. She had no idea if Marko had escaped via the roof she'd seen when she was in the garden, and was long gone, or if he had been caught in time.

An ambulance arrived and Kelly assessed her wounds. Her body ached all over and she shivered as she realised that it could have been much worse. Gabriela was escorted out of the house, and Kelly spotted Phillips in one of the cars. They were listening to the command exchange between the armed response and their seniors.

She heard a shout and her gut turned over as she recognised the command to lower a weapon. So Marko isn't giving up, she thought.

'PUT YOUR WEAPON DOWN AND STEP AWAY FROM THE WOMAN!'

A final request to shoot came over the radio and Kelly closed her eyes.

'WE WILL SHOOT! PUT YOUR WEAPON DOWN, SIR!'

A single deafening shot penetrated the night, followed by silence.

'Property secure.'

For Kelly and the medics, this was their signal to go in. She and Phillips entered and got to work on processing the site for their undoubted mountain of paperwork they'd have to write later. Kelly went upstairs and found Teresa Joliffe being attended to, next to the lifeless body of Marko Popovic.

'He cocked his weapon, ma'am.' She'd guessed as much.

'Ma'am?'

'I'm all right. I want to see if the girl is OK. There was another girl too, I don't know where she went.'

'I think we've got several girls downstairs, ma'am. They were in rear annexes.' He fired various codes into his radio and carried on his duties. Kelly went back downstairs. 'I think you should get checked out by the medics,' Phillips said.

Kelly knew her wrist was broken, and her ribs screamed in agony on her right side, but she was alive.

'I'm all right.'

'Still need to get you checked out. Come on.'

'Where's the girl?' Kelly asked.

'Which one?'

'The one who was in the kitchen.'

'In an ambulance, being checked over.'

They found Gabriela being treated for shock.

'Is she OK?' Kelly asked a medic.

'Shaken up. Superficial. She'll be fine.'

Phillips helped her climb into the ambulance and she lay on the other bed, opposite Gabriela. As she did so, she heard shouting outside and recognised Curtis's voice. She was glad she hadn't killed him; he'd suffer more in prison. She remembered Curtis standing over Gabriela and couldn't understand why this aspect of the evening had been so important to Marko; was it just to screw with her head? He could have been long gone. She couldn't comprehend it and didn't think she ever would.

'You need to go to the hospital,' the medic said. Kelly began to shake, and he rooted around in a bag and pulled out a chocolate bar. 'You're in shock.'

As Kelly devoured the bar, her injuries began to throb. Her cheekbone stung and every joint felt as though it was on fire. Tomorrow will be worse, she thought. Phillips backed away as the ambulance made its way along the private road and on to Penrith.

Two hours later, she discharged herself from the Penrith and Lakes Hospital with her wrist bandaged, and went home for a shower. She'd have to go back for a cast when the swelling went down.

Her mother bombarded her with questions.

'Mum, I'm OK! I need to get back to the office.'

'What? Are you crazy? It's almost nine o'clock at night!'

'You know the score. I've got reports to write and probably several irate senior detectives wanting answers to some tricky questions. It's only a broken wrist. Don't wait up.'

At Eden House, her team was stunned to see her. They'd made excellent headway and Kelly listened as they brought her up to speed. No one mentioned the fact that she'd made the decision to actively enter the residence on her own. Phillips called it a dreadful coincidence: no one could have possibly known what was in there. Their suspect, Marko Popovic, could have been at any one of his many addresses, and the suspects had given multiple addresses in a direct attempt to confuse police.

And that was how it was written up.

Chapter 60

In a house in Leyton, a man watched the news on TV as he stuffed pork chow mein into his mouth with chopsticks.

'Seven people have now been detained by police and one is confirmed dead in one of the biggest raids in UK police history connected to people-trafficking,' the reporter said. 'The international community has praised Cumbria Constabulary for their handling of the case and for cracking a global money-laundering ring. Two senior cashiers and a manager of the Onchan Island Bank on the Isle of Man have been arrested and charged with money-laundering offences across several different countries. The government have launched an investigation into how the group managed to keep the operation going despite new anti-money-laundering legislation.'

'Shh!' the man hissed at his wife, who'd come in to collect his bowl. She looked at the TV and rolled her eyes. She didn't understand a word of it. Until a picture of Marko Popovic came onto the screen. Then she stopped what she was doing, and covered her mouth with her hand. She pointed at the screen.

The man said something in his native tongue and his wife left the room.

He went back to watching the news.

'If found guilty, the gang could face life imprisonment. It is not yet clear how many people the gang successfully trafficked, but the police have released this statement.' The newsreader looked intently into the camera and a video was played. Nedzad watched carefully, amused that Marko Popovic had finally got what was coming to him. It looked as though someone was needed to take over where Marko had left off, but he'd have to wait for a while until the dust settled. He had contacts in Manchester and Liverpool who all thought Marko Popovic was an egotist who took too many risks.

He and Jovana had finally made their way to London after he'd managed to get a message to her in the hospital. It hadn't been hard: he'd worked out where she was and waited outside the nearest toilet window. She was distraught to leave the boy, but they had no choice. She'd cried all the way to London. She still cried every day.

He'd get their son back, he'd promised her.

On the TV, a senior uniformed policeman made a statement outside a large red building in Penrith. The cameras flashed.

'The investigation has brought to light several criminal allegations, including illegal trading of persons aged as young as one year old. We urge the public to come forward with any information that might lead to the rescue of such persons, as we have evidence to suggest that the trade has been going on for some time. There are also allegations of five counts of homicide being investigated. Special helplines have been set up for the public to contact us.'

The officer read out the numbers and other ways of getting in touch, and the information travelled across the bottom of the TV screen. The story would be on a loop for days, possibly weeks, while they investigated every angle of the alleged crimes.

Journalists screamed questions, but the police officer turned and went back inside the building.

Chapter 61

Kelly rolled over and smiled. Her broken wrist was still in a cast. It ached constantly after being smashed in three places. Two operations later, it was expected to make a full recovery.

The hotel was quiet and understated, but well run. She deserved a break. They had three whole days to themselves, and they walked, ate and drank, and chatted about stuff that didn't matter and stuff that did.

She'd said goodbye to Gabriela for the final time in Penrith with the girl's future uncertain, but last week she'd received a letter telling her that she was home in Lodz with her mother and brother.

Kelly had wanted to arrange for her to come back to the UK to go to art college, but Gabriela said she'd never leave home again. Her drawings, however, had been fundamental to the inquiry and, so far, thirty-two more people had been found living in servitude at addresses across Cumbria. Colin Day's laptop – the one Gabriela had hidden in her room – together with that used by Tom Day in prison had made the case watertight.

'What shall we do today?' Kelly asked.

'Last night you said you wanted to climb a mountain; were you a little drunk?' replied Johnny.

'I can climb a mountain in a cast, and no, of course I wasn't drunk. You'll just have to carry more.' She smiled at him.

'Where shall we go?'

'Skiddaw. It's got to be Skiddaw on a day like this, and it involves no scrambling.'

It was a cool November day, but the sky was bright blue and the view from the oldest mountain in the National Park would be spectacular.

'Deal.' He high-fived her good hand.

'I think I'll need help dressing,' she said.

Epilogue

In Manchester, Carl Bradley smiled to himself. The scoop was complete and the *Daily Telegraph* had offered him a job. He'd been there when the extent of Colin Day's business affairs was announced and used as an example by the Organised Crime and Corruption Reporting Project, the non-profit making investigative platform for global organised crime. It was the biggest case in Western Europe for quite some time. Colin Day, Barry Crawley and Harry Chase had been trading in desperate illegal travellers, charging them ludicrous amounts and either selling them on or using them for prostitution or slavery. The cash was funnelled through the tanning salons, as well as taken by speedboat from Workington to Douglas and on to the Onchan Island Bank. From these legitimate sources, with placement complete, it was then invested in countless other schemes purely designed to deceive and head off any interest: a process known as layering. Afterwards, the now clean money was integrated back into the monetary system by trading in luxury items and paying wages. Tomb Day, the watertight shell created by the genius of Tom Day, was at the centre of the mind-bogglingly complex scheme, and he'd almost got away with it. It had taken five weeks to crack the firewall in his computer, but it was all there. Darren Beckett's compliance in revealing the whereabouts of Anna Cork's body saw his term reduced to nine years; he wouldn't last one.

Carl had been asked to cover the trials for his new employer. When the attention had died down a little, he'd turned his attention to Lottie Davis.

The DNA on her body had been matched to that of a fifty-one-year-old banking director from London. He'd used Snapchat to arrange to meet a twelve-year-old in a hotel room for sex. When he'd gone to the rendezvous, he'd been greeted by officers from the Met, who had been trying to close a paedophile ring for months.

After the years of waiting, the news was bittersweet.

–

It was Kelly who introduced them after Carl had covered the trafficking case. It was a thank you for his meddling that had turned out to be very useful in the end. But there was no way she would allow him to meet with Jenny alone. He was still a journalist after a story, after all.

The details of the case were harrowing, not least because the banker denied the charge and they had to go to trial, despite the concrete forensic evidence. Jenny had to sit and listen to lawyers argue that the integrity of any evidence found on such a decomposed body would not stand up in court. In the end, it was payments to Colin Day's bank account that clinched the guilty verdict. He'd paid ten thousand pounds for the girl.

Carl brought a photographer and she clicked away, catching Kelly and Jenny in an embrace: it was a scoop and would look great on the front page. A photograph of the portrait that hung in Jenny's living room would also be used.

After Carl left, the two women sat for a long time in silence. Closure was a funny word; it meant to stop, to finish, to shut, to cease or conclude, but that wasn't the case at all. But at least Jenny now had a name and a story, a chain of events that she could use to explain what had happened, and that was something.

Kelly had names too.

But she had yet to get her peace of mind back.

Acknowledgements

I would firstly like to thank my agent, Peter Buckman, for his never-ending encouragement and faith; also Louise Cullen and the team at Canelo for their passion and meticulous attention to detail. For their fascinating insight, Harry Chapfield, Cumbria Constabulary (ret'd), Inspector Paul Redfearn, London Met Police, and DI Rob Burns, Beds Police. I want to thank the Lemons: you know who you are, I love you. And finally Mike, Tilly and Freddie for being neglected at odd times of the day; I couldn't have done this without you.